PRISONER'S PLEA

When Fred Fellows, Chief of Police in Stockford, Connecticut, received a strange letter from a condemned man awaiting execution for the murder of his wife, the chief was inclined to be skeptical—for the prisoner professed his innocence and sought the policeman's help to clear his name. Remembering the case, Fellows is convinced of the man's guilt, but finds himself drawn into re-opening the investigation. He uncovers new evidence which points to the man's innocence, but time is short, as the execution is due to take place in only a few days . . .

PRISONER'S PLEA

Hillary Waugh

ATLANTIC LARGE PRINT

Chivers Press, Bath, England.
Curley Publishing, Inc.,
South Yarmouth, Mass., USA.

Library of Congress Cataloging-in-Publication Data

Waugh, Hillary.
  Prisoner's plea / Hillary Waugh.—Large print ed.
    p.   cm.—(Atlantic large print)
  ISBN 0–7927–0316–2 (lg. print)
  1. Large type books.   I. Title.
[PS3573.A9P73   1990]
813′.54—dc20   90–35228
                                                                          CIP

British Library Cataloguing in Publication Data

Waugh, Hillary
  Prisoner's plea.
  I. Title
  813.54 [F]

  ISBN 0–7451–9868–6
  ISBN 0–7451–9880–5 pbk

This Large Print edition is published by Chivers Press, England, and
Curley Publishing, Inc, U.S.A. 1990

Published in the British Commonwealth by arrangement with Victor
Gollancz Ltd and in the U.S.A. and Canada with Ann Elmo Agency, Inc.

U.K. Hardback ISBN 0 7451 9868 6
U.K. Softback ISBN 0 7451 9880 5
U.S.A. Softback ISBN 0 7927 0316 2

PRISONER'S PLEA

CHAPTER ONE

The letter bore the postmark, 'State Prison, Midland, Conn. Jul. 17 1963' but it wasn't on official prison stationery. The address on the face of the envelope was a formal, 'Chief of Police, Stockford, Conn.' and in the corner was written the word, 'Personal'.

Fred C. Fellows, the chief to whom it was addressed, said, 'Must be from the warden. Wonder what he wants,' and tucked the envelope behind the others he was sorting.

Detective Sergeant Sidney B. Wilks, sipping from a container of coffee in the chief's office, said, 'What warden? Where?'

'Joe Curry, the warden at Midland. Letter from there and he's the only guy in those parts I know even slightly.' He tossed a direct mail circular into the wastebasket without bothering to open it.

'If you want to find out what he wants, read the letter.'

'I'd rather get rid of the junk mail first.'

The squawkbox in the outer room came to life with an unintelligible remark and Sergeant Unger, holding down the main desk, said back, 'I gotcha.'

Fellows tore open another envelope, studied the contents briefly and unfolded a sheet that bore pictures of revolvers. He

1

looked it over, then consigned that to the wastebasket. He tossed another envelope onto the pile of papers that littered his desk without opening it and was left with the Midland Prison letter with the legibly written address and the 'personal' notice.

When he finally opened that, Wilks swirled the coffee in his cup and said, 'The mystery of what Joe Curry wants will now be solved.'

The chief smiled but as he started to read a quizzical frown crossed his face and he exhaled noticeably. He went through to the end with the frown in place and a disbelieving light growing in his eye and then he said, 'Well I'll be God damned.'

'What's Curry want, some new prisoners?'

'It's not from Curry.' Fellow looked at the front and back of the sheet and read the envelope again. 'I don't get it. It must be some kind of gag.' He handed the letter to Wilks. 'What do you make of it?'

Wilks took the paper, sat back and read aloud. '"Dear Chief Fellows: My name is Ernest Sellers and I am in Death Row at Midland State Prison. I have been unjustly convicted of killing my wife. Appeals have been in vain and there is little if any hope of clemency from the Governor. Three weeks and one day from now I am to be executed, but I am an innocent man.

'"I was convicted not because of any evidence against me but only because there

2

was no one else to pin the murder on. All that can save me now is the uncovering of some kind of evidence pointing somewhere else or supporting my own innocence. It is for this reason that I turn to you. Your great detective ability is well known. You can find things that ordinary policemen can't and if anyone can save an innocent man from dying in the electric chair for a crime he did not commit, you are the one.

'"Please take pity on a poor working man who has not only lost his wife of fifteen years to a most brutal murderer, but who has spent the past two years of his own life in a death cell and will soon lose his own life as well if something isn't done and done quickly.

'"I know that you are a humane man and one interested in justice. I know that your life as a policeman has been dedicated to helping fellow citizens in distress. I ask please that you give me your help now while there is still time.

'"Your most obedient servant, Ernest Sellers."'

Fellows tipped back his chair. 'Isn't that the damnedest thing you ever saw?'

Wilks nodded and returned the letter. 'You going to do anything about it?'

'Do anything about it?' Fellows tossed the letter onto the desk. 'What could I do about it? What does he think, I'm retired or something? I've got a police department to

3

run. I've got a job. He's out of his mind. What does he think I am?'

Wilks shrugged and smiled. 'Apparently he thinks you're a super-sleuth.'

'That's a lot of baloney. If he wants somebody to investigate something for him, let him hire a private detective agency. That's what they're in business for.'

'He calls himself a "poor working man". Maybe he means he doesn't have any money.'

'So he comes to me? Isn't that nice!'

'But he says he's innocent.'

'Of course he says he's innocent. I never heard of a killer yet who said he was guilty.' Fellows straightened up. 'He got a fair trial and he got convicted. I remember Sellers now. Very jealous man. It was up in Banksville about three years ago. He said he came home one evening and found his wife dead on the floor. The prosecution said he beat her to death before he went out and the jury decided the prosecution was right. I know the case.'

'Juries have made mistakes before, Fred. So have prosecutors.'

The chief shook his head. 'What are you trying to do, Sid, be my conscience? There's nothing I can do. I work here, or maybe you forget it.'

Wilks smiled. 'You live here, you mean. You're so convinced the police department can't get along without you you can't even let

4

your days off go by without dropping in to see what's going on.'

Fellows sighed. 'All right. My hobby is the police department. You know it and I know it. It's also my job and I can't go off investigating complaints way out of my jurisdiction at the other end of the County just because somebody asks me to. Even if I could, can you imagine what would happen if I did? You'd need a truck to handle the appeals that would come in for free service investigating things for people.'

Wilks sat back and gazed idly into space. 'When'd you take a vacation last, Fred?'

'What's that got to do with it?'

'If you wanted to look into this thing, I don't suppose the police commissioners would object to your taking a few days. They said you could have off when you wanted when they approved the vacation schedule.'

Fellows made a face. He clapped a hand on the arm of his chair. 'Sid, you're a policeman, for Christ's sake. You know what police reaction would be to some nosey outsider wanting to re-open a case that's been settled! Suppose I did look around. What kind of cooperation do you think I'd get? Not only does something like that throw extra work on the police involved, it's a slap in their face. It's saying, 'I don't think you did your job.' I'd make myself good and popular with that Dennis Acton, the chief up there in

5

Banksville.'

'You running for office or something?'

'How's that?'

'I was wondering why you were worrying about being popular.'

Fellows said irritably, 'Cut it out, Sid. What're you needling me for? You think I should go off on a wild goose chase? You really think so?'

'I'm just wondering what you think.'

'I think I'd be a damned fool. If you're sold on this guy's innocence, why don't you go look into it?'

'I didn't get asked. Besides, I'm no super-sleuth.'

'No, but something's bugging you. I think you'd really like to see me do it.' Fellows heaved a sigh. 'It wouldn't be any use, Sid. There isn't anything I could do and you should know it even if this guy Sellers doesn't. In the first place, the original police investigation would have been as thorough as possible. In the second, the trail is nearly three years old and if nothing's turned up in that time it's certain I wouldn't find anything.'

Wilks stared into his coffee cup and then drained it. 'Of course I know you're right, Fred. Maybe I'm just a sucker for sob-stories.'

Fellows nodded. He drew his tobacco from the breast pocket of his shirt and chewed off a

6

piece. 'I am too,' he said. 'That's one of my troubles. I don't like suffering and I'm in the field where, outside of a hospital, you're going to see the most of it. Every disaster, every family quarrel, every burglary, everything where somebody gets hurt, that's where we are. Everybody who ever walks in here has a problem. Maybe that's why I worry over the force so much. We're the ones who have to try to ease the hurts, patch up the quarrels, find the stolen goods. I want to see us do the best we can at it. But, Sid, I think this is a sob-story and nothing else. I remember, when I was following the trial in the papers, I figured the guy was guilty. Didn't you?'

'Me?' Wilks laughed. 'I wouldn't even know what the case was about. I'm no file system on crime in the United States. I don't memorize all these things the way you do.'

'What's wrong with studying things like that?' Fellows challenged. 'Every so often you come across some new gimmick some crook has pulled somewhere and if you tuck it away in your memory, you're that much better prepared for what happens here.'

'You're wasting your talents in Stockford. You ought to hire yourself out.'

Fellows smiled. 'That's what Sellers thinks I ought to do. Except he wants it for free.'

'And you think he's guilty.'

'Sure I think he's guilty. That's what the

jury said. And if all his appeals have been turned down, then there was nothing wrong with the way the jury got persuaded. And what's more, they wouldn't have come out for the death penalty if they hadn't been dead certain.'

Fellows picked up the letter and scanned it again. He shook his head and tossed it back on the desk, then went out to the squawkbox to hear what Leroy Manny, in car one, was reporting.

CHAPTER TWO

The next day was a Friday and Fellows was in an hour early. He kept to the hot confines of his office till time for muster at quarter of eight and he ran through the roll and carried out inspection with even more than his accustomed severity. 'When did you last polish your buttons, Harris?'

'Yesterday, sir.'

'What do you call that?'

'I think a little polish got caught in the design.'

'You clean it out of the design before you go on duty. One gig for Harris.'

The men held themselves at taut attention when he read off the duty schedule and they relaxed but little when he dismissed them and

8

stalked back to his office. They eyed each other and murmured as they started out that it was going to be one of those days.

The chief was notoriously a stickler for personal neatness and courteous attendance to duty and he cracked down hard on errors. Other than that, he generally ruled with a relaxed hand and morale on the force was high. The chief didn't permit familiarity on the part of the men except with Sergeant Wilks and, to a lesser degree, with Sergeants Unger and Gorman, but that was as it should be if a chief were to have the respect of his men. He made them toe the line for he wanted a sharp, well-knit organization, but he also understood that the men were human and he allowed whatever latitude he could within the limits of the line.

Now and then, though, like today, he drew them up sharply and landed on them hard and these were the days when the men went out with an uneasy gnawing in their stomachs, a keen eye out for the chief's sudden appearance, and special efforts to make not even the slightest mistake. These were the days when they worried about the chief's home life and what his wife or children might have done to set him off.

The moods and the worries which caused the crackdowns were never due to his family, however, though Wilks was the only one close enough to the chief to know it. Fred and

9

Cecilia Fellows were devoted and their four children well trained. When the chief was bothered, the reason lay elsewhere.

Wilks went out that morning to investigate a case of vandalism which had been reported the preceding evening. Three windows had been broken in a new house nearing completion on Nightshade Lane. He talked to the neighbors, checked some tire marks in the soft dirt of the graded area beside the unconstructed driveway and asked questions of the workers on the job. When he returned to headquarters at half past ten he had a pretty good idea as to the boys responsible. It was now a question of picking them up after school and having a talk.

The door to the chief's office was closed when he got in and Wilks didn't try to enter. He gave Lerner, subbing on the desk, a quick rundown then got out the portable typewriter and started on his report.

He was halfway through when the door opened and Fellows came out. 'Want to get some more coffee, Lerner?' he asked. 'Black, this time. No sugar.'

Lerner nodded and departed without a word, going out through the open door and up the steps into the sunshine. Fellows said to Wilks, 'Got a lead?'

'A woman across the way heard the glass breaking and looked out. There was a car in the drive with the headlights on and at least two, possibly three youths. One ran back to the car in front of the lights and she described him. I think it's the Braslin kid from what she says and from the other things I found out. If that's right, I can guess the others.'

'Any motive?'

'Possibly. One of the workers said there was a kid hanging around the job two days ago. They caught him trying to swipe some tools. The contractor pushed him around a little. He fits Braslin too.'

'You going to talk to Braslin's parents?'

'First I'm going to talk to him.'

Fellows smiled. 'I hope he doesn't retaliate by throwing bricks through our windows.'

Wilks said, 'Well, you're turning human again. I thought you were going to chew a hole in the wall a couple of hours ago.'

'Did it show that much?'

'It showed. What's the matter, no sleep last night?'

Fellows scratched his neck. 'Not a hell of a lot. I'm bothered.'

'About that letter?'

Fellows paused in his scratching and lowered his hand slowly. 'Yeah. How did you know?'

'I'm a detective.'

'What have I been doing, dropping clues?'

Wilks sat back and grinned. 'Well, let's see. First the chief, hereinafter called the suspect, says it's a lot of hogwash, this request for his aid, and he throws the letter away. But he doesn't throw it in the wastebasket, he throws it on his desk. That means that's not the end of it. Suspect is further known to be a bleeding heart with an overdeveloped sense of justice and a feeling of personal responsibility for righting all the wrongs in the universe. He protests so vigorously about the futility of looking into the matter that he sounds like he's trying to persuade himself. Then he shows up an hour ahead of time with circles under his eyes which spell insomnia. He's got a chip on the shoulder that has nothing to do with the lack of sleep since he can go thirty hours on duty at a stretch without forgetting his manners. The chip says he's mad at himself because he doesn't know the answer to a problem and all the rest of it points out what the problem is.'

Fellows shook his head and said wryly, 'Damned if I knew I was so transparent.'

'Oh, you aren't—except to me, the rest of the force, the Police Commission, the Town Administration, your family and friends.' Wilks smiled and then added, 'And maybe a guy named Sellers.'

Fellows grinned wryly again. 'You mean he's trying to use me for a fall guy?'

'He knows a sucker when he sees one.'

'Listen, yesterday you were the one trying to persuade me I should look into it.'

'That was when you didn't want to. I like

12

being contrary.'

Fellows hooked a leg over the end of the table. 'What do you really think I ought to do?'

'What's it matter, Fred? You know damned well what you *are* going to do. You're going to take a look into the thing far enough to satisfy your curiosity. You hope a quick look will convince you he's guilty and you can forget the whole business. But until you are convinced you aren't going to be able to leave it alone.'

'Well,' Fellows admitted, 'I guess it wouldn't hurt to at least go pay the guy a visit. Monday's my day off and I could drive up to Midland and see what Sellers is like and hear what he has to say.'

'That is if the warden up there will do you the courtesy of letting you see Sellers. You aren't his lawyer, his priest, or his family.'

'He'll let me.'

'Yeah? What makes you so sure?'

Fellows said with another twisted smile, 'Because I already called him.'

CHAPTER THREE

Midland State Prison was up near the Massachusetts border, a mile north of the road to the town of Midland. It was a sullen, gray stone fortress accessible only by a patchy macadam road which bored a straight path through an equally sullen and swampy forest. The prison itself stood in the middle of the forest and was centered on a vast field of fill which held the trees back a hundred yards in all directions to give the roaming guards on the parapets a clean shot at anyone scaling the battlements. Exposed as they therefore were, the forbidding walls always burst like a sunlit surprise after the gloom of the swamp.

Fred Fellows had been there once before when Warden Curry had taken a group of police officials on a tour. That had been some six years before but on this Monday in July he got the same sense of instant depression at sight of the place that he had got then. The sun was bright, the day was hot and the sky cloudless. Still, and all the dank and putrefying woods were dark and sad, chilling the brightest spirits. Even worse, however, was the monstrous prison on its island of sand. It was bleaker and sadder and more chilling because it was a place where people lived. To Fellows it made little difference whether a man stayed there because he was sentenced to or whether he was paid to. A prison would be the last place on earth he'd want to call home.

The main gate was a huge wooden door twenty feet high with an arched top. It was well painted and sturdy and Fellows drove up to it across the stretch of barren ground, under the eyes of the armed guards patrolling walls which rose ten feet higher still. He stopped and honked in obedience to the word 'Honk' painted on the face of the door while, above, the guards saw and ignored.

After a minute, the door was swung out by an old man in an olive drab uniform and Fellows could see through to the barred gate twenty feet beyond which opened onto the prison grounds. He drove into the passage and halted while the old guard closed the wooden door behind. From an office at one side another guard came out and approached the side of the car. 'Pass?' he said when Fellows failed to produce anything.

'I don't have a pass. I'm Chief Fellows from Stockford. Warden Curry is expecting me.'

'You have identification, Chief?'

Fellows produced a wallet from his hip pocket and showed his driver's license.

The man pursed his lips, turned and went back inside the stone doorway to the little office. Fellows waited and the old man passed by the car, entering the office himself. He looked as gray and depressed as the prison he tended.

The younger man was a while in there and then came out again. 'The warden is expecting you. You have a gun, Chief?'

Fellows said he did.

'You'll have to check it here.'

The chief unstrapped his holster and the guard said, 'You should know better than to come with a gun.'

Fellows let that pass without comment. As a police officer he lived with a gun. It was a part of his clothing and it was as automatic to strap it in place as it was to put on his shoes. He handed it over and though he hadn't drawn the gun more than three or four times in his life, he felt naked without it.

The guard took the gun inside the office and there was another wait before he reappeared with a receipt. He handed it through the window then went around the front of the car and climbed in the passenger side.

'Guard of honor?' Fellows asked.

'We don't take chances.'

The old man came out of the office and pressed the lower of two buttons in a switchbox. The steel-barred gate slid noisily aside on a wheeled track and the guard said, 'Drive ahead.'

Passing out from under the arch they came onto a sandy hard-packed yard separating the outer walls from the inner buildings. The buildings, a complex making up living and eating quarters, workshops, and the rest, were all of stone and joined as one unit. The architecture was plain and utilitarian, devoid of fancy touches and empty of inspiration.

16

The aim was to meet the requirements as economically as possible and the aim showed.

'Drive over there,' the guard said, pointing towards the right. 'Park in that parking area.'

Fellows did as he was bid, pulling to a stop beside half a dozen other cars close to an oak door. He got out without being reprimanded for doing so but the guard moved quickly so that he was beside the chief by the time he was free of the car. Now that Fellows was standing, the guard had his first full length look at him and his eyes wandered over his gray shirt and gabardine pants, the summer police costume in Stockford. There was an itchy quality to the guard's manner, as if he longed to run his hands over those clothes for concealed weapons, but he didn't quite dare. Besides, Fred Fellows filled his clothes fully and there was no place to put a gun where it wouldn't show.

'This way,' the guard said and opened the door. Fellows turned for a look around as he followed. The yard shimmered in the sunlight like a desert. There was no blade of grass to be seen, no tree, no little patch of flowers, no soil. There was only the hard-packed sandy clay, devoid of charm and life. Nothing moved but the scattering of guards stalking the walls between the bulletproof searchlight housings and machinegun mounts.

The guard led Fellows through the door to the administrative section of the prison.

There were offices and typewriters and a number of secretaries and clerks, all of them men. The guard took Fellows through another door marked 'WARDEN' and said to a man at a desk, 'This is Chief Fellows who has an appointment with Mr. Curry.'

The man at the desk was young and cleancut, an FBI agent type. He gave Fellows a smile and came to his feet. 'The warden said to send you right in,' he said and opened the sanctum door.

Fellows nodded and passed through and for the first time was free of the guard who didn't take chances.

Warden Curry was a middle-aged man with gray curly hair and a serious, lined face. He rose from behind a large oak desk and extended a hand soberly. 'Yes, Chief. We met before. I believe I remember you.'

'That tour,' Fellows said, shaking his hand. 'We talked some.'

'I know. You asked most of the questions. Have a chair.'

Fellows chose a leather seat which faced away from the glare of the window. He cast a glance around the room, at the paneling, the bookshelves and cabinets. It was a masculine room and even the drapes had a heavy, male quality about them.

'So you want to see Ernest Sellers,' Curry said, pushing a cigar box in the chief's direction. 'I must admit I was surprised at the

18

request though, of course, I have no objection to granting it.'

'In a way I'm surprised myself,' Fellows said. 'What kind of a man is he?'

Curry pulled the box back when the chief shook his head at the offer and selected a cigar for himself. He rubbed it between his palms for a bit and stared at the walls. 'That's hard to say. Like most people, I suppose. Seems like an ordinary type. But then, most murderers do.'

'How does he get along?'

Curry shrugged and put the cigar in his mouth. 'He doesn't beat his head against a stone wall if that's what you mean. He's smart enough, you might say, to accept the inevitable.'

'Meaning his execution?'

Curry ignited the cigar with a large desk lighter and blew out smoke. He leaned forward to replace the lighter and said slowly, 'I don't mean that. I don't think anyone is ever capable of accepting his own death. We, all of us, think we're immortal and even though, intellectually, we know we're going to die, emotionally we always think it'll be tomorrow. And, of course, tomorrow never comes.'

'That's because we don't know the date. Sellers is in a different position. He does know.'

'He does know, but like all people who are

19

to be executed, he doesn't think it's really going to happen. Death is too terrible a thought for a man to stand and his mind creates a mental block to protect him from it.' Curry leaned back and blew out another mouthful of smoke. 'Even when they get strapped into the chair in many cases the mind still refuses to allow the man to believe it. When the man walks stiffly forward and takes his position without a murmur, it's a sign his mind is blotting out what's going to happen to him.

'Of course there are the cases when the mind doesn't function that successfully and the criminal does come to a full realization that his time is up. Those are the bad ones. That's when the man goes into hysterics. His mind cracks under the impact and he becomes insane. Sometimes they fight, sometimes they plead and beg. They cry or they go berserk. At such times they have to be forcibly carried to the chair and held while they're strapped in and there have even been times when a sedative has had to be administered.' Curry looked thoughtfully at the glowing ash of the cigar. 'The human being is able to cope amazingly and he can face up to some pretty appalling situations. But he can't face that.'

Fellows said, 'Well, I suppose you're right, though I guess Sellers doesn't have much to keep hope alive with now except prayer.'

Curry shrugged again. 'He never had anything else going for him anyway from what I hear. His lawyer's been fighting delaying actions but that's all they are. There was never any serious chance of upsetting the verdict.' He struck the cigar against the ashtray to knock off an ash and went on. 'I don't know why people cling to existing like that, though. Look at this guy Sellers. He's been sitting alone in a cell twenty-four hours a day for nearly two years. The only people he ever sees are the guards when they bring him food or when they take him out for exercise. Once in a while his lawyer comes to pump a little hope into him but that's all. He's got no family, or if he has they never come here. The chaplain's available, of course, but Sellers isn't interested. So there the guy stays like a vegetable and his lawyer fights to keep him there. Personally I'd rather be dead than live like that.' Curry sighed. 'Well, it won't be much longer, anyway. Another couple of weeks and he'll be well out of it.'

Fellows said, 'There's no question about his guilt, I gather.'

'I don't know of any, but then I'm only a glorified jailer. They bring the prisoners in and I take care of them. What they did that got them sent here I only know from the reports that accompany them. The reports say Sellers murdered his wife and that's all I know about it outside of what I read in the

21

papers when the trial was going on.' Curry swung around in his chair. 'You think he's innocent?'

'I have no opinion.'

Curry arched a quizzical eyebrow. 'Now you didn't come up here to see a condemned man just because you want to know what a condemned man looks like. Something's going on to make you take a personal interest. Hell, he doesn't come from anywhere near where you operate. Of course it's none of my business but it sure is curious about the sudden interest being taken in this guy.'

Fellows became more alert. 'Sudden interest?'

Curry took another puff. 'Of course we always have interest, especially when the execution date draws near. There're the bleeding hearts, there're those who're opposed to capital punishment. You also get the crackpots who'll blow up the jail and stuff. They all write in. But you're the second guy who's wanted to *see* the man.'

'Second? Who was the other?'

'I don't even remember. I got a phone call from him on Saturday and I didn't really catch his name. Jones or something. He wanted to know if he could talk to Sellers. I said nothing doing. He was probably a reporter trying to pull a fast one.'

Fellows frowned. 'I suppose so,' he said.

'So, like I say, I don't know what your

interest is. It's not going to make any trouble, is it?'

'My interest?' Fellows shrugged. 'I don't really know that I have any. Maybe I won't even know after I talk to him.' He made a move to get up. 'O.K. to see him now?'

Curry sighed. 'Yeah. Sure,' He pressed a buzzer and sat back. 'I guess I'm just the jailer—not that I expect confidences, of course. You want to have lunch here after you talk to Sellers?'

'Depends on how long it takes and what happens.'

'He's going to tell you he's innocent, Fellows. I might as well warn you.'

The chief smiled and rose. 'I'm hardly expecting him to confess his guilt.'

The bright young man entered from the outer office and Curry waved. 'I'm giving Chief Fellows permission to visit Ernest Sellers in his cell. Make me out a pass to sign and take the chief to McCarthy.'

CHAPTER FOUR

Death Row in Midland Prison was just what the name implied. It was a series of five cells, side by side along a corridor in a special building well separated from the main cell block. There was a heavy oak door at the far end of the corridor and though there was nothing about that particular door to distinguish it from many similar doors in the prison complex it stood as an ever-present and ominous reminder. The door didn't need signs or special markings. Its location was sufficient and no prisoner consigned to Death Row needed to be told that that was the door through which he would one day pass and never return.

Perhaps for humane considerations—since the door couldn't be seen from the first cell in the corridor—perhaps merely for convenience sake, Ernest Sellers was in the cell adjacent to the other door. This was the one through which his food was brought, through which his paltry list of visitors came and went, and through which he passed for his daily period of exercise in the small, private yard close by.

It was this door that the guard named McCarthy unlocked and pushed open for Chief Fellows. He stepped through after without bothering to relock it and said, 'You got company, Sellers.'

Fellows was already at the barred cell gate looking through into the small confines. There was a bunk folded down on chains from the wall on the right, a small barred window flush with the ceiling, a stool upon which a man would have to stand even to reach the bars of the window, a sink in one corner, toilet in the other, and not a great deal of light.

Sellers was lying on the bunk with his head towards the bars, nor did he stir at the sound of opening doors. A magazine lay forgotten on the floor and he rested with his hands behind his head.

It wasn't till the word 'company' that he displayed any sign of life. Then it was merely to turn over on his side and lift his head. His eyes met Fellows' and he said, 'Yeah. Great. Come into the parlor.' He made no move to rise from the bed while McCarthy unlocked the door and pulled it back, but he kept watching the chief as he entered. 'Sit down,' he said. 'The stool's very comfortable.'

McCarthy relocked the door and said through the bars, 'Just holler when you want out. I'll be back down the hall.'

Fellows said, 'Thanks,' and stood on the stone floor looking down at Sellers. He was in his late forties, Fellows guessed, though the prison pallor and haggard lines of his face made him appear, to a casual glance, middle fifties. His hair was brown but graying and his build moderate to slight. He looked as if his stay in prison had cost him some weight. As for his face, it was drawn and diffident, neither handsome nor ugly. It was an undistinguished face that could be readily forgotten.

Sellers did a similar appraisal of the chief until the corridor door was locked and the

25

guard presumably out of hearing. Then he pushed himself to a sitting position and placed his feet on the floor. 'Well,' he said, 'it appears the stool doesn't suit you. Should I know you?'

Fellows, still regarding the man with calculating eyes, said, 'You wrote to me. At least the letter had your name on it. I'm Chief Fellows.'

Sellers' manner warmed appreciably. 'Chief Fellows.' He got up and held out a hand. 'Please pardon my lack of hospitality. I really didn't think you'd come.'

Fellows took the hand and noted that Sellers was a good five inches below his own six feet plus. He seemed still slighter when he was standing.

'Maybe,' the chief said, 'you want to tell me about it. Your letter was pretty cryptic.'

Sellers let himself down onto the bunk again and turned blue eyes up at Fellows. 'Cryptic? I thought it was pretty clear myself. I'm going to be executed for a crime I did not commit.'

Fellows remained on his feet. He folded his arms on his chest and his manner was forbidding. According to due process of law the man before him was a murderer and the chief had little sympathy for killers. 'You made that part clear,' he said. 'What you didn't make clear was why I should believe you.'

26

'I see.' Sellers looked at the floor and his face was downcast. It remained so only for a moment before he brightened again. 'But you're here. That means you at least think I might be telling the truth. I'm right about that, aren't I?'

'There's the possibility. Yes, that's why I came. I'll tell you, though, if you couldn't convince a jury, you've got two strikes on you right there. What is it that makes you think you can convince me?'

Sellers ran a hand over a smooth chin. 'I suppose I haven't really worked all that out yet. When a man's about to die unjustly he gets a little desperate. I've read about you. You've got a pretty good press, you know. You've cracked some pretty tough cases and the write-ups have been pretty good. I guess I figured if you were as good as the papers say you are, you'd be the one to turn to.'

'Turn to for what?'

'Help. To get me off the hook. When the last appeal got turned down and the execution date was finally set, I got frantic trying to think what to do. That's when I decided maybe you could help me.'

Fellows pulled the stool over at last and sat down. 'Now you'd better understand a few things, Mr. Sellers. You were given a fair trial. You were convicted on the evidence. This was two and a half years ago and presumably your lawyer's been doing everything he can for you. If he'd been able to uncover any new evidence, there'd be a new trial. Since he hasn't got you a new trial it's obvious there's been no new evidence. All he's been able to do for you is appeal on legal technicalities and the courts have ruled against him. There was nothing wrong with your trial, there's been nothing since the trial to indicate the jury made a wrong decision. Now you claim there *is* something wrong with the decision. It's going to take a good deal more than your sayso to back that up. And if you've got more than a sayso, you should be giving this information to your lawyer. He's the one you should talk to, not me.'

Sellers bit his lip and tears came into his eyes. 'I was convicted on circumstantial evidence,' he pleaded. 'There was no proof.'

'There doesn't have to be proof so long as the jury is persuaded beyond a reasonable doubt.'

'They had no *right* to be persuaded beyond a reasonable doubt,' he said, his voice coming up with emotion. 'I had no reason to kill her! I loved her.'

Fellows said, 'I'm here. I'll listen to your story. I want to hear what you have to say. But I also want to warn you not to think this means I'll do anything for you or that I could if I wanted to.'

'Then what did you come for if you aren't going to help me?' Sellers wailed. 'What do you want to do, just hear me beat my gums?'

Fellows sighed. 'Sometimes,' he said, 'there are miscarriages of justice. Fortunately it's not often, but since justice is meted out by human beings there are going to be occasional errors. I came up here because there is the possibility—I'm saying just a possibility—that this might be one of the cases where justice went wrong.'

'Just a possibility?' Sellers said shrilly. 'You believe I'm guilty, don't you? Where's that All-American tradition about a man being innocent until proven guilty?'

'You've already been proven guilty,' Fellows answered quietly. 'The shoe's on the other foot. It's up to you, now, to prove to me you're innocent.'

'If I could prove it do you think I'd be here?'

'If you can't prove it what are you calling on me for?'

Sellers jabbed a stabbing finger at the chief. 'Because I want *you* to prove it!'

Fellows blinked. 'Me?'

'Yes. You! You're the only one who can.'

'What the devil do you think I can do that hasn't been done?'

Sellers was speaking earnestly now. He leaned forward, elbows on his knees. 'Look, do you know the one reason I was convicted? The one and only reason? it was because nobody could point a finger at anybody else.

29

They had no case against me. They had no motive, they had nothing. But the cops, they didn't bother to look for anybody else. I was the handy one. Why bother looking? One quick glance and they see one suspect and only one suspect. Why complicate things by digging? If they dug they might come up with another and then they wouldn't know what to do. Let's tag the husband with the crime and close the file on it. That's the way they were thinking. They didn't give a damn about justice, they just didn't want to work. It doesn't matter if an innocent man dies. Not to them it doesn't. It's not their skin. Wrap it up and be done with it. That was their attitude.' He stopped and nervously ran a hand over his face. 'But I care. It's my skin. It's my life they're playing with.'

Fellows said, 'What about your lawyer? If there *was* anybody else he'd be pointing fingers all over the place.'

'My lawyer.' Sellers snorted. 'He was appointed by the court to defend me. Maybe if I had dough he'd have done a little work, but I didn't have dough. I didn't have enough to pay for a lawyer so the court gave me one. A lot of good that does. He was working hand in glove with the prosecutor. I'd've been better off without any lawyer.'

Fellows said, 'Sellers, you don't know very much about policemen and you don't know very much about lawyers.'

'I know more than I want to, I can tell you that.'

'Your lawyer did his best for you, you can rest assured of that. The court wouldn't have appointed him if he wouldn't.'

'His best? Look where I am right now. If he did his worst for me I couldn't be in a worse fix. What's he going to do for me when he's not getting any money?'

'Lawyers work for other things than money, Sellers. One thing about lawyers, they don't like to lose cases. It's not good for their reputation. Especially, they don't like to lose cases they could have won. If he could have won, he would have and if you think otherwise, why do you think you're still alive? Because he's been going to bat for you, pulling every legal trick he knows to keep you from going to that chair.'

'The hell with his legal tricks. If he wanted to keep me out of the chair why didn't he find somebody else besides me to point a finger at?'

'Maybe there isn't anybody.'

'There you are,' Sellers said heatedly. 'There you go again. You're so damned sure I'm guilty too. Listen. Somewhere, somehow, there's somebody who wanted my wife dead. I don't know who and I don't know why but I do know there is somebody somewhere. Because *I* didn't want her dead and *I* didn't kill her!'

31

CHAPTER FIVE

Fellows sat for a moment in silence, digesting Sellers' outburst. The man was slumped, staring dispiritedly at the floor. Fellows regarded him uncertainly and finally said, 'All right, Mr Sellers. I gather what you want from me is this somebody else you can point a finger at.'

'That's right,' Sellers said emphatically.

'That's a tall order, you know, assuming there is such a person. Your lawyer couldn't find him—or her—the police couldn't find him, and now, nearly three years later, you want me to.'

'I suppose it is a tall order,' Sellers admitted in a subdued tone, 'but that's why I wrote you. From what I've heard about you you've filled some pretty tall orders.'

'I don't work miracles, Mr. Sellers, and that's what it would take right now.'

Sellers nodded. 'I'd like to think you tried, though,' he said. 'I admit you could have done it better three years ago and I admit there isn't much time any more—only seventeen days, in fact—but it's never going to get any earlier than it is right now.' He looked up. 'Maybe it's too late. Maybe nothing can save me, but at least I don't want to go down without a struggle.' He was very pale and drawn but he managed a wan smile. 'Who knows? Maybe the age of miracles isn't quite past.'

'Maybe,' Fellows said without a great deal of enthusiasm. He shifted his position on the stool. 'Let's start at the beginning, Mr. Sellers. Tell me about yourself and your wife and everything that happened the night of the murder.'

Sellers looked at him warily. 'You're really willing to listen?'

'That's what I came for.'

Tears came suddenly into the convict's eyes. 'This's the best break I've had in three years,' he said, his voice choking.

'I can't promise anything,' Fellows said uncomfortably. 'I just agreed to listen. Now you'd better go ahead. We've wasted enough time.'

'Yes, fine. All right.' Sellers even managed a smile of relief. 'Now let me see. You want to know about Sheila and me. Where'll I begin?'

'Start with Sheila.'

'Oh, yes, well, Sheila was a beautiful girl. Make no mistake about that, Mr. Fellows. She was seventeen when I met her and very mature for her age. I was older. I was nearly thirty and I'd been living at home with my mother who was an invalid, caring for her and working. I worked in a job shop—job printing—and was in line for the foreman's position. Sheila and I met at a church social. I went to church in those days. It was about the only social life I had. I wasn't much with girls, my mother being ill so long and all. So, anyway, there was this social. Actually it was sort of a young people's supper and some of the Pilgrim Fellowship kids were there—high school kids. Sheila was one of them. I might've seen her before, in church or something, but I never really noticed her—not till that night. She was the prettiest girl in the lot and she was smiling and having a good time. She wasn't exactly vivacious, really, more on the quiet side you might say, but she was young and happy and gay and it made you feel gay and happy just to watch her and that was kind of a new experience for me who hadn't had much to be gay about for a long time.

'She was plenty popular too. Like I say, she was the prettiest of the lot and it was easy to see the boys liked her the best. They were all the time hanging around and fooling with her. Of course at that time I wasn't thinking anything except that it was nice to watch her and the fun she and the boys were having—and the other girls, but you kind of think of it as kid stuff, that they were, all of them, kids.

'I don't really know if any more would've come of it if it hadn't been that I helped out in the kitchen when the supper was over,

34

cleaning up dishes and coffee things with some of the women. I was used to dishes and things with taking care of mother and I was on the shy side anyway and I felt better if I was doing things. So then she came out with some cups and saucers and said to me, "Here, what are you doing? That's woman's work." I told her I didn't mind and she said that was nonsense and then she said that I was blushing and she insisted on taking over the dishes and said that if I was so stuck on doing something, I could wipe. It was better for a man to wipe than to wash.

'So I wiped the dishes with her and she teased me a little about my blushing and about being shy and she said girls weren't something to be afraid of, they didn't bite. That got me saying about my mother and taking care of her and how I didn't get much chance to be sociable and she got more serious and said she was sorry about all that, that it didn't sound like I had much fun.

'I don't know. We talked along and you could see she had a heart as well as good looks and she got thinking I was a pretty decent person because I stayed home looking after mother instead of going out for good times myself. Then she asked me if I was going to dance after when they had the square dancing and I said I didn't know how. So she told me she was going to see to it I had a good time this one night anyway and she made me get

35

out on the floor and into the square dancing with her.

'It might have ended there except the boys didn't like it much, her spending this time with me. They kept trying to get her away but then she got mad at them. I told her she didn't have to stay with me but she said the heck with them. They wanted to leave and go someplace else but she wouldn't go so there was really nothing for me to do afterward but take her home.

'We had a long talk in the car in front of her house and she was very intelligent and understanding and we got along fine. I could talk to her and she could talk to me and that's when I found out she wasn't just frivolous, but had her serious side too. I don't know how I got up enough nerve but I asked her to the movies and then suggested we could have dinner first. She said she'd never been taken out to dinner before and she liked the idea.

'I took her out several times and then, in a month or so, my mother died and I was left all alone. That's when I started thinking about marrying Sheila. We'd been going together and while I knew she had other dates and nothing had been said, I still felt I was the one she liked. She used to say how mature I seemed alongside the other boys.

'Anyway, one thing led to another and we could see we were the people each of us wanted to spend our lives with. We didn't

36

wait the traditional year after my mother's death because it didn't seem sensible. We were married only a few months after, in the summer after Sheila's graduation from high school.

'I sold Mother's house and we started life together fresh and new in a house we bought at 36 Wellington Street in a new development. We lived quietly and happily, or as happily as we could without children, and that's the way things were for fifteen wonderful years. That's the way they were right up till the night I found her dead.' He paused and brushed a hand over his forehead. 'Since that time it's been a life of loneliness and hell, and I guess I don't have to tell you that.'

Fellows said nothing. He unbuttoned his pocket, took out his notebook and pencil and wrote briefly. Sellers watched and remarked, 'You aren't putting down much.'

Fellows didn't comment on that. He looked up and said, 'Anything of importance you've left out?'

'No, not that I know of.'

'As I recall the case, the prosecution made much of jealous rages you threw anytime anyone looked twice at your wife.'

'Oh, that.' He made a bitter face. 'That was the prosecution again, building the whole thing up out of all proportion. My wife was a beautiful woman and she attracted attention.

I didn't like it when men got too damned attentive.' His voice came up angrily again. 'That's where my lawyer was supposed to help me. He should have interrogated those witnesses and got the whole thing put into perspective. That was the only thing the prosecution had to build a case on. That was the only motive they could dream up for me to kill my wife—because other men got out of line sometimes! The prosecution made hay on that and my lawyer let them. Can you imagine a jury convicting a man of killing his wife because she was so beautiful she attracted other men? Yet that's the motive the prosecution put across and my damned lawyer let them get away with it!'

Fellows said quietly, 'Did your wife encourage these attentions?'

'No she did not!'

'Then why did you get upset?'

'Because a man doesn't let other men make passes at his wife. That's why.'

Fellows made more notes and switched subjects. 'Now I'd like you to tell me what happened on the murder night. Tell me everything.'

Sellers rubbed his neck. 'All right,' he said, getting himself under control. 'Let's see, it was a Thursday night in October three years ago. The twentieth, it was. You see, I'm a chess player. Maybe I don't look like one, but I like the game and I belonged to this club in

Banksville. We had a room in the Good Fellows Club where we met once a week on Thursday nights. Some people like bowling, I happen to like chess. Good mental exercise.

'So on this particular Thursday I got through work at the shop at five o'clock, same as usual. I came home about five thirty and Sheila and I gabbed about what we'd done that day like we always did. Then I read the paper and she got the supper.

'We sat down to eat about quarter of seven, which was the usual time, and finished around quarter after or a little later. She cleaned up and I got ready to leave and I asked Sheila what her plans were for the evening and she said she thought she'd take a bath and go to bed. Sheila liked to read in bed. She often went to bed early to read while I stayed in the living room and worked a chess problem or played out a game or something because I couldn't sleep well with the light on and if she wanted to read in bed she read before I came in.

'So this night that's what she decided she'd do. As for me, I went out and got the seven-forty bus downtown to the chess club. We didn't have a car because we never went anywhere and there was a bus right at the corner.

'I got there around eight, and while we're on the chess club, if I'd done what they say, how could I have possibly gone to that

39

meeting? It would have stuck out all over me that I'd done something. But I went there and I was perfectly normal because I hadn't done *anything*! Sheila was still alive!' His voice was up with emotion again.

'All right,' Fellows said soothingly. 'That doesn't help any. Just tell me what happened.'

Sellers got himself back under control. 'Where was I?' he said, breathing heavily for a moment or two. 'Oh, yes, the chess club. All right. I got there around eight. So I played three or four games until eleven—somewhere around there, and then came home again. I got home about half past eleven and I found what happened was I forgot my keys. There I was at the front door and the door was locked and I couldn't get in. The lights were on in the living room but you couldn't see in because we always kept the shades drawn at night. Of course Sheila always left a light for me but there was more than one light on this time. The lamp near the window was on besides the table lamp Sheila would leave on. I didn't think anything about it at the time except I probably thought Sheila hadn't gone to bed but was reading in the living room. I don't know what I thought except I thought Sheila was still up and maybe it was the extra lights made me think so.

'Anyway, I didn't have my keys so I rang

40

the doorbell. I rang it two or three times but nothing happened. Sheila didn't come to let me in. So I guess then I thought she was asleep and didn't hear. Then I went around to the back door but that was locked too. Sheila—well it wasn't that there were any burglars in the neighborhood or anything like that, but Sheila always locked up the house when I was out. Other times, when I was home, we wouldn't lock the doors till we went to bed. But anyway, there I was, locked out of the house with Sheila not answering either door.

'I didn't know quite what to do. I thought of maybe going to a phone and calling her up but if she didn't hear the doorbell she might not hear the phone either. So I thought the best chance would be to try getting in a window.

'Well, there were lights on in the house next door. This was the Baxters. So I went over and rang their back doorbell and told them about being locked out and did they have a stepladder or something I could get in a window with. They said sure, of course, and they told their son, Mike, who was in high school but was still up, to help me. He brought a stepladder over and his folks came out to see if he could get in and he found the kitchen window was open and he went through that. He turned the light on in there and I went to the back door expecting him to come around and let me in.

'But he didn't come and the next thing I know he's back at the kitchen window and he's scared to death and shaking and he can hardly talk. He said something like, "My God, my God, it's terrible." Right away I wanted to know *what* was terrible and his folks asked what was the trouble and he said, "She's dead. Mrs. Sellers is dead!" He could hardly talk.

'I thought he must be kidding. I couldn't believe what he was saying. I thought he must have seen her sleeping or something. I said, "Where? What are you talking about?" or something and he said she was in the living room and there was blood.

'I just about went out of my mind, Mr. Fellows. I went just about stark staring crazy. The Baxters, they were stunned and the boy looked ready to faint. I said, "Let me in, let me in," and finally he came around to the back door and opened it and I rushed right through the house to the living room.'

He swallowed. 'She was dead all right. The boy knew it and Mr. and Mrs. Baxter, who followed me, they knew it the minute they looked at her. I guess I knew it too, except I couldn't believe it. She was lying in a pool of blood and her head was smashed and she wasn't wearing anything except a robe. You wouldn't hardly have known who it was from all the blood and what had been done to her head but it was Sheila because I'd been married to her for fifteen years and if I saw nothing more than her little toe I'd know it was hers.

'After that everything is all kind of jumbled. I hollered something about get a doctor, I guess, and I went to her. I don't know if I thought I could give her artificial respiration or what but I wanted to do something to keep her from being dead. I don't know where the Baxters went, or the boy, except I didn't see Michael again. I guess Mr. Baxter called the police from my phone and somehow Mrs. Baxter was around and they were trying to say, "Don't get excited," or something about help being on the way and all I remember was kneeling beside her and not knowing what to do for her and saying things like "call a doctor, call a doctor."

'Then there were a lot of people around, policemen and detectives and doctors with stretchers. One detective asked me questions about what happened as if I should know what happened. There was a lot of questions but there wasn't nothing I could tell them.'

Fellows interrupted. 'Did they ask about any enemies she might have?'

'I guess they did, but that was ridiculous. She wouldn't have any enemies.'

'No enemies? And there was nothing taken from the house?'

'Nothing that I know about. The detectives had me look all through the house, but I couldn't find anything missing.'

'All right, then what?'

'The Baxters wanted me to stay overnight with them but I wouldn't do it. I was staying right in my own house. They wouldn't let me go with Sheila to the hospital or wherever it was they were taking her. They told me I had to stay home. The doctors, they wanted to give me an injection or pills or something and I took the pills they gave me so they wouldn't argue about it but I didn't swallow any.

'Then it was the next day and I didn't go to work. I hung around the house waiting for something to happen, waiting for the police to come and tell me who killed Sheila.

'In the afternoon two detectives came to the house and asked me more questions only these were about me and Sheila, how we got along, how long we'd been married and all kinds of things like that. I asked about who killed her and they said they were still trying to find out.

'The next day they came back to find out what I wanted to do about the funeral and we went through all that. She was buried on Monday and she had a nice service in the church but nobody was allowed to see the body.

'I went to work on Tuesday and when I came home those detectives were waiting again and they asked me some more questions and then on Thursday they came for me at work and brought me down to the County Seat—down to the courthouse in Pittsfield—and the prosecuting attorney there told me I was going to be held and tried for murder and I should get an attorney. I didn't know anything about attorneys and I didn't have any money so they said the court would appoint one for me if I'd rather.

'They appointed this Leonard Mills and he's the one who represented me. He's still supposed to be representing me but all he's ever got me is stuck in the death house for two years and all my appeals turned down. A kid in law school couldn't have done any worse for me than that.'

Sellers sighed and gestured a conclusion. 'So that's it, Chief. Somebody killed Sheila and I don't know who. I don't know anything except they're going to electrocute me and I didn't do anything. Now do you see why I need help?'

CHAPTER SIX

Fellows sat in silence for a moment and rubbed his chin reflectively. 'No enemies,' he said slowly. 'You're still sure that Sheila had no enemies?'

'Of course. How could she have enemies? We lived a quiet life.'

'You didn't have any friends?'

'We knew some people. We didn't have any close friends.' He glowered in sudden anger. 'That's the hell of it. We should've got around more. That's the thing the prosecution made so much of at the trial. They tried to claim we weren't happy together and, because Sheila and me didn't get out a lot, we couldn't prove we had been.'

'Seems to me,' Fellows said, 'it would have been up to the prosecution to prove that you hadn't been. However, that's not the point right now. You're certain Sheila had no enemies, nobody who hated her?'

Sellers spread his hands. 'Well, how can anybody be sure of something like that? I mean maybe some clerk in a store didn't like it because she looked at him crosseyed once or something.'

'But she never mentioned having trouble with anybody?'

'No.'

'Nobody made passes at her?'

'She wouldn't let anybody do that.'

'People did, though. You got violently angry on several occasions.'

'Well, yes, but that's because Sheila was a beautiful woman. Of course men tried to get fresh with her, but they didn't get very far.'

'You know for a fact that they didn't?'

'She would have told me if they had and, believe me, I would've fixed their wagons.'

'Might that have made her afraid to tell you?'

'Well, hell—' He paused. 'You think it might have?'

'I'm asking you.'

'Well, hell, if somebody'd got fresh with her, she'd want me to do something about it, wouldn't she?'

'I suppose so—if she objected.'

'Why wouldn't she object?'

Fellows said carefully, 'Let's try it another way. Was your wife faithful?'

Sellers didn't hesitate over that. 'Of course she was. Why?'

'You know this?'

'Well—' He stopped again. 'You keep asking these damned questions. I suppose she was. I always thought she was.'

'But she could have been unfaithful without you knowing about it?'

Sellers shrugged. 'I suppose she could. But she wouldn't have had any reason. We were happy.'

'Did she enjoy this quiet life you led?'

'Certainly. Why wouldn't she?'

'She was a lot younger than you. Young people like to get out and kick up their heels, especially when there're no children to tend.'

'She wasn't that type. She liked our snug little home.'

47

'The prosecution sought to show that you and she weren't happy, that you had a motive for killing her? What was the motive?'

'Jealousy.' He leaned forward and went on heatedly, 'They kept saying I killed her because I thought she was carrying on with men and that's ridiculous. She wasn't.'

'They produced no evidence that she was?'

'Not one bit! That's what was so wrong about the trial. They couldn't produce any evidence she was carrying on but they go and tell the jury I killed her because I *thought* she was carrying on! Now what kind of a case do you call that?'

Fellows scribbled another note or two. 'What about the fact that she was found in the living room clad only in a robe?'

'Well, what about it?'

'What's your explanation of it?'

'She was taking a bath. The coroner's report came out that she was killed between seven o'clock and eight-thirty. Well, I left at seven-thirty and she was very much alive then. In fact, she was getting ready to take a bath, like I told you. You take the mid-point between seven and eight-thirty and you get quarter of eight. Figure at quarter of eight somebody rings the doorbell. She's either in the bath or getting ready for it. In either case she's got no clothes on. So what would you expect her to do but put on a robe to answer the door. Whoever was at the door is the one who killed her. Maybe he was some admirer and when he made advances she resisted and he went off his nut. Then, after he saw what he'd done, he got scared and ran. That's the way I figure it.'

'Would she be likely to answer the doorbell with nothing on but a robe?'

Sellers waved an uncertain hand. 'Well, hell, I wouldn't know. I suppose so. Why not? It was a regular robe. She wouldn't've been showing anything.'

'Any idea who might have been ringing your doorbell at that hour of night?'

'Nobody, except some unknown admirer like I said.'

'Was your porch light on?'

Sellers nodded. 'We kept it on for when I came home.'

'And a woman alone in a house, especially one with nothing on but a robe, would look out to see who was at the door before she opened it, wouldn't she?'

'I suppose so.'

'So whoever she let in would have to be somebody she knew—and trusted?'

'I suppose so.'

'Or perhaps somebody she was expecting?'

'She would've told me if she was expecting somebody to drop in.'

'Even if it were a man?'

Sellers wet his lips. 'I suppose not in that case,' he said reluctantly. He peered at

49

Fellows. 'Is that what you think—that she was carrying on behind my back?'

'I'm just wondering if it's possible. I gather it is.'

'Yeah, except that I wouldn't believe it. Not when we've been married fifteen years.'

'It's one possibility,' Fellows said. 'Now what about you? Tell me about your enemies.'

'My enemies?' Sellers widened his eyes in surprise.

'You're the patsy in the case, aren't you? Isn't it possible someone deliberately framed you?'

Sellers said in some wonder, 'Well I'll be damned. Now that's one angle that dumb lawyer of mine never came up with. The love affair business, of course, everybody thought of. The detectives questioned me about that right away. But nobody asked me about something like that. Not directly, like that.'

'How about answering it, then. Is there anybody who would profit by your dying, or who'd like to see it happen? Better yet, is there anybody who'd like to see both of you dead?'

Sellers pondered but could think of no one. 'Damn it,' he said. 'That's a nice twist you've come up with. That's the subtle approach all right, but what's in it for anybody? My insurance policy is all cashed in, not that I had much to begin with. I sold the house after

50

I got sent up so I got some money from that but the nearest relative is my mother's sister and she's in a nursing home.'

Sellers was equally at a loss trying to think who would like to see him or both of them dead even if there were no profit to be gained. He got along well enough with the men in the shop and with his neighbors, he said, and those two groups formed his total circle of acquaintances. 'There isn't anybody I know well enough, really, to want something bad to happen to me.'

'Is there anybody you'd like to see something bad happen to?'

'Me?' He spread his hands. 'No. I like everybody. What made you think of that?'

'Somebody you didn't like might not like you.'

'Well, then, that's out. The only person I've got anything against is the one who killed Sheila and brought me to this fix and him I don't even know.'

'You think it's a him, though?'

'I guess it never occurred to me it wouldn't be. What would a woman want to kill Sheila for? I think it's got to be a man who had a yen for her that I didn't know anything about and she didn't either. If she did, she wouldn't have let him in.'

Fellows had about reached the end of his questions. He did, however, get from Sellers a list of everyone he knew, the names of all the neighbors, the people in the nearby stores, the men in the job shop. There were twelve people in the neighborhood whom Sellers could name, two in the stores, and twenty-one in the shop. Fellows folded his notebook and stood up. 'I can't promise anything, Mr. Sellers,' he said. 'I'll take a look around and see what I can find. That's the best I can do.'

Sellers came to his feet and shook hands. 'That's all I can ask, Chief. All I know is there's got to be somebody somewhere and the way you've already come up with an angle nobody else thought of makes me think you'll find him.'

Fellows called out for McCarthy and turned. 'Don't hope for too much, Mr. Sellers. Remember, it's a cold trail.'

It was like telling a starving man not to eat. 'You'll do it,' Sellers said with new strength in his voice. 'I've got my fingers crossed on that. But don't forget, it's got to be done before the eighth of August. That's the day they pull the switch.'

CHAPTER SEVEN

Fellows stopped in at the warden's office to pay his respects to Curry but he turned down the luncheon invitation. As Sellers had

52

pointed out, there wasn't much time and even a luncheon could be costly when there was an unknown amount of work to do.

He did, however, stay long enough at the prison to make a phone call. Leonard Mills, defending attorney in THE STATE OF CONNECTICUT VS. ERNEST SELLERS, headed the list of those to see and the call was to make an appointment.

Leonard Mills, a corporation lawyer in the firm of Blakesley, Blakesley, Mills & Young, had offices on Bittner Avenue in Pittsfield and he told the chief he could see him at two o'clock. Fellows, driving directly to Pittsfield from Midland Prison, arrived in town far enough ahead of time to grab a hamburger and milkshake at a luncheonette nearby and he was up in Mills' waiting room fifteen minutes early.

Mills was still out for lunch according to his secretary and Fellows thumbed through the waiting room magazines till the lawyer strode through the door promptly on the dot. Mills was a big, gray-haired man with a pink face and prosperous clothes. 'Fellows?' he said as the chief rose from his cushioned seat. 'Nice to meet you.' He shook hands. 'Go on into the office. I'll be with you in a moment. I have to run through a couple of things with my secretary.'

Fellows entered the private room and looked around. The furnishings were elegant

53

and the walls were panels interspaced with loaded bookcases. The door behind him opened and Mills came through, strode around behind his desk and sat down with his back to the window. 'Help yourself to cigars. Would you like a drink?'

Fellows refused both offers and waited while Mills read a note on his desk and tucked it away. Mills smiled benignly, tilted back his chair and pressed his fingertips together. 'You said this was about Ernest Sellers, I believe. What about poor Ernest?'

'That's what I've come to ask you. What do you think he is, innocent or guilty?'

'Oh, I think he's innocent. After all, I defended him.'

'You were appointed to defend him.'

'Of course. Defending clients for nothing is something all of us lawyers have to take our turn at. It's our contribution to society, you might say.'

Fellows frowned. 'Do you believe he's innocent because you're supposed to or because you're convinced?'

Mills frowned too. 'You're not making much sense, Chief. I don't believe anybody's innocent or guilty because I'm *supposed* to.'

'Maybe I didn't express myself. I'm wondering what your personal conviction is in this case.'

'My personal conviction is that he's innocent. If I'd thought he was guilty, I'd have handled the case differently. I'd have concentrated on mitigating circumstances, on possible insanity, that sort of thing. Since I believed him innocent the defense was on the grounds that he hadn't done the deed at all.'

'The jury found him guilty, though.'

'Juries and I have disagreed both before his case and since. That doesn't make them right, you know.'

'You think they were wrong here?'

'Yes, I do. I don't think there was any case against my client in the first place. The prosecution had no business even bringing it up for trial.' He waved both hands in an expression of helplessness. 'But that goes to show you about juries. You get a case you should win hands down and they vote against you. Another time you think you've got no chance at all and they go and find for you.'

'But in the Sellers case you think they made a mistake?'

'I do. I most certainly do. But it's not the first time and it probably won't be the last.'

'Except,' persisted Fellows, 'on this particular occasion when the jury made what you regard as a mistake it was a man's life they were playing with.'

'It's not the first time that's happened either, you know. You seem kind of naive to me, Chief. Stockford you're from? Pretty hick town, I imagine.'

'Yeah,' Fellows said. 'It's a pretty hick

town. We get a little bit concerned down there about the idea of justice going wrong. Especially when a man's life is at stake.'

Mills lifted his chin. 'I don't think I care for the implication, Mr. Fellows. I'm concerned too. What do you think I've been doing for the past two years? Why do you think Ernest Sellers is still alive? Because I've kept him alive, that's why. I've used every tactic in the book. I've appealed everything I could appeal on all the grounds I could appeal on. Right now I've got an appeal for clemency on the Governor's desk. I'm asking him to commute the sentence to life imprisonment, using all the arguments against capital punishment I can rustle up, plus all the data I could produce to show there's question of Sellers' guilt, plus even the teary refrain from Abraham Lincoln about how it's better to let twenty guilty men go free than punish one innocent man. So don't suggest I'm not doing everything I can for my client.'

Fellows said, 'All right, Mr. Mills. I didn't mean to imply you weren't. But what good would a commutation do if the guy's innocent? He'd still be in jail for life.'

'Not for life—only till parole time came by. It's next to impossible to keep a man in jail for life. Look at the Leopold-Loeb case. Life plus ninety-nine years only came out to a total of thirty years. Sellers would do much better than that—fifteen at the most.'

56

'Fifteen years is a long time for an innocent man.'

'It's better than the chair, isn't it?'

'I don't know. I'm not too sure that it is.'

Mills leaned forward on the desk. 'Now look, Fellows. It's not going to do any good being a bleeding heart about all this. Innocent men go to jail. Innocent men get hung, gassed, electrocuted, shot or guillotined, depending on where you are. It's one of the facts of life. All right, you accept it, just the way I accept losing a case because the jury doesn't like my tie or my face or the way Ernest Sellers combed his hair or whatever it was that made them vote the death sentence for him. All right, it's water under the bridge. Unless the Governor moves to save him, Ernest will die on August eighth. When he does, I'll be sorry but at least I'll know I did everything I could for him. It just wasn't in the cards, that's all. If the law made a mistake, you don't condemn the law. Mistakes happen and if you're a lawyer you know this and accept it. So you put it out of your mind and go on to the next job.' He sat back and regarded the chief critically. 'I can tell you, Fellows, you'd make one hell of a lawyer. You'd take everything personally. Which brings up the question, what's your personal interest in this case?'

'I'm not sure he's guilty myself.'

'See?' Mills said as if the chief had just

proved a point. 'That's what I mean. It's not even your case but here you are worrying about it. You'd be one hell of a lawyer. You wouldn't give your next client a fair shake because you'd still be worrying about the last one. Forget it, will you? That's what you have to do. Look at it this way. Maybe we're wrong and the jury's right. You ever think of that?'

Fellows said, 'Of course I've thought about it. It's the 'maybe' that bothers me.'

Mills waved his hands to dismiss the statement. 'Well there's nothing that can be done about it in any event, so what's the point in being bothered? What you can't do anything about you might as well put out of your mind.'

'Put it out of your mind, sure—unless something *can* be done about it.'

Mills eyed the chief critically. He sat forward again. 'If you're thinking of going to the Governor yourself, I wouldn't advise it. My appeal says all there is to say and the Governor wouldn't like being pestered. You'd only make things worse.'

Fellows said, 'I was thinking of another way of saving him.'

'There isn't any other. What do you mean?'

'How about new evidence?'

'New evidence?' Mills burst out laughing. 'Pardon me, Chief, but you really are naive. Nearly three years after the fact and you

58

think you're going to turn up new evidence? What kind of new evidence do you think you'll find?'

'If Sellers didn't kill his wife, somebody else did.'

'Oh. You mean the *real* murderer? That's expecting quite a lot, don't you think, considering the fact the police couldn't find even another suspect at the time that it happened?'

'How hard did the police look?'

'You'd know the answer better than I. You're a policeman.' Mills slapped his hand down on the desk. 'Now look, Fellows, I don't know what kind of ideas you've got about this case, but I can tell you they're all wrong. You think the police picked the handy man and nailed him for the crime rather than do a little digging? You think the State's Attorney prosecuted the case believing Sellers was a fall-guy? You think I sat back on my hands and did nothing to defend my client except shout, "you haven't proved a thing" at Jack Heligman? You're wrong on every count. You can take my word for that!'

Fellows remained undaunted. 'If somebody other than Sellers murdered Sheila, that somebody exists, doesn't he? Just because nobody's found him doesn't make him disappear.'

Mills said bitterly, 'Maybe he exists. I tried to make him exist for the jury but they wouldn't buy it.'

'If he exists, there has to be a connection between him and the woman.'

'Does there? If you think that, then go right ahead and try to find one. You'll only be going over ground the police and I—and the State's Attorney—went over way back three years ago. If you want to make the effort, go right ahead but I can save you the time by telling you what we found. Nothing. We found absolutely nothing.'

'But you still think Sellers is innocent?'

'Didn't I say I did? Look. You want to know what I really think happened the night of October twentieth? I think Ernest Sellers went off to his stupid chess club meeting at half past seven and his wife got undressed to take a bath. I think that somebody came to the door—a man with lust in his heart. I think it was somebody who knew Sellers played chess Thursday nights. I think he was probably loitering around the neighborhood watching for Sellers to leave. I think he might have waited just long enough to see Sellers onto the bus and then he hurried to the front door and rang the bell.

'I think Mrs. Sellers put on a robe and went to the door. I think she either took it for granted it was some woman neighbor wanting to borrow a cup of sugar or collect for the Community Fund or something—the Fund drive was on that week in case you didn't know it—and she opened the door—'

'Had the Sellers been solicited before the date for a contribution?' Fellows interrupted.

'No, they had not. But you can forget about that angle. No money for a contribution was found and there was no check made out or anything like that. It's something that I think might have happened but it's something for which there's not one shred of evidence whatsoever.' He went on, 'So she opened the door expecting someone else and got this guy with the yen for her instead.

'The other way of looking at it is that she *did* look out to see who was there and recognized the man and opened the door to him thinking he was harmless. That would make him somebody like a delivery boy or a clerk in a store where she shopped.'

'Or the boy next door?' put in Fellows.

'You mean Mike Baxter? Yeah, him too, except he was doing his homework.'

'And all these people were investigated?'

'They were and they were all cleared, every last one of them. We couldn't find a man in all her acquaintances who *might have*, let alone would have come to her house. I'm afraid that part is out. So what was I left with? I think it was a stranger, maybe some crackpot who'd seen her on the street and followed her and found where she lived. Maybe it was even more freakish than that

61

and just a stroke of chance that a certain type of guy rang a doorbell for some reason we'll never know—maybe to ask directions or to use the phone to get a flat fixed—and happened to get the doorbell answered by a very lovely, well-built lady wearing nothing but a robe. He goes berserk, kills her and flees and is never seen again.

'Now,' he said, 'that's the kind of thing that *can* happen. It's possible—only barely so, but possible. But when I try to pull that as the alternative to Sellers killing her himself, you can imagine how far I got. How do you explain her answering the door and letting in a stranger when a robe is all she's got on? Sure, maybe she *did* think it was a woman from the Community Fund, or maybe some friend had called her up with plans to drop over that evening and she opened the door thinking of course that's who it is. That might have done it if we could've found somebody in the Community Fund who was going to call on her that night, or some woman who had planned to drop in. Or, for that matter, anybody at all who'd had any contact with her that day.

'We might even have got away with the stranger at the door deal if some other woman somewhere around had got killed the same way—like the Boston strangler thing. But no other woman had been attacked, just this one.

'So you can guess what the prosecution did

with that "mysterious stranger" angle. That's so old a dodge it has whiskers.' He leaned forward. 'So, Mr. Chief of Police, if you think you're going to dig up something the rest of us have overlooked, you go right ahead and dig and good luck to you.'

Fellows said ruefully, 'It doesn't sound too hopeful, I'll admit. What about the lover angle?'

Mills grinned. 'You mean it's not a stranger at the door, it's the boyfriend and that naked-but-for-a-robe business was her costume for the party? You think we never thought of that? That's the first thing the police did think of. What do you think they are, a bunch of nitwits? She wasn't lying so near the door when she was found that it had to be she let somebody in who slugged her as he stepped through. She was lying five feet away and from the position of the blows and the fact there were no signs of a struggle it looked like whoever did it was already in the house with her and wasn't somebody she was fighting off. So, in that garb, what do you think was the first thing the cops thought of? They thought of the lover deal even before they thought of the husband. It was only because they couldn't find even a smell of a lover that they turned the spotlight *on* the husband. They figured it had to be one or the other.'

'But you don't?'

Mills spread his hands. 'It might be a lover, if we could find a lover. It might be the sex maniac telling her he's got a telegram—that "mysterious stranger" everybody likes to pass the buck to. It might be Sellers himself. He's the only one you could prove opportunity for and the only one who might have had a motive. Just because I happen to think he's innocent doesn't mean much. It's a minority opinion held by him and me—and now, apparently, by you.'

'What about a woman for the job?'

'Sure. That's as good a bet as any. Find one with motive and opportunity and I'll push it. Find anybody with motive and opportunity and we can get Sellers out of the death house and back to the courthouse for a new trial. Anything else you want to know?'

'You said the prosecutor was a Jack Heligman? Is he still around?'

'He's probably in court but I'll have my secretary ring his office if you want to see him.'

'I'd appreciate that.'

'Sure.' Mills depressed the intercom button and gave the message. He sat back and said, 'But if you think you're going to get any encouragement out of him you'd better think again.'

CHAPTER EIGHT

State's Attorney John J. Heligman was in court, Fellows learned, but was due back in his office fairly soon. Since the office was also in the courthouse, the chief went over and sat in on the last few minutes of the case being tried. Heligman, representing the State of Connecticut, was arguing a criminal case on a grand larceny charge.

It was the tail end of things and before Fellows was comfortably seated the matter was over. Heligman, a dark-haired brisk man in his late thirties, stuffed his papers in a briefcase amidst a cluster of people and came up the aisle with two hangers-on still with him. Fellows went out to the vestibule and caught him at the staircase as he parted from his entourage. 'Got a minute, Mr. Heligman?'

Heligman turned and took in his uniform. 'Police? Not from around here.'

'Stockford. Chief of Police there. Fellows is the name.'

Heligman smiled. 'You didn't have to tell me. Stockford was enough. You don't really think we haven't heard of you in this town, do you, especially after the Partridge kidnapping? Come on upstairs.'

Heligman moved up at a brisk clip for he was vigorous and didn't pack the chief's weight. He turned in at the first door on the second floor and said to his secretary, 'Meet Chief of Police Fred Fellows, Vivian. That ought to make your day.'

The secretary looked up and smiled. 'Don't mind him, Chief,' she said. 'But it's true. You're quite a celebrity around here.'

Fellows said, 'At least he's trying to make me feel like one,' and followed the younger man into a fair-sized, ugly office with the cream-colored walls, varnished woodwork, and tall windows that go with old county buildings. Heligman threw his briefcase on a battered desk, slumped into his swivel chair and clumped his feet onto the desk top. 'Just sit anywhere, Chief,' he said. 'Make yourself at home. What have you got, another murder down in Stockford?'

Fellows made himself at home. He sat down in a worn leather chair and took out his chewing tobacco. 'No,' he said. 'This one took place in Banksville.'

'Banksville? Another one? When? I haven't heard about it.'

'Not another one. The same one.'

'Sheila Sellers? That who you mean?'

'Sheila Sellers. You remember the case?'

Heligman clasped his hands back of his head. 'Sure I do. It's still my biggest and best. I'll remember that one on my deathbed. Her husband did her in with a still undiscovered blunt instrument on the basis of

66

an all-consuming jealousy and the conviction he could get away with it.'

'You sound pretty sure of yourself.'

'I am.' Heligman cocked his head. 'Why? Are you doubting me?'

'I'm curious about the case.'

'What for? That's a long way from your stamping grounds.'

'I was invited to get curious,' Fellows said. He went on to tell about the letter he'd received and the details of his talk with Sellers. Heligman took his feet down from the desk to listen and one corner of his mouth twisted. 'You're not buying his story are you?'

'Not yet I'm not. I don't know that much about it. I'm trying to find out.'

'Well you won't find out listening to him. He'll lie you to death. Like that bit about us railroading him on a motive of jealousy. We didn't even produce a motive in court. We only showed the jury what the guy was and what kind of a marriage it was and let them pick their own motive. Jealousy is only what I *believe* the motive to be and, judging from the way his mind worked talking to you, jealousy is what he *knows* it to be. Forget it. Sellers is looking for a shoulder to cry on. He knows you've got a soft heart, Chief. Don't waste your time or your pity on him.'

'He doesn't want to cry, he wants out, Mr. Heligman.'

'They all do. And what's more, they've all been robbed and cheated. To hear the people behind bars talk, our courts are wrong one hundred percent of the time. They never convict guilty people, only innocent ones.'

'I know that. What I don't know is what the story is in his case.'

'I can tell you that in one word. "Guilty".'

'His lawyer thinks differently.'

'His lawyer didn't do any kind of a job impressing his convictions in the matter on the jury.' Heligman tilted back his wooden swivel chair and propped his feet on the desk again. 'Let me ask you, Chief. Do you think a jury would recommend the death sentence for any man unless they were convinced, not only beyond a reasonable doubt, but beyond any doubt whatsoever that the man was guilty? And do you think that sentence would stand up in the face of all the appeals Leonard Mills has filed? Don't you think some judge, somewhere, would have some doubts about the justice of the verdict if there were doubts to be had and would set the verdict aside? I put that to you, Chief, and what do you say?'

'It's convincing, I have to admit.'

'You're damned right it's convincing.' Heligman twisted and reached for the cord to adjust the windowshade. 'Don't let Sellers snow you,' he said, turning back. 'Let me tell you a few things about the case that he conveniently overlooked when he saw you,

68

O.K.? In the first place, there's the little matter of the time element. The autopsy revealed that Sheila Sellers died between seven and eight-thirty in the evening. Those are the absolute outside limits. It couldn't have been one minute earlier than seven nor one minute later than eight-thirty. Now the way that time period was arrived at was through various things, temperature of the body, rigor mortis, stomach analysis, you know. Witnesses can lie but these things don't.

'O.K., now according to the stomach analysis, Sheila Sellers died about an hour after eating. If we only knew when she ate her supper, we'd be all set. Unfortunately, the only living person who can tell us is Ernest Sellers himself and he says they ate around quarter of seven.

'Now, of course, if this is true, then he's completely in the clear. But suppose—just suppose for a minute, that Mr. Sellers and his wife follow the custom that is more general among people in their particular status. The guy comes home from work. There's no cocktail hour or anything like that. He's tired and he's hungry and he wants his meal. Place him coming in the door at half past five and sitting down to eat at quarter of six instead of quarter of seven and now where are you? Give her half an hour to eat and an hour to digest and you have her being killed at quarter past

69

seven, at a time when her supposedly ever-loving husband is getting ready to go to his chess match.'

Fellows laughed. 'Now there's circumstantial evidence if I ever heard any.'

Heligman took his feet down and sat forward, picking up a pencil and pointing. 'Circumstantial? Sure it's circumstantial. Inasmuch as most murders aren't committed in front of eye-witnesses, all the evidence in a murder case is going to be circumstantial. But you haven't let me finish. The stomach analysis said an hour after eating but that doesn't pinpoint anything if we don't know when she ate. That seven to eight-thirty maximum time limit was arrived at by other means too, you know. And those times are the absolute outside. You can be sure she was killed well within those limits, well after seven and well before eight-thirty. You know what the experts testified to as their best estimate for the time of the killing? Half past seven—give it five minutes either way. And that leaves you with only Ernest Sellers as the murderer.'

Fellows shrugged. 'Very convincing, Mr. Heligman, but I'm sure you didn't build your case on that. That kind of testimony doesn't mean a thing.'

'No,' Heligman said, shaking his head. 'I didn't build my case on that. That was just another strand in the rope around Sellers' neck, just that added touch that helped get a maximum conviction. I built the case around the solid stuff, the business about the locked house, for example.' Heligman gave a fire-eating grin. 'I love it when they pull something like that. They think they're so clever and it's just like an open confession.'

'What about the locked house?'

'He forgot his keys. All the other times in his life that he's gone to the chess club he's been able to get into the house when he's come home. But on the one night when his wife is murdered, that night of all the nights in his life, he forgets his keys. As a result, he goes next door for help and the boy there gets a stepladder and goes in through the window. How happy this is for Sellers. He doesn't have to say to a curious crowd "Look what I found!" He doesn't want to do it that way, naturally, because the first thought that would go through everybody's mind would be, "Did you *find* it or *do* it?" He doesn't want anybody having thoughts like that in their head when that body's discovered so he conveniently arranges for someone else to do the discovering.'

'And, of course, there's the kid's parents right there handy too so, when he sees his wife's dead body lying on the living room floor, he can throw his fit of grief with an audience to watch. He equips himself with three witnesses to testify how hard he took her death.' Heligman waved a hand. 'He did a good job on that. Clever boy, Sellers. I shook Mr. and Mrs. Baxter on the stand on the genuineness of that grief and made them concede it could have been faked, but I couldn't shake the boy. Mike was really sold on it. Sellers did a good bit of acting there.' Heligman grinned again. 'He knew he could, of course, or he would have worked it another way.'

Fellows leaned back against the cushions and regarded Heligman through narrowed lids. 'I see you don't believe in coincidence.'

'Coincidence?' Heligman looked sharply at the chief and then laughed with thorough enjoyment. 'Sure, Chief. Sure I believe in coincidence but there's a limit to the extent of my imagination. Just one time in his life Sellers forgets the keys and that's the one time his wife gets murdered? The one time somebody else has to go into the house for him is the one time there's a body to be found? Come on Chief, that one's so obvious even the jury could see through it. Don't tell me you don't.'

'How do you know it's the only time he forgot his keys?' Fellows asked. 'He might have forgotten them every other week only he didn't have to bother the neighbors about it because Sheila was there to let him in.'

'You think he forgot them every other week, Chief? You really think so?'

'I'm mentioning the possibilities.'

Heligman sat back. 'Then let's consider that possibility. His wife locks up the house when he's out. That's her custom and that claim is in his own testimony. But how come she fails to lock the kitchen window? The house was checked by the police, you know. Every window was locked but that one.' Heligman shook his head. 'That guy Sellers was so dumb or so cheap he didn't even set up a situation where he'd have to break the glass. He made it a snap for young Mike to enter the house. He only made it tough for himself to get in.'

Fellows, still reclining, said, 'You still haven't shown me that Sellers couldn't have habitually forgotten his keys.'

'I can't prove he didn't habitually forget them,' Heligman said with a touch of sharpness in his voice, 'but let's put it this way. How often do you forget yours?'

'Is that what you asked the jury?'

'Yes, and I'm asking you. How often do you forget your keys?'

'I'm not Sellers,' the chief reminded him.

'No, you're not, but you're certainly bucking for him. What makes you think he's innocent?'

'Seems to me,' Fellows said, 'that it would be quite a feat for a man to murder his wife and then go out and face the members of his chess club, all of whom knew him well, and

73

behave as if nothing had happened.'

Heligman's eyes grew sharp. 'Is that what he told you? That he acted as if nothing had happened?'

'That's what he says. I suppose members of the club testified?'

'You bet they did.'

'And they said he acted normal?'

'They did. The guy's an actor, let's face it. A guy who could put on a display of grief in front of the Baxters could put on a "normal" act in front of the chess club.'

'A man who wasn't an actor and who hadn't killed his wife could have done the same thing.'

Heligman grinned with a certain fiendish glee. 'I said actor, Chief. Sellers was very clever. He pulled that bit off neatly. Four members of the club came in and testified he behaved normally. Mills thought he had a good point for his client there until I got up for cross-examination. You know what the cross-examination uncovered? Ernest Sellers was one of the top players in the club. So that night he played three games, all against members he consistently beats. And what happened on that particular night? He lost all three games. It was, to quote the testimony, "most unusual". In fact, not in the memory of any member of the club had it ever happened before. And chess, mind you, is not a game of luck. It's one hundred percent

74

skill. I think you'll have to agree, Chief, that his mind wasn't on the game that evening. When he looked at the board during those three games he lost, he wasn't seeing chessmen, he was seeing his wife's body.' Heligman rubbed his hands in pleasure at the recollection. 'I got a lot of mileage out of those three lost games of chess, Chief. I can tell you I did. He didn't just lose, he played badly. In fact, for my own interest I got copies of those games and compared them with others he'd played and there's no doubt about it in my mind. He was *way* off. Never mind how he acted on the outside, those chess games showed what was going on inside. It was as plain as a fever chart or a polygraph. If I'd any doubts in my mind at all, playing out his games removed them.'

Fellows was silent and Heligman waited a bit watching. The prosecutor said, 'What are you thinking? Are you still convinced an innocent man is sitting up there in Death Row?'

'I'm thinking,' Fellows said, moving his eyes to Heligman's face, 'that the prosecution had a very sharp attorney going for the State.'

'Thanks. I'm not going to pretend it was an easy case to get a conviction on. Frankly I had my doubts.'

'I'm also thinking that the prosecuting attorney had it all over the defense attorney.'

Heligman gestured. 'Mills did all right. He

didn't have anything to work with.'

Fellows struggled up to a sitting position once more. 'I'm not so sure he didn't,' he said. 'I'd feel happier about the verdict if I thought he'd given the effort you did.'

'He did his best.'

Fellows got to his feet 'Yes, and I think his best is a good bit below yours. Where would I find the trial record?'

'Room thirteen on the first floor. You going to look it over?'

Fellows nodded. 'Today I've heard three different versions of what went on and three interpretations of the trial. I think it might help me to go to the source.'

Heligman tipped his chair back and put his feet on the desk once more. 'More power to you, Chief. I'll tell you, though, if that doesn't convince you Sellers killed his wife, nothing will.'

CHAPTER NINE

Detective Sergeant Wilks was in the cellar of his home Tuesday night working on his model trains when Chief Fellows clumped down the stairs into the dust and cobwebs to join him. Wilks, poking through a tray of various-sized screws, said without looking up, 'Sounds like the Chief of Police himself, back from the dead. You know, this is the first Monday and Tuesday in history that you haven't poked your nose into headquarters at least once.'

'What do you do, keep records?' Fellows said, ducking under a hanging bulb.

'It was obvious from the high morale of the men these past two days. So now you've spent forty-eight hours on the Sellers case and you don't know where you stand, right?'

'Some detective,' Fellows growled.

'Nothing to it,' Wilks said, peering at the tray and bending closer. 'When you come down those stairs like an old man it means you're in trouble. Sellers got you puzzled?'

'I don't think so. Why don't you get a magnifying glass and a pair of tweezers for those screws?'

'My eyes aren't that bad yet.' Wilks examined one screw and tossed it back. 'So your mind's made up, huh? What is he, innocent or guilty?'

Fellows leaned against the worktable and gazed off at the cellar walls. 'Let's put it this way. I don't think the case was ever satisfactorily solved.'

Wilks straightened and stared at the chief with a twist to his mouth. 'What the hell does that mean? I ask you a simple question, "innocent or guilty?" and you give me a conundrum.'

'All right,' Fellows said, turning and

77

matching the twisted grin. 'I'll say "innocent" if it'll help your mind.'

Wilks turned and spit tobacco juice into a pail. 'Help my mind? You think it's going to help my mind to tell me an innocent man's sitting in Death Row waiting for the chair?'

'You wanted an answer, I gave you one. You want to know what I really think and I tell you I don't think the case was satisfactorily solved.'

Wilks abandoned screws and trains and hitched a hip on the edge of the table. 'Explain. Stop the suspense, will you?'

'That's what I came to do, and the answer isn't as simple as a mere innocent or guilty.' Fellows took his chewing tobacco from a pocket and bit off a piece. 'I talked to the guy yesterday morning and heard his side—'

'Innocent as the driven snow, no doubt.'

'Naturally, which means nothing by itself. So then I talked to his lawyer and to the guy who prosecuted.'

'And his lawyer said he was innocent and the prosecutor said he was guilty.'

Fellows shook his head. 'I don't know how you ever got to be so clever, Sid. It beats me.'

'I practise late at night. So two say innocent and one says guilty, only the opinions aren't exactly unprejudiced and now you're in a quandary. What next?'

'That's what I've got to figure out.'

'You mean that's what you want me to help

78

you figure out, don't you. You're not here to watch me play with my trains.'

'Have it your way.'

Wilks laughed and then he said, 'You know something, Fred, I don't think you've learned a damned thing these past two days. You knew what everybody was going to say before you ever left Stockford—or at least you should have.'

'Oh,' Fellows said, 'I've learned a *few* things.'

'Such as?'

'I don't think Sellers was given as good a defense as he could have been.'

'Who says so?'

'Nobody. This is just an overall impression.'

'What, for example, gives you the impression?' Fellows pursed his lips. 'You know the story of the squirrels?'

'How am I supposed to know the stories you make up until you make them up?'

The chief smiled faintly. 'Well, all the squirrels in the forest were starving to death one winter because somebody had stolen their hoard of nuts. So they were roaming the forest in search of food when one squirrel spied a lone acorn way at the top of a tall oak. He started scampering up the trunk of the tree and the other squirrels immediately spotted what he was after and there followed the doggonedest race you ever saw with squirrels scrambling, clawing and fighting their way up the tree for that one acorn, all except, that is, for one squirrel named Jasper who remained on the ground.

'When the fight was over, all the other squirrels came back down and they said to Jasper who hadn't got into the race, 'Why didn't you go after the acorn too?' Jasper replied, 'I didn't want to get my fur all scratched.' So all the squirrels promptly went around to Jasper's house and there they found all the stolen nuts. I think we can end the story there and not go into what those squirrels did to poor Jasper after that.'

'Crime doesn't pay,' said Wilks. 'Is that what you're trying to tell me?'

'Nope. The moral of that story is: He who isn't hungry doesn't fight for food.'

Wilks said slowly, 'I see. And you don't think Sellers' lawyer was hungry?'

'Sellers' lawyer isn't sitting in Death Row. He's lost a case but it's not costing him his life or even his career.'

'You're saying he's a bum lawyer?'

'No. I think he's a very competent lawyer. He did all the right things, made all the right appeals and the like, but most men don't run into the burning house to save another man's stocks and bonds. Sellers' lawyer is like that. He's thorough and he knows his law and he's making all the moves in Sellers' behalf that are open to him. But he's a corporation lawyer and he hasn't dealt in human life before. Sellers is just a case to him, one he happened to lose. What happens to Sellers the man doesn't bother him even though he claims to believe him innocent.' Fellows shook his head. 'What he was up against, on the other hand, was a prosecutor who was one hundred percent convinced of Sellers' guilt. Not only did Heligman, the prosecutor, want to win the case for his own reputation, but he wanted to win it to see justice done. He gave it the old college try and this was too much for a guy who only defended with his head and not his heart. I don't think Sellers had an even break in the matter. That's why I say the case was never satisfactorily solved. At least it hasn't been to my satisfaction.'

Wilks shrugged and bent over the tray again. 'You're not telling me much, Fred. That's all in the realm of the intangibles. What determines whether Sellers is innocent or guilty is evidence.' He straightened again. 'You can't say Sellers didn't murder his wife just because his lawyer didn't go into court with fire in his eye. In fact, when a competent lawyer doesn't have his heart in it it's the other way around. It makes it sound like the lawyer, deep down, felt Sellers really *did* do it.'

Fellows rubbed his chin. 'Don't think I didn't think of that, Sid. Heligman's conviction that Sellers murdered his wife was impressive and Mills' conviction that he hadn't was not impressive. So what I did after talking to them was read the transcript of the trial. I spent a couple of hours on it yesterday and the whole of today up there in Pittsfield and that's where my conclusion that Sellers didn't get any breaks comes from.'

Wilks sat on the edge of the table again. 'All right, tell me about it.'

Fellows produced his notebook and flipped to a turned down page. 'The trial started, of course, with the usual preliminaries,' he said. 'It was established that Sheila Sellers was killed by an unknown blunt cylindrical instrument, probably a piece of two-inch pipe, in the living room of her home when she was wearing nothing but a robe. She was struck from behind and the series of blows was more than enough to kill her. Over objections it was put across to the jury that she was killed in anger which, of course, was an important point since it helps knock out any theory that she surprised an intruder. It was further established that the house was locked, except for the kitchen window, and that there were no signs of breaking and entering. Nothing was stolen, nor were there any signs of a struggle. She was killed where she lay and had not been moved. The time of death was set at between seven and eight-thirty in the evening on Thursday, October 20, 1960.'

Wilks compressed his lips. 'Was anything made of the unlocked kitchen window? That's one way a burglar could have got into the house.'

Fellows shook his head. 'The defense didn't go into that. The defense never tried to present the argument that she was killed by an unknown burglar.'

'She hadn't been sexually attacked?'

'No.'

'What about blood?'

'There was a lot of it around.'

'Some would have gotten on the murderer. Were Sellers' clothes checked?'

'Of course. There was no blood. That comes out later. The prosecutor sold the jury on Sellers stripping before committing the crime, washing up and dressing and going to his chess club.'

'Pretty smooth operator if he could do that.'

'That's what I'd have to say. I don't know that I buy it but the jury did. And once you do, then it's a cold and calculated crime and no wonder they gave him the death penalty.'

'O.K., let's hear the rest.'

'After establishing that murder had been committed, Heligman then went about the business of showing that Sellers was capable of murder. He put three witnesses on the stand to testify that Sellers, at a party three years earlier, had created a violent scene

83

because a man named Kenneth Landon showed attention to Sheila. He wanted to fight Landon and the whole affair was embarrassing. The witnesses claimed there was nothing at all to get excited about, that the two were just talking together.

'Mills objected that the witnesses were drawing conclusions. He wanted to leave the idea with the jury that maybe there was more going on there than appeared, that Sellers' action might have been justified. He didn't press that too much, though, because he was, admittedly, in a bind. The more he tried to show Sheila up as a flirt—the more he tried to picture her as a girl who'd entertain a man while wearing nothing but a robe, the more he gave Sellers a motive for killing her. His whole defense was based on the line that Sellers and his wife were a happily married and devoted couple and Sellers had no reason to want her dead.'

'So,' said Wilks, 'both the prosecution and the defense were interested in showing Sheila up as pure?'

'Yep.' Fellows shook his head. 'I'm afraid Mills was playing right into Heligman's hands there. Heligman put Landon on the stand himself and he testified that he never saw Sheila Sellers again after that night. In fact, the Sellers were never invited back after that little episode.'

Fellows referred to his notes. 'Then

Heligman produced a Banksville delivery boy, a kid of twenty named Nick Daggett, who said he was abused by Sellers when he delivered groceries to Mrs. Sellers and merely made a few pleasant remarks in the process.

'Mills really went after him on cross-examination trying to force him to admit his remarks were offensive or suggestive but he couldn't shake the kid. I can't tell so well from the written record as I could have being at the trial but I think that hurt Mills pretty badly. He *really* wanted that one and he really went for it and he didn't get it. That put him in a worse spot than if he hadn't tried.

'Heligman then put eight witnesses on the stand to tell about Sellers' behavior at a block party when he attacked and struck one George Walker for dancing with his wife. Walker testified himself about the matter and Mills, still smarting from the whipping the delivery boy gave him, went after Walker. He got Walker to admit he was a bachelor, got him to admit he was a salesman, and tried to make him appear unsavory to the jury. He questioned the guy's morals and made some headway trying to justify Sellers' attack on him. He showed Walker up as a man with an eye for the ladies and certainly put the impression across that Walker wouldn't exactly be stopped by a wedding ring.' Fellows nodded. 'Mills was at his best there.'

'Score one for Mills.'

'Score zero for Mills,' Fellows retorted. 'Heligman wrecked him on re-direct examination. Heligman established that this apparently unsavory characer, living in the neighborhood, could hardly go through life without ever seeing Sheila Sellers. He did see her to talk to on subsequent occasions, including one other block party, and Ernest Sellers didn't kick up any fuss at all. Sellers only seemed to object to Walker dancing with his wife. He didn't regard Walker as too unsavory to speak to her.'

'He objected to that guy Landon speaking to her,' Wilks said.

'Right, and what does that do but show Sellers up as emotionally unstable? Then, right after that, Heligman puts Michael Baxter, the boy next door, seventeen at the time, on the stand to testify that Sellers had lit into him and bawled him out for helping Sheila spade her garden the previous spring.

'And, of course, through all of this, Heligman brings out how miserable and upset Sheila was at these flare-ups. He further shows that they seldom went out and never had anybody in and that they, in effect, had no friends. He subtly gets it across that Sellers' jealousy is the cause of this withdrawal and he works very effectively at establishing that there was no basis for the jealousy. Sheila didn't flirt. Sheila didn't lead men on.'

'And,' put in Wilks, 'Sellers' lawyer goes right along with it.'

'That's right. So, anyway, Heligman very carefully isolates Sheila and her husband from the rest of the world thereby leaving nobody to kill her but the husband himself. He did it extremely well and then he got testimony to the effect that Sheila seldom smiled and seldom put her face outdoors except to shop. He showed the jury that she was not a happy woman and that, therefore, it was not a happy marriage. He scored a beat on Mills on that for, of course, Mills' whole line of defense was that it *was* happy.

'Then he got psychiatrists on the stand to testify that a man throwing the tantrums Sellers threw, who had so little emotional control, was capable of committing murder. See the pattern?'

'Yeah,' Wilks said slowly. 'I'm not much on law but I can see that. First you show nobody but Sellers could have done it, then you show that he was capable of doing it. Then you show he had motive.'

'Well, you can't show motive very well. Heligman wasn't fool enough to try to say Sellers killed his wife for this or that specific reason. It's enough to show the marriage wasn't happy and leave it to the jury to wonder about the particular circumstance that brought the murder about. You know, husbands have killed their wives because their eggs weren't cooked properly, stupid things like that. But those are only the overt, final straws. The real reason for such killings lies way deeper and is almost impossible to probe. And that's one place where Heligman knew what he was doing. He got it from the psychiatrists that Sellers' jealous flare-ups were symptomatic of some deep-seated trouble.'

'Uh-huh. I can see Heligman knows his business. Go on.'

'Well,' Fellows said, 'this is one place where Mills did score a point. He showed that in all of Sellers' jealous rages he never said or did anything to his wife. It was always the man in question whom he attacked, not Sheila. Mills made as much of that as he could, particularly in the summation.'

'It's a good point,' Wilks said.

'Sure it is, but it wasn't enough to outweigh all the points Heligman made. For example, now Heligman gets to the murder night. On what he's shown already, it becomes quite evident that Sheila is the shy, retiring type. Thus it is hardly likely that she'd open the door for anybody while wearing nothing but a robe. Since the house was locked, the only other way someone could get in would be with a key. And who has keys but her husband?

'Then Heligman had the bus driver testify

88

that he picked up Sellers at twenty minutes of eight. Mills asked how Sellers behaved and the bus driver said, "normally"—'

'Another point for Mills.'

'Yes, but Heligman then forced the bus driver to admit he wasn't in a good position to judge Sellers' condition. Sellers steps on the bus, pays his fare and takes a seat. No words passed, the driver wasn't paying attention. He didn't do more than glance at Sellers.

'After that there's testimony about Sellers arriving at the chess club at eight and then the Baxters are called on to tell about Sellers coming to them for help getting into his house because he forgot his keys. It seems that he pointed out the kitchen window as the first place to try and that was the *one* window that was unlocked. Heligman made a lot of that and even more about the forgetting of the keys, showing how this gives Sellers what he needs—a witness to the discovery of his wife's death. And there, for the most part, you have the prosecution case.'

Wilks said, 'I don't know, Fred. It's not exactly conclusive. If I were on the jury I'd lean towards his guilt but not enough to recommend the death penalty.'

'That's right,' the chief answered. 'But Heligman didn't win on the prosecution case, he won by bombing the defense. First off, Mills gets members of the chess club to testify Sellers acted normally that evening.

Heligman threw grave doubt on that idea by showing that Sellers, one of the top players in the club, lost three games, all to inferior men, something without precedent. 'He wasn't thinking about chess that night,' was the way Heligman put it.

'Then Mills gets police officers to testify that examination of Sellers' clothes showed no blood on any except the ones he wore when he discovered his wife and knelt down beside her. So Heligman cross-examined and got the admission that if Sellers were naked he could kill his wife without getting his clothes stained. Then, just to back up that play, he showed that there was nobody to say just how many clothes Sellers had and if the weapon hadn't been found it was equally possible for blood-stained clothes not to have been found.

'The trouble with Mills was that the only real witness he had was the defendant himself and he, like a fool, put Sellers on the stand. Maybe he had to because there was nobody else—except some old friend of Sheila's from way back who testified Sheila told her how happy she was in the first years of her marriage. Anyway, Sellers was a sitting duck for Heligman and Mills lost the case right there.

'In the first place, Sellers, under Mills' examination, said he forgot his keys quite frequently but had always, in the past, rung the doorbell and been let in by Sheila. Next he said he saw a man lurking in the vicinity when he went for the bus, but he wasn't able to give any good description of this man. As for the unlocked kitchen window, Sellers said he had Michael try that one first because he thought he remembered noticing it was unlocked. And, of course, he told how happy he and Sheila had been—fifteen years of marriage without an argument. Why would he kill her? If he wanted to be free of her he could always get a divorce, but he wouldn't have waited fifteen years. He gave a very touching description of their life together and said the reason they didn't go out much was because they were so happy alone by themselves.'

'Possible,' Wilks said. 'Quite possible.'

'Yeah,' Fellows said, 'but Sellers made the mistake of lying on the witness stand and that's what killed him. Heligman got up for the cross-examination and went right after the business about the man "lurking" in the neighborhood. If the man was lurking, why hadn't Sellers mentioned his presence to the police after the murder? Why did he go off and leave his wife alone and unprotected if he noticed a suspicious character hanging around? In no time he gets the admission from Sellers that maybe he wasn't "lurking". In another minute he has Sellers conceding that this mysterious stranger had nothing to do with anything. In fact, the jury's well convinced by now that Sellers made the whole thing up, which he undoubtedly did.

'Then Heligman goes after the key business. How often did he forget his keys? Since his wife was asleep when he got home from the chess club, he'd have to wake her up to let him in. That wasn't very considerate, was it? To spare her this, didn't he make some effort to remember to take his keys with him?'

Wilks said, 'Brother. He should never have taken the stand!'

'Heligman had him coming and going,' Fellows agreed. 'Sellers was fumbling badly in here. Then there was the business of the unlocked window. Since it had been established that Sheila kept the house locked up when Sellers was out, why didn't Sellers lock the window when he noticed it was unlocked? Since it was the kitchen window and Sheila was nervous about an unlocked house, how come she didn't notice it if he did? She was in the kitchen more than he.

'So,' said Fellows with a sigh, 'that was the way it went. Heligman put it to the jury in his summation that Sellers did the job, that he deliberately unlocked the window himself and deliberately went off without his keys so Michael could discover the body and he'd have an audience to witness his display of grief. The jury decided he was right in about five hours.'

Wilks said, 'But you think otherwise? You think he's innocent?'

'I think as I said before. His defense left a lot to be desired.'

CHAPTER TEN

Sid Wilks spat into the pail. He said to Fellows, 'All right, Fred. The defense wasn't good. What does that prove?'

'It doesn't prove he's guilty.'

'It doesn't prove he's innocent either.'

'No, but let's just suppose he is. Let's take the whole thing from the standpoint that he did not kill his wife and see what we've got.'

'We've got him lying about a mysterious stranger lurking in the neighborhood. We've got him lying, or apparently lying, about forgetting his keys and we've got him not giving any good explanation as to why he didn't relock the kitchen window when he found it unfastened. How are you going to explain that away?'

'That's not hard, Sid. The guy is scared. He's on trial for his life. He's got almost no defense at all. So, unwisely but naturally, he tries to build a defense. He makes up the lurking stranger as a means of throwing suspicion away from himself. He makes it up that he forgets his keys often because it looks so bad, his forgetting them this one time. He makes it up about noticing the window unlocked because he happened to go to the nearest window to try to get in and finds it the one open one in the house. In other words, the truth—that nobody was hanging around, that this was the only time he forgot his keys, that he just happened to hit the one window that hadn't been locked, makes him look so bad he doesn't dare rely on the truth.'

'All right, so you assume that. Now where does that leave you? How are you going to get around the fact that nobody else had a key to the house and nobody broke in and the woman wouldn't let anybody in when wearing nothing but a robe, to say nothing of the fact that she was killed in rage and hatred?'

'Who says they're all facts, Sid?'

Wilks stopped, his mouth slightly open. 'Pardon me,' he went on. 'Maybe I'm just assuming that when both the prosecution *and* the defense agree on something, that it's pretty well established to be a fact.'

'I told you the defense relied on the happy marriage angle. That doesn't mean it *was* happy.'

'All right, come on. What are you thinking?'

Fellows pointed a finger, jabbing it at the air. 'If,' he said, 'Sellers is innocent, somebody else is guilty. Where I think the defense made a mistake was in ignoring the second part of that statement. Somebody else is guilty. Mills tried to convince the jury that Sellers was innocent but I don't think it can be done in his case without showing who the guilty man is, or at least the direction where one should look for the guilty party.'

'What's the direction? You got one?'

'Sure. The obvious one. The lover.'

'I thought there wasn't any.'

'So does everybody else.'

'Everybody else says there's no lover. Nobody can produce a whisper of a lover. Everything that's said about the woman's character says there's no lover. But you say there is.' Wilks shook his head in wonder. 'Would you mind, Mr. Detective, telling me how you arrive at that fascinating conclusion, three years after the fact and contrary to all available statements and evidence?'

'I wouldn't call it a conclusion, Sid.'

'What would you call it, a hunch?'

Fellows shook his head. 'It's not even a hunch. All I can say is this. *If* Mr. Ernest Sellers did not kill his wife, then the only person I can see who possibly could have would be a lover. Thus, if I want to help Mr. Ernest Sellers, that is the avenue I have to follow. If there's a lover, then the husband may be innocent.'

'And if there is not?'

Fellows lifted his shoulders and let them drop. 'Then I think Mr. Sellers is going to go to the chair.'

Wilks turned away. 'If you want my opinion, Sellers is going to the chair whether there's a lover or whether there isn't, whether he killed his wife or whether he didn't.'

'How so?'

'Simply because he's only got a couple more weeks and if the police and the state's attorney and the defense lawyer and Sellers himself could not produce any sign of a lover three years ago in all the weeks before the trial, I don't see how the hell you think you can in fifteen or sixteen days.'

'Well, I'm going to try.'

'Good luck to you. What about the Stockford police department?'

Fellows said, 'I called up the police commissioners and laid the problem in their laps and they said I could have my vacation right now. The Stockford police department, starting tomorrow, is going to be run by one Detective Sergeant Sidney Wilks.' Fellows grinned. 'Think you can manage?'

'Yeah,' Wilks said sourly, 'but I wish they'd give me a chief's pay for the job.'

'Maybe they'll make you a captain. I put in a good word about that.'

'Thanks. Meanwhile, what're you going to do?'

'I've already made a reservation at a motel in Banksville. That's the scene of the crime and that's where I'm going to dig.'

CHAPTER ELEVEN

It was ten o'clock in the morning on Wednesday July 24th when Fred Fellows, in civilian clothes, drove his dusty Plymouth into the area of the Bulldog Motel just outside of Banksville and walked into the office to register. The sign outside said there was TV in all the rooms and a swimming pool for guests and the pool itself was sunk close to the road where every driver could see it. Three women, one of them lithe and pretty in a yellow bathing suit, added to the lure of balmy waters under a hot, up-state sun.

The manager, a heavy man with gray hair and a sport shirt with perspiration stains under the arms, handed the chief a card and said, 'We've reserved room twenty-four for you, Mr. Fellows. I guess you'll want to get a swim pretty quick.'

'It's a good day for it,' the chief said noncommittally. 'How long's the motel been here? It looks pretty new.'

The manager who, according to the nameplate on the counter, was Martin Rose, said, 'It's very new. This is the second season.' He turned Fellows' card around to read it, deposited it in a drawer and picked the key to room twenty-four from the set of hooks behind him. 'Not a place for full-house business,' he said. 'Banksville isn't on any main route to anywhere, but we do all right if you aren't trying to get rich fast.'

Fellows nodded, took the key and walked out into the hot sun. The rooms formed a U opening onto the road with the office and a cafeteria set in the center. Twenty-four was beside the road at the end of the leg of the U that had the swimming pool behind it. It was a pleasant room, clean and new, with a space heater and a bathroom but no air-conditioning. Through the back wall could be heard the splash of water and the voices of the women frolicking and loafing at the edge of the pool. Only two other cars were parked by two other rooms.

Fellows opened the cowhide suitcase his wife had given him the previous Christmas just in case they should ever get to have a vacation. He unpacked carefully and methodically, tucked the suitcase in the closet and rinsed his face in the bathroom. The morning sun threw patterns of light across the bed but though the windows facing the dusty court were open, no breeze came through. He left the room then, latching the door behind him and climbing into the Plymouth, headed for town. With him was a notebook, an address, and the thirty-five names Ernest Sellers had produced.

Banksville, formerly a dot on the map, was a rapidly swelling town of 16,000 according to the last census. Farmlands still filled most of the western section so that the center, now bustling and populous, erupted suddenly and with little warning. East of the center was where the expansion had taken place and after the section of large houses with upwards of a century behind them came the newer and smaller residences and after them, in mass production, the developments. Near the end of these, a mile and a half from the center of town, was the particular section of development where, on Wellington Street three years before, a woman had been murdered in her living room.

Wellington came into the main road from the north and was three blocks long. Fellows, who learned its location from a traffic policeman downtown, reached the spot shortly before eleven and turned onto the street to reconnoiter. He found the murder house, number 36, in the second block, seven houses up from Solomon and four short of Finch Street. It and all of its neighbors for blocks around were identical in all but color, a mass of cheek-by-jowl small, two-floored, one-family dwellings with a fifty foot frontage, a driveway to the left, and a two-car garage at the back.

Fellows made a turn at the corner of Finch and came back, parking on the far side opposite number 36. He got out and crossed the street to the sidewalk in front and looked it over. The Baxters, according to what Sellers had told him, would be in 34; but where the other eleven neighbors who had known Sheila lived he had still to find out. From the sidewalk he could see the nameplate under the bell at the head of the tiny brick stoop and he advanced up the walk till he was close enough to read the name, 'Sharkey'. Whoever the Sharkeys were, they didn't mind buying a house in which a murder had been committed.

Fellows suddenly felt under observation and turned slowly. A dark-haired man in a white sport shirt was standing watching him from the stoop of the Baxter house, his hand still on the knob of the closed door. Fellows met his gaze but the man still stared. Then as the chief turned and started back, the man came down the brick steps and approached. He was in his early thirties, tall and lean with dark hair and he walked briskly. 'You looking for something?' he said, coming up.

Fellows, a little taller and a good bit huskier, pursed his lips. 'Do you have some particular interest in what I'm doing?' he asked.

'I might have.'

'Such as?'

The man changed his manner a little and permitted a smile. 'It so happens I'm in real estate. You thinking of buying something around here?'

'Is something for sale?'

'Yes. Quite a few places. You interested in this house in particular?' he gestured towards the Sharkeys' front door.

'I'm just looking,' Fellows answered. 'Are you Mr. Baxter?'

'No,' he answered promptly. 'I'm not Baxter. My name is Jones.'

'Jones?'

'One of the Jones boys. Raphael Jones to be exact.' He waited a moment expectantly and then said, 'And your name?'

'Fellows,' the chief told him. 'Fred Fellows.'

The man's eyes flickered a moment and then he held out his hand. 'Nice to meet you, Mr. Fellows. You planning to move in around here?'

'I'm looking around,' the chief said carefully. 'If you want to give me your card, I'll get in touch if I decide anything.'

Mr. Raphael Jones touched his pocket, then said, 'I don't have any with me. I left my wallet home. No matter. I'm in the phone book. Just remember the name. Jones. One of the Jones boys.' He turned and went to the car parked in front of the Baxters', started up and drove off with a wave. It was a dusty, white Ford Anglia and it carried Massachusetts plates.

Fellows watched him go and tightened a corner of his mouth. 'Which phone book?' he

101

muttered under his breath and headed for the Baxters'.

CHAPTER TWELVE

Mrs. Baxter was a slender, attractive woman with dark hair and a ruddy face. She wore an apron over a light summer dress but housework didn't affect her grooming. Her blue eyes met the chief's and she seemed to conclude he was not a salesman for her 'Yes?' held more curiosity than a salesman usually merits.

Fellows introduced himself as the chief of police in Stockford and asked if he could bother her for a minute. Her curiosity deepened and she said, 'Why, I guess so,' and held the door wider.

He took a seat on the couch at her bidding and she lowered herself into a facing chair. She said, 'I can't imagine why the police in Stockford would be coming here.'

'It's with regard to your erstwhile neighbor, Ernest Sellers.'

'Oh?' Her eyes clouded slightly. 'Is he supposed to have done something in Stockford too?'

Fellows smiled. 'No. What I'm doing is investigating what he's supposed to have done here.'

She said, 'That's very interesting. So was another man, just a few minutes ago. There's been nothing since the trial and now, suddenly, two people in one morning want to discuss that awful thing.'

'Did the other man tell you why he wanted to know about the matter?' Fellows asked, displaying only idle curiosity.

'Yes,' she said. 'He's doing a book on it. He's a writer, it seems. He writes about true murder cases.'

'Did he give you his name? Maybe I'm familiar with it.'

'Jones, he told me. Raphael Jones.'

'What sort of things did he want to know?'

Mrs. Baxter pursed her lips. 'Oh, what kind of a woman Mrs. Sellers was. Who her friends were. Whatever I could tell about both her and Mr. Sellers.'

Fellows nodded. 'And what kind of a woman *was* Mrs. Sellers?'

'Attractive,' Mrs. Baxter replied. 'Quiet, withdrawn. I really felt sorry for her.'

'Sorry for her? Why?'

'She seemed to have so little in life. No children. Few friends. No interests.'

'Did you know her well?'

'Not especially. We were friendly when we met in the back yard. We didn't associate socially. She didn't do anything socially.'

'She just stayed in the house from morning till night?'

Mrs. Baxter smiled a little. 'Just about. Oh, she went shopping. There's a shopping center a couple of blocks from here. Now and then I drove her. They had no car, you know. She'd walk to the store two or three times a week so she wouldn't have to carry so much. I tried to tell her she could go with me when I did my shopping but she wouldn't accept the offer. She said it gave her a chance to get out.'

'She didn't like being cooped up all the time?'

'I really couldn't tell you. It was hard to tell what she did like. She didn't open up very much.'

'Do you think she was happily married?'

Mrs. Baxter shook her head in perplexity. 'Again it's hard to tell. She didn't speak about her marriage. Of course she would sometimes refer to "Ernest" and say things like he didn't like her in shorts and things like that. I think he might have been a little too old-fashioned for her taste but I don't know that she was actually unhappy.'

'At the trial the impression was created that she was.'

Mrs. Baxter said, 'I think that impression went a little too far. I don't think she was as unhappy as the prosecution tried to make her appear. I remember the summer before it happened—when she was out more—and I would see her in the back yard and pass the time of day with her occasionally. She certainly seemed happy enough. I don't mean she was bubbling and effervescent or anything like that for she wasn't that kind of person, but for the kind she was I'd say she seemed happy. I certainly didn't suspect there was any trouble.'

Fellows nodded at that and took out his notebook to record the data. 'You weren't prepared for what happened, then?'

'Prepared? I was shocked beyond belief. The idea of anything like that was too horrible to expect at all.'

Fellows looked at her frankly. 'Tell me, Mrs. Baxter. Do you think he killed her?'

Mrs. Baxter flushed under the direct stare. When she spoke she stammered a little. 'I don't really know.' She met his gaze. 'I really don't know, Mr. Fellows. I—I suppose I accepted it at the trial, I mean that he did kill her, but I can't say what I really believe. I don't suppose I've thought about it. I put it out of my mind.'

'You were with him when he found her?'

'Yes, I was. We all were. My son Michael was the first to see her. He let Mr. Sellers in and my husband and I went in too. It was'—she shuddered—'horrible.'

'Did the idea that Mr. Sellers had killed her occur to you at that time?'

'No. Not for a moment. He was so—so stricken. All I could think was what a horrible thing for him to come home to. What

105

a horrible thing for someone to have done.'

'Who did you think did do it then?'

'I don't know. I had no idea. I suppose vaguely I assumed some robber or somebody. I never thought it was him himself.'

'But at the trial you changed your mind?'

Mrs. Baxter looked unhappily at the chief. 'I don't know what changed my mind or if it really was changed. I suppose when he was arrested I began to wonder. I suppose then I began to think about the possibility that he did it. I guess I got used to it after a while—I mean that he *might* have done it—so when the jury said he did I guess I wasn't too surprised.'

'But you've never been sure in your own mind?'

She wet her lips. 'I didn't think about it. I said, "This is what the jury decided and I'm not going to think about it any more." I haven't.' She leaned forward a little. 'Is Mr. Sellers still alive? They were going to execute him. Have they done that?'

'They haven't yet,' Fellows said slowly. 'But they're going to.'

'The poor man.'

'Do you say that believing him guilty?'

She looked up quickly. 'I don't know why I say it,' she answered, seeming puzzled herself. 'I guess I don't like to see people die. I wish they didn't execute people. You can never be sure they've done the things they're accused of. It would be so awful to make a mistake.'

'It would be,' the chief agreed. 'That's why I'm investigating it.'

Her eyes widened. 'You think he's innocent?'

'I think there's a possibility.'

'But if he is, then who *did* do it?'

Fellows smiled faintly. 'Let me ask you this, Mrs. Baxter. How was Mrs. Sellers around men? Did she seem to like men?'

The woman gestured helplessly. 'I wouldn't have the faintest idea. I didn't know her that well. We never talked about men. I mean, why would we?'

'You did see her with men. There was the block dance when Mr. Sellers got upset about a man named George Walker dancing with Mrs. Sellers.'

'Well, yes,' she said tentatively. 'I do remember that. But all they were doing was dancing.'

'Does Mr. Walker still live around here?'

'Over in back. But all he did was dance with her. Mr. Sellers turned away and Mr. Walker grabbed Mrs. Sellers and said, "Let's show them how to do it," or something like that. Mr. Baxter and I were standing with them at the time. So then Mr. Sellers turned back and saw Sheila was gone and when he saw her in the arms of Mr. Walker, he ran over and pulled her away and when Mr.

Walker tried to say something, he struck him. He gave Mr. Walker a bloody nose and he was much smaller than Mr. Walker. Mr. Walker would have beaten him up something terrible except other people jumped in and stopped it. Mr. Walker was very angry.'

'What kind of a man is Mr. Walker?'

Mrs. Baxter said carefully, 'I don't know him well. He lives around the corner and I never see him except sometimes shopping. He's a bachelor so he does his own shopping. We say hello and that's about all. I really wouldn't know what kind of a man he is.'

'At the trial an attempt was made to show him as lecherous. Do you think that description fits?'

Mrs. Baxter shook her head vigorously. 'I wouldn't say that at all. I know there's talk about him, that he has women to his house—girlfriends and such—and they stay overnight sometimes, but he's never been anything but polite to the women around here. We're all married, you know.'

'And you can be certain he's never been fresh with any of these—ah—married women?'

'Oh, absolutely. Why it'd be all over the neighborhood in an hour if something like that happened. People talk, you know. In fact, this is a very gossipy neighborhood.'

'And you gossip about George Walker?'

'Oh, no. We don't talk much about him.

108

You expect a bachelor to have ladyfriends and we don't know who they are anyway. They shouldn't have tried to call him lecherous at the trial just because he was a bachelor. He's not the only one, after all.'

'There are other bachelors?'

'Two on this block. There used to be. Gordon Henry, around the corner on Finch Street. He lives with his mother and there's nothing lecherous about him, I can tell you. And then there was John Davins down the block, who lived with his sister, only they moved, way back around the time of the trial.'

Fellows made note of that and checked back. Sellers had given the name of George Walker as known to Sheila but hadn't mentioned either of the other two. 'Would you know if Mrs. Sellers knew Gordon Henry or John Davins?'

'Oh, I'm sure she at least knew who they were. We all know everybody in this neighborhood. Of course she didn't circulate very much so she might not have, but there are these block dances we have a couple of times a year when the weather gets good. She must have known who everybody was even if she practically never saw them. And she'd hear about them because after all, what else do we women have to do except have coffee klatches and gab about the neighbors? Of course Mrs. Sellers didn't do that very much so she wouldn't, maybe, hear as much news as the rest of us.'

'What kind of gossip was there about *her*, Mrs. Baxter?'

'About Mrs. Sellers?' Mrs. Baxter laughed. 'Why there wasn't any about her. There was nothing about her to talk about. She was probably the least interesting person in the whole neighborhood. She never did anything.'

'If she ever entertained anybody in the house while her husband was away, would you know about it?'

'Oh, certainly.'

'How? Do you keep that close a watch?'

'Well, no, of course not, not I. But somebody would be sure to see someone coming to her house in broad daylight and the word would get around mighty fast, I can tell you.'

'How about at night—say while her husband was away?'

'He never was away, except for those nights he played chess.' She thought about that a moment, then shook her head. 'No. Their stoop light was always on when he went out. Somebody would have seen. We pretty well know anytime anybody entertains anybody around here.'

'Suppose,' Fellows persisted, 'she didn't want you to know she was entertaining?'

Mrs. Baxter smiled faintly. 'I know what

you're after, Mr. Fellows. You're thinking of a secret love affair. I can tell you it wouldn't go on long before she'd be found out.'

'How would she be?'

'In the first place, there's that business about calling. It wouldn't be long before somebody'd see him ringing her doorbell. And then there'd be the car. Everyone would notice a car parked in front of the house.'

'The caller would hardly park it there.'

'He'd park it on the street, wouldn't he? It would be noticed no matter what house it was in front of and people would wonder whose it was—particularly the person whose house it was in front of. And if he parked it in the driveway, I'd be noticing it. No, it simply couldn't happen.'

'He could arrive on foot and go to the back door.'

'He still couldn't do it more than a few times without somebody seeing him on the street and noticing he was a stranger; without somebody seeing him turn in the driveway. You have to realize, Mr. Fellows, that we all live close together and nobody can do very much for very long without the neighborhood knowing about it. Why, you take young Dick Spencer, for instance. He got himself involved with a girl—got her pregnant, in fact. She didn't even live around here but it got out. It was all over the neighborhood and the Spencers, they up and moved. That's what happens. You live in a place like this and you've got to watch your step.'

Fellows nodded and made more notes. 'About the night of the murder,' he said. 'Did you hear anything?'

She shook her head. 'That was October. We had the windows closed. We had supper around half past six and Michael went upstairs to study and my husband and I watched the television most of the evening. We never knew a thing was wrong till Mr. Sellers knocked on the back door and we all went out to help him get in the house.'

'If Mrs. Sellers had screamed—'

'The police tested that,' Mrs. Baxter interrupted. 'They tried screams and shots and all kinds of noise but with the windows closed neither we nor the Castles on the other side could hear a thing—except, very faintly, a gun.'

Fellows made another note and looked at the page. There was nothing on it that helped in the hunt for a lover but he hadn't expected there to be. The police had gone into that question thoroughly three years before without results. If a lover existed, he lay far below the surface and only a search in depth, based on the conviction he existed, could uncover him. For that purpose the scanty list of twelve neighbors given him by Sellers seemed insufficient. If a lover existed it was more than likely he was a man Sellers was unaware his wife even knew. He turned to that subject next and asked Mrs. Baxter for Sheila's male acquaintances.

'Men?' Mrs. Baxter said. 'Why Mrs. Sellers didn't know *any* men.'

'She knew George Walker.'

'She danced with him once. I wouldn't call that knowing.'

'I understand she spoke to him on other occasions.'

'Yes, I remember that she did, but that was only polite conversation, same as she'd have with anybody.'

'And she knew your son Michael.'

'Well, certainly. And my husband.'

'And a delivery boy named Nick Daggett.'

'She talked to him. I remember that. I suppose if you want names like that, you could say she knew every man in the neighborhood. Or, at least, it's likely she did.'

'Can you name every man in the neighborhood—who was living here three years ago, of course?'

'Why I think I could,' she said, smiling at the challenge. 'Let's see, starting at the corner—'

She went all around the block, family by family, twenty-six in all, including those who had moved out and those who had moved in. Then, to top it off, at Fellows' request she listed the families on the opposite side of

Wellington Street and threw in three extras who weren't that close but who were involved in the block dances. Her impressive feat further included the first names of husband and wife and the number and approximate age of the children. After that she added the clerks of the stores in the shopping center and the manager of the supermarket where Mrs. Sellers had bought her groceries. Her only uncertainty lay in whether one clerk or another had been around three years before.

When she finished she was proud of herself but she was also amused. 'You don't really think one of those men I mentioned made love to Mrs. Sellers, do you? You're not really serious about that, are you?'

Fellows smiled back. 'I have no idea,' he said. 'You never can tell.'

'I can tell,' she said smartly. 'Mrs. Sellers could never have gotten away with it. She didn't have the experience and her husband kept too close an eye on her. She never would have had a chance.'

'It doesn't seem so,' Fellows had to admit but he didn't add that one reason was having Mrs. Baxter next door. He rose and thanked her and as he left, said, 'By the way, when would your son be around? I'd like to talk to him about the murder if I may.'

'He won't be around at all, I'm afraid. He's got a summer job as counsellor at a camp in Pennsylvania.'

'I see. And your husband?'

'He usually gets in at half past five.'

Fellows thanked her again and stepped out into the broiling noonday sun.

CHAPTER THIRTEEN

Fellows drove into the motel yard at six o'clock, tired and hot. It had been a long afternoon and he'd spent it at the job shop where Ernest Sellers had once worked, checking on the long list of twenty-one co-workers. The chore had been successful from one standpoint. The chief could pretty well eliminate them all from complicity in the murder of Sheila Sellers, but he learned little else. None of them had known Ernest in any way other than as their foreman. They had liked or disliked him according to their nature but he was only a figure in coveralls in their minds. What kind of a man he was outside the shop they did not know and did not care. They had accepted without question that he had killed his wife but they would have accepted the opposite just as readily.

The results were not unexpected by the chief. This was an area, however, that had to be covered and he had tackled it first to get it over with. The tackling had been thorough, nonetheless, for one idea Fellows had was that the reason no lover had been uncovered might have been because the police had looked for such a man only in the immediate area of the home. A job-shop Romeo might have escaped their notice. This no longer appeared a possibility and the chief returned to the motel with the opinion that it hadn't been a very good idea to begin with.

He took a long cool shower to refresh himself for the evening's chores and dressed in fresh clothes, putting on a sport shirt that hung outside his trousers to conceal the inevitable gun on his hip. When he crossed the dusty motel grounds to the cafeteria he noted that the rooms were getting filled. Six cars were angled before the string of identical doorways along the back and the one in front of room 14 was a white Ford Anglia with Massachusetts plates. Fellows made a face as he opened the screen door. There could hardly be two such cars in Banksville.

The cafeteria was air-conditioned and felt almost chilly after the heat of the day. It was also nearly empty and only half a dozen people were scattered among the two dozen tables. There was the lithe young girl who'd worn the yellow bathing suit in the morning sitting against a wall flanked by two older women. A middle-aged couple was in a corner near the plate glass rear wall and two men sat at separate tables poring over their day's sales records between mouthfuls. The man who

116

called himself Raphael Jones wasn't there.

Fellows collected a meat pie, a salad, ice cream and iced coffee from the woman behind the food counter and picked a table close to the glass wall where he had a view of the white Anglia, the six other cars, and the row of rear rooms. It wasn't an enchanting sight and he dipped into his food and let his thoughts run through and discard the possibility that Sheila had been slain by neither her husband nor a lover but by somebody else. Burglars, rapists and mysterious strangers might be possibilities because almost anything was possible but the objections to all of them were too strong. None of those alternatives fit her being struck from behind and beaten viciously. No, it had to be a lover, Fellows decided, if it wasn't Sellers himself. He got out his notebook and started going through the scanty information and the host of names he had collected to see what he could make of it all.

His concentration was so great that he was unaware of what he ate and it wasn't till a voice said, 'I trust this seat isn't taken,' that he realized anyone else was around. He looked up and found himself staring into the rather quizzical eyes of Raphael Jones.

Fellows kept his own expression bland and folded his notebook shut. 'I don't suppose so,' he said.

'Good thing.' Jones placed his plates on the

117

table and set the tray on another, then sat down opposite the chief and spread a paper napkin. 'I hope this stuff is edible,' he said for conversation and tried a mouthful. 'Well, not too bad.'

'How's the real estate business?' Fellows asked him.

'It's coming along.'

'You're roaming a little south of the border I notice. Can't you sell in Massachusetts?'

Jones smiled. 'I forgot you're a detective. Silly of me.'

'You know I'm a detective?'

Jones said, 'Don't you read your own press notices? All I ever see in the papers when there's a tough case to crack is Fred Fellows to the rescue. Let me know the name of your press agent one day, will you? He's got the word.'

'You in need of a press agent?' Fellows asked.

Jones sighed and put down his fork. 'Typical cop thinking,' he said. 'Literal to the point of sarcasm. Which reminds me, aren't you a little far afield yourself today? I thought Stockford was your hangout. What brings you up to Banksville?'

Fellows said, 'I thought we had it worked out that I was house-hunting.'

'More cop stuff,' Jones said sourly and picked up his fork again. 'Never give out information. Save it all for the newspapermen.' He let his eye go to the notebook. 'You wouldn't want to let me see what you've got in there, would you?'

'Not particularly.' Fellows picked it up and tucked it in his shirt pocket.

Jones shook his head and said chidingly, 'You aren't going to fool anybody going around with something like that. It spells cop. Even if I didn't know your name when you gave it to me this morning I would have known what you were. The job stamps you. You know that?'

'So I'm stamped. There're worse occupations in the world. A phony real estate agent is one of them.'

Jones laughed. 'You don't make me bite, Fellows. I'm not one of your suspects. So you don't want to tell me what you're doing here? Why don't you let me guess?'

'Go ahead.'

'Well,' said Jones with an elaborate display of cogitation. 'Let me see. You're a cop so it must have to do with crime. And since you were standing in front of a house in which a crime was committed, it would be the Sellers killing. And what's with Ernest Sellers? He's waiting execution day which is the eighth of August. So let's just suggest to you that Mr. Sellers, seeking to escape the chair, appealed to your kind heart and interest in justice and pleaded with you to come save him.' He looked pleased with himself. 'How's that?

Did I hit it close?'

'Almost,' Fellows said, 'but not quite. It's really that a convict I sent up appealed to my good nature to get him some drugs and that house on Wellington Street is a front for an opium den. I was waiting outside while they approved my credentials.'

Jones nodded. 'Well, you're quite a character, Fellows. I'll say that. Trouble is, you left something out. For instance, you left out that after I drove away you rang the doorbell of the Baxter house and were admitted by a certain Mrs. Baxter. And I don't really think you'll find any opium in Mrs. Baxter's house. She doesn't strike me as the type.'

'I can see you're very observant.'

'Nothing to it. I stopped the car around the corner and took a look back.'

'Curious, eh?'

'Sure I'm curious. I'm a writer and writers are curious. Didn't Mrs. Baxter tell you?'

'Yes, she told me you're a writer. And you told me you're in real estate.'

'And you don't believe her either?'

'Oh, it's not her. It's you I don't believe.'

'You got any better occupations for me?'

'Well, yes,' the chief replied. He imitated Jones's display of cogitation and said, 'Offhand I would say you were a private detective who wasn't doing too well and then, presto, there comes a letter from a certain

Ernest Sellers who's going to be executed on August eighth and he appeals to your better nature to help save him from the electric chair.'

Jones paused in mid-mouthful and gave Fellows a wry smile. 'You're pretty curious yourself, it seems. So you've been checking up on me.'

'Just putting two and two together, that's all. What're you doing about your business while you're down here trying to save Ernest?'

'I've got a partner. If you checked that far you ought to have found that much out.'

'I didn't check on you,' the chief said, pushing his dishes aside and drawing over the ice cream. 'What difference does it make to me?'

'Come off it, Fellows. You didn't pull that detective business out of the sky. You looked me up. That's how you found out. Admit it.'

'Have it your way.'

'If you didn't, then how did you know?'

'Well, I'll tell you, Mr. Jones. It's sort of like the story of the little girl who went to her mother and told her that a big bad robber had stolen all the cherry jam out of the jar her mother had carefully hidden in a secret place especially so her daughter couldn't get to it. You know what the mother did? She spanked the daughter. This was, I might add, to her daughter's very great amazement.'

'Pardon me if I suggest that your interesting story eludes me.'

'Don't tell me you're as amazed as the daughter? I should think it would be obvious that the mother correctly calculated that the daughter had found the secret hiding place and had eaten the jam herself.'

'That,' Jones said haughtily, 'is rather evident. What I want to know is what that's supposed to have to do with the price of eggs in Banksville.'

'Oh. Well, simply put, there's only one logical explanation for your astonishing surmise that Ernest Sellers sent me a letter pleading for my help. That would be if you'd received such a letter yourself. If you did, then you must be in an investigative occupation, quite obviously a private investigator. If you're willing to drop everything and come here for no pay—Ernest Sellers is pretty close with his money, I notice—then you must have time on your hands.'

Jones looked at the chief for a long moment. Then he said, 'I think we might as well quit sparring, Fellows. All right, we both know what we're here for. Let's compare notes.'

Fellows smiled. He said, 'I suppose I should have expected something like that from Sellers. I don't know why I assumed he wrote to no one but me. I wonder how many

122

pleas for help he did send out—and how many answers he's getting.'

Jones relaxed for the first time and laughed. 'I know a guy at Pinkerton's and he says they heard from him. He probably went through the directory.'

'Maybe he'll have an army in here trying to clear him.'

'Aah. Nobody'll come unless you get some small outfit like mine that's in need of publicity. Who's going to be that much of a fool?'

'Fool?'

'Trying to clear the guy. Let's face it, Fellows. This is a waste of time.'

'You mean you think he's guilty?'

'I mean I don't know what he is and I don't particularly care. If I'm lucky, I might stumble on something that would throw just enough doubt on the matter to cause a new trial. If I do that, I'm in clover. My firm will get a raft of publicity and business will come rolling in. If I don't, at least I'll get *some* publicity. It won't all be down the drain. Hell, see the deal? "Condemned criminal pleads for help to prove his innocence." That's quite a gimmick to begin with. Then you follow that up with "Jones and Strathmore Investigation Agency leaps to the rescue, free of charge, in the interests of seeing justice done." We cash in on that publicity right there and if we should by chance latch onto something and get him a new trial, that's even better. If we could prove he didn't do the job, man, we'd be set for life. So no matter how it turns out you've got to admit it's too good to pass up.'

Fellows said dryly, 'Yes, I suppose so.'

'Yeah,' Jones answered, with less pleasure in his voice. 'So then I start investigating and here's this guy staring at the murder house and it turns out he's Fred Fellows and that he's up here for the same purpose and where does that leave us? Let the papers in on this little gimmick and the reporters will all be hanging around Chief Fellows waiting for him to make with his great deductions. A fat lot of good that's going to do Jones and Strathmore.'

'I think you overrate my reputation,' Fellows said.

'Yeah. Man, you must think I'm naive. Listen, I'll tell you what I'll do. You give me a break and I'll give you one.'

'Such as?'

'You don't hog all the headlines and I share information. We can shorten the job if we both work together.' He paused and added, 'After all, we want to clear Sellers, don't we?'

'I want to find out whether he's innocent or guilty. I don't want to clear him if he did it.'

'Oh, hell,' Jones sighed, 'save that for the newspapers. You believe he's innocent or you wouldn't be here. O.K., that's good enough for me. So what do we want to do? We want to find some evidence. Two can do it better than one. So what do you say?'

Fellows hesitated. 'I don't suppose I can find any objection,' he said. 'It depends on the way you work. I have my own system and we might clash.'

'We'll play it your way. How's that?'

Fellows said reluctantly, 'You've got all the answers, don't you?'

Jones didn't let him off the hook. 'I always do.' He drained his coffee cup. 'O.K. Let's go over to my room and talk about it.'

CHAPTER FOURTEEN

Jones' room was a carbon copy of the chief's and he led the way in, tossing his jacket onto a chair. 'Like a drink?'

Fellows, closing the door, said, 'Your room come equipped with alcohol?'

'Not the room, but all good private detectives come equipped with alcohol.' He produced a pint from the bureau drawer and unscrewed the cap. 'I got glasses in the bathroom. No ice, though. I'm afraid you'll have to take it warm.'

'Just a short one. Police chiefs can't afford that kind of equipment.'

'Financially or workwise?'

'Both.'

Jones came out with two glasses and poured a couple of fingers into each. 'Water?'

'Half and half.'

Jones got the water, gave Fellows a half-filled glass of amber fluid and sat down in the chair by the bureau. 'Well,' he said. 'What have you got, Fellows? Or maybe I should say "chief" since you're boss of this operation.'

Fellows sat on the bed and his actions were a little stiff with reluctance. 'Let's hear what you've got—since I'm the boss of this operation.'

Jones gestured with his own glass. 'Nothing much yet.'

'What have you been doing all day?'

'Familiarizing myself with the case. There was that talk with Mrs. Baxter and in the afternoon I went through the newspaper files.'

'Newspaper files? Have you read the trial transcript?'

'Nope. That would be down in Pittsfield and I can't afford the time. Remember, if something doesn't turn up before the eighth of August it's all for nothing. So I got what I could from the newspaper office instead.'

'And let them know why you were here?'

'Well, I did hint at it of course. After all, I'm hoping to cash in on the publicity when this thing's over.'

'And what that means is that all the time this thing is "on" you're going to be working harder on the publicity angle than on the evidence angle?'

Jones shrugged and waved his glass again. 'Let's face it, Fellows. If there wasn't any evidence three years ago there's not going to be any evidence now. Evidence doesn't grow with the years, it shrivels. Like I say, I'm not really expecting to find anything. And if you are, you're a bigger fool than I take you for. We give it the old college try then pack it in and go home. Let's be realistic.'

Fellows took a sip of his drink and set the glass on the bedtable. 'You're right,' he said, rising. 'We should be realistic. The reason you want to tie up with me is because you figure there's a better chance of my finding something than you and you want half the credit if something is found. You're trying to cover yourself both ways, Jones, and I'm not about to play patsy for you.'

Jones came up off his chair. 'Hey, now, don't take it like that. Don't go off in a huff. It's still to your advantage for us to work together. You want evidence, don't you? Two can find it better than one. If Sellers really should be innocent, you'd be chancing sending an innocent man to the chair if you balk at combining forces. You need me and I need you. There's no point in our fighting each other.'

Fellows didn't move to the door. He remained standing and said, 'I'm not so sure I *do* need you, Mr. Jones. I think you might prove more of a liability than an asset.'

Jones grinned. 'Well,' he retorted, 'there's one way to find out, isn't there? Try me.' He picked up Fellows' glass and put it back in the chief's hand. 'What've you got to lose talking it over but a few minutes of your time? You haven't found out enough about me yet to know what I'll be.'

Fellows reluctantly sat down again and watched Jones resume his chair. Jones took a large gulp of his drink and smiled. 'What do you want to know?'

'First,' Fellows said tightly, 'what kind of evidence do you think you're going to look for?'

'Oh, that?' Jones gestured with his glass and took a long swallow, finishing the drink. 'We've got to find some clue somewhere that someone else could have done the job.'

'What kind of a someone?'

'That's the key point.' Jones sat up straighter and grew more sober. 'I regard it as very significant that Mrs. Sellers was wearing nothing but a bathrobe. I also regard it as significant that she was struck from behind.'

'So?'

'So the big question is, who does she know well enough to appear in a bathrobe in front of and who does she know well enough to

128

turn her back on?'

'Ernest Sellers.'

'Very funny. Who else?'

Fellows said, 'Don't ask me. I don't know who else.'

Jones sat back. 'Well, if we don't know who else, then we'd, by God, better damn well manufacture someone else pretty quick because we don't have a hell of a lot of time.'

'Who would you manufacture?'

'A lover would be best. I suppose if that falls flat we could come up with some peeping tom who couldn't resist trying to grab what he'd been peeping at.'

'How's your peeping tom going to see through drawn curtains?'

'The curtains were drawn, huh? That wasn't in the papers.'

'It was brought out at the trial.'

'You've read the trial transcript?'

'That's right. And I talked to Sellers.'

Jones' eyes widened. 'You did?' He sat back. 'It goes to show you what influence will do. I tried to and the warden said "no dice".' He brightened again. 'That doesn't matter, though. The lover angle is best all around. That's the one I'd figure on playing for. She's got a lover, see? He's been trying to break off with her. Maybe he's got a new sweetie. She's not going to stand for it. She'll go to her husband and her husband will do some pretty terrible things to the lover. He did some pretty violent things to men who even talked to her so you can imagine what he'd do to somebody who climbed into her bed. So the lover is on the spot. He hates her guts now because she won't turn him loose. He comes over for a final talk and she threatens and he loses his head and kills her in a fit of emotion. How does that strike you, Fellows?'

'There are a few holes in your story but it could have happened something like that.'

'Oh, holes? Where?'

'He must have had the weapon with him because he took it when he left and Sellers found nothing in the house missing.'

'Better yet. That makes it first degree. He didn't intend to try to break it off, he really meant to kill her. She opens the front door to him and turns her back to head for the bedroom and, wham, she's dead before she hits the floor. He whacks her a few more times for good measure and then walks out.'

'Through the front door?'

'What else?'

'The outside light was on.'

'What of it, if nobody's around?'

'Pretty risky for a murderer to use the front door, isn't it? Somebody *might* be around.'

Jones reached for his bottle and poured himself another shot. 'Man, Fellows, you sure can get bogged down in trivia. We don't care how he got in and out or how he and she came to end up in the living room. Let him use the back door, let him climb in a window. The point is, he's her lover and he killed her while her husband was off playing chess, a habit that was very well known to both of them.'

Fellows said, 'All right, we'll discard the trivia for the time being. It's a lover. So who is this lover?'

'We don't know and we don't care. All we have to do is show that there was one.'

'The defense stayed away from the lover angle, Jones, because all that does is give Sellers motive. You have to do more than show a lover. You have to show the lover killed her.'

Jones sipped a little of the whiskey straight. 'I swear I don't know how you ever solved anything, Fellows. All you do is block the paths to a solution. You keep pointing the finger *at* Sellers, not away from him.'

Fellows shook his head. 'I'm merely trying to show you what we're up against, Jones. I like the lover theory myself but Sheila having a lover isn't going to keep Sellers from the chair unless we can show the lover did it. And to show the lover did it, it's almost imperative that we find who the lover is and stick him with it. The least we have to do is show that he might have done it.'

Jones looked glumly at the floor for a moment, then up at the chief. 'A real big order, isn't it?' he said dryly. 'Well, like I
131

say, we give it the old college try and make as much hay as we can and then, when they throw the switch up at Midland Prison on the night of the eighth, we pack up and go about our regular business.' He sipped more of the whiskey and said musingly, 'It would be kind of a neat trick, though, if we could pull the whole thing off. It would really create a sensation.' He smiled at Fellows. 'I know you're thinking I'm visualizing the publicity, but it'd be fun for a lot of other reasons. It'd be fun just by itself.'

Fred Fellows visibly relaxed for the first time since Raphael Jones had stopped by his table. He picked up his glass and held it up in a toast. 'Shall we try to have a little fun, Mr. Jones?'

Jones lifted his own glass. 'I'm all for it, Mr. Fellows. Let's try to make it a ball.'

CHAPTER FIFTEEN

'The first thing,' Fellows said, opening his notebook on the bed, 'is that we've got nothing to go on. The only hope we've got, therefore, is to do a lot of guessing and pray that the guesses pay off. All right, the first guess is that Sheila, if she wasn't killed by Sellers himself, was killed by a lover. The second guess is that the lover lives in her neighborhood. Those two are probably the safest guesses we can make.'

Jones moved to the bed beside the chief and looked at the notebook. He flipped through several pages. 'What are all the names?'

'Possible suspects.'

'Great. Just great. It looks like a telephone directory. Where'd you get them all?'

'Thirty-five of them I got from Ernest Sellers. There are fifty-one others, including duplications, that I got from Mrs. Baxter.'

'How'd you rate so high with Mrs. Baxter? You romance her?'

'The fifty-one,' Fellows said, ignoring the crack, 'are males that Mrs. Baxter thinks Sheila might have known.'

'I don't believe it. She was supposed to be the retiring type.'

'She was, but it's a chummy neighborhood and everybody knows everybody.'

'Mrs. Baxter might know everybody but I'll bet Mrs. Sellers didn't. Not according to the way the newspapers pictured her.'

'She probably didn't, that's true. But another guess we're going to have to make is that everybody she did know is included here, however many it may be. And that includes the unknown lover. These fifty-one names we'll call our master list.'

'Fifty-one men?' Jones shook his head. 'And all living around Sheila?'

'Figure it,' Fellows said. 'There are ten houses down the block, front and back, and three houses on each width. That's twenty-five families not counting the Sellers right there. Then there are ten families across the street. There's a man in each family plus, in five cases, a teen-age son. That's forty. There are three other families on the other block that Mrs. Baxter thought the Sellers knew and there are eight male store employees whom she also probably knew. There's your fifty-one.'

Jones winced. 'And we have to find a lover from that list? That's a regular needle-in-a-haystack deal. Man, did I say it would be fun?'

'It's groping in the dark,' Fellows admitted, 'but I've done that before. We roll up our sleeves and go to work.'

'So who do we hit first? Do we close our eyes and stick a pin in the page?'

'No, we try to cut the list down. That's what I was working at during supper, dividing it into probables and improbables.'

Jones brightened. 'What about the ones Sellers had fights with? Seems to me they'd be likely lovers. He may have had more reason to fight than people knew about.'

Fellows shook his head. 'If he did he didn't tell me about it. He assured me his wife was faithful.'

'Don't be such a wet blanket. Take that

guy, what's his name, the salesman—George Walker. He's a bachelor, right? He's got a yen for the women, right? He danced with Sheila and got punched by Ernest, right? There's a come-on if I ever saw one. That's just the kind of challenge an old rake would eat up.'

'It's a nice revenge on Sellers,' Fellows admitted, 'but there are a few things wrong with Walker for the job.'

'What's wrong with him? To me he's the obvious suspect.'

'That's one of the things wrong. He's too obvious. Don't forget the police were looking for a lover three years ago.'

'But cops never see the obvious. You don't sell me anything with that line.'

'Then, too, we don't know what kind of a rake he is—'

'We find out.'

'I'm going to. Then another thing wrong is what's to keep him in the neighborhood? If you killed a woman and got away with it, wouldn't you move away before you tripped yourself up? And lastly, of course, is Sellers' belief his wife was faithful.'

'So he thinks his wife was faithful. We think she wasn't so what does his opinion mean?'

'Quite a lot, I believe. The men he fought with would be the men he had his eye on. These are the men he's expecting trouble

135

from yet he never even scowled at Walker after the fight even though Walker was known to have said hello to his wife. If Sellers thinks his wife was faithful it means he's sure he foiled all these people. If she wasn't faithful, then, I'd guess the lover would be someone he never suspected.'

Jones mulled that over. Finally he said, 'All right, you've got the ball. You carry it.'

Fellows nodded. 'The first thing I'd do,' he said, 'would be to concentrate on the people who lived in her block.'

'Yeah? Why?'

'If there was a lover, he was so secretive nobody knew a thing about him. If he got involved enough with her to have to kill her to get her off his back, this was no one-night affair. This must have gone on for some months. If he lived in her block he could make his way to her back door through back yards after dark. If he lived anywhere else, he'd have to approach the house in the open. In that neighborhood, from what Mrs. Baxter told me, this couldn't go on very long without somebody seeing him and then the rumors would fly.'

Jones thought about it. 'All right, I'll go along with that. That cuts the list in half then.'

'I count twenty-nine. Twenty-five families and four teen-age sons.'

'Twenty-nine, huh? Can we cut it down

some more?'

'There's the moving busines,' Fellows said. 'Nine families have moved out since the murder. Six from her block and three from across the street.'

'And you figure if a lover had done the job, chances are he'd be one of the ones who moved? That sounds logical.'

'I think there's a good chance of it. Therefore, one of the first things we should do is find out when these people moved, where they moved to, and why.'

'And if it's to California what do we do?'

Fellows shrugged. 'If it's to California we have to hope the guy wasn't a lover, I guess.'

'But that's where the lover would be most likely to move to—as far away as possible.'

'No,' Fellows answered slowly. 'Actually, it seems to me, if a man moved away solely because of the murder, he wouldn't be changing jobs, he'd only be changing neighborhoods. I think he wouldn't be far away at all.'

'Good. Good.' Jones was perking up. 'Then we're looking for people who moved from her block to a place near by and when we find them we turn on the heat.'

'They're the most probable,' Fellows corrected, 'but we can't limit ourselves that much. We have to go after everybody who moved from any block as our first step and everybody who lives on her block as the second.'

'And what are we going to ask them—"Did you have a love affair with Sheila Sellers?"'

'What we're going to try to find out, first off, is why, when and to where all the nine families who moved, moved to. The six on Sellers' block are Kligerman, Spencer and son, Roberts, Justin, Davins and Williamson. Across the street there is Hensen, Benton and Strauss.

'Secondly, we can guess that the only time a lover could approach Sheila Sellers unseen would be at night and the only time Ernest was away at night was Thursday when he played chess. Therefore we're going to want to find out, without being too obvious about it, what people in the whole neighborhood had some kind of business that took them out of the house Thursday evenings.

'The third thing, of course, is to try to find out what everybody was doing between seven and eight-thirty the night Sheila Sellers was killed.'

'Oh come on,' Jones said. 'You expect those people to remember what they did one night in October three years ago?'

'I want to know who doesn't remember, I can tell you that.'

'Nobody'll remember. What do you mean "who doesn't"?'

'Just that. I remember what I was doing Pearl Harbor Day. I'll bet you do too and that was more than twenty years ago. They'll all remember exactly what they were doing when they heard the news an acquaintance was murdered. Anybody who doesn't is suspect.'

'Well, you may be right. So tomorrow—'

'Tomorrow?' interrupted the chief. 'What do you want to waste tonight for? This is the time the men will be home.'

Jones sighed. 'I was afraid you'd see it that way. Ah, well. Tonight it is. By the way, what's our approach going to be?'

'Approach?'

'Yeah. Like my telling Mrs. Baxter I wrote true crime stories. I got to admit you don't look much like a writer, Fellows, but then a lot of writers don't look like writers either.'

'Why be writers?'

'Why not? We've got to be something to make these people open up. What's your suggestion?'

'Policemen. What else?'

'What else?' Jones struck his forehead. 'My God. What an imagination. I admit "copper" sticks out all over you and there's probably not much chance anybody'd believe you if you told them you were anything but a cop, but why not at least figure some excuse for quizzing people? Tell them you're doing it for the policemen's ball or something. You want these people to clam up on you?'

Fellows arched an eyebrow. 'It'd be kind of interesting to see who *does* clam up, don't you

139

think? We could start wondering why.'

'They'll all clam up, you jerk. Don't you know people and what they think of cops?'

'Mrs. Baxter didn't. I'll tell you, Mr. Jones, we might get some interesting results by letting it be known there's a question about Sellers' guilt. Let those people think there might be a killer living in the neighborhood and all kinds of things are apt to come out.'

'Sure. Great. But why tell them we're cops? That's the last thing we should tell them.'

'I imagine they already know,' Fellows said. 'I expect Mrs. Baxter got on the phone the moment I left her this morning.'

'Well,' Jones grumbled, 'then I guess we're stuck with it. Make me a list of the people I should see and let's go get clobbered.' He poured himself another shot and downed it quickly.

CHAPTER SIXTEEN

Fellows assigned Jones to work the back of the block down Xavier Street from the Penny house on the corner of Finch and his instructions were specific. Jones was to pick up all the information he could about those who had moved; he was to suggest the possibility that Sheila's murderer was still at large; he was to get each man's recollection of the murder night and he was to prod each family to talk about its neighbors, especially with regard to men who were away from home evenings. He was also to keep an ear out for any interesting tidbits; rumors and scandals that had swept the neighborhood and opinions as to who might have been glad to see Sheila dead.

He himself started at the opposite corner and worked along Solomon Street. He skipped the corner house since the Justins, who had had it, had moved. The Polin place was dark but the next had lights and Fellows was pleased. That was the home of the questionable George Walker and Walker's reputation made him best-suited for the role of lover. Though he was "too obvious," as Jones had said the police sometimes missed the too obvious. Perhaps the hypersuspicious Ernest Sellers had missed the too obvious, too.

Walker opened the door on the first ring. He was a husky, sandy-haired, gray-eyed man in shirt sleeves, capable and self-assured. 'Well?' he asked.

Fellows introduced himself by holding out his badge and saying, 'I'm Fred Fellows, a police officer. I wondered if I could have a few words with you, Mr. Walker.'

Walker didn't note that the badge was for a police department far from Banksville but reacted instead as people inevitably react when approached by the law. His face sobered and he racked his brains for what crimes he might recently have committed. He stepped back with a murmured invitation to come in and closed the door behind the chief.

An attractive woman with an apron on appeared from the kitchen and stopped dead. She was about thirty, brunette, and tan of skin with an occasional dark freckle. She looked from the chief to Walker with bright green eyes, said, 'Oh, excuse me,' and disappeared back into the kitchen again.

Walker hesitated, decided to ignore the event and motioned. 'Take a chair, officer. Make yourself comfortable.'

Fellows made himself comfortable but he took a chair that would give him a view down the short hall where the woman had been. Walker shifted his feet. He appeared to be in his middle thirties and his waist showed an appropriate thickening. 'What's the trouble?' he finally asked as Fellows was slow getting out his notebook and finishing his preparations.

'Nothing's the trouble, Mr. Walker. Not recently, anyway. I'm investigating the murder that took place here three years ago. The murder of Sheila Sellers.' He licked the tip of his pencil. "Let's see now. You're in the insurance business, that right?'

Walker was watching him warily, a fact the

chief observed without appearing to. 'Yes, insurance,' Walker said. 'What do you mean, the murder?'

'Sheila Sellers,' Fellows told him again. 'You must remember the murder. Three years ago.'

Walker eased himself down onto the couch. 'Yes, of course.' He darted one quick glance at the empty doorway and said, 'But what do you mean you're investigating it? It's over and done with.'

Fellows met him with an open stare. 'Oh, I wouldn't say that, Mr. Walker. Murder cases are a long time dying. They have a way of coming back.'

'But that fellow Sellers. He killed her. It's all been settled.'

'He was convicted of killing her,' Fellows corrected. 'Convicted. That doesn't necessarily mean that he actually did it.'

Walker's eyes widened. 'You mean you think he *didn't* do it?'

Fellows smiled at him. 'Now you've got the idea, Mr. Walker. So if he didn't do it, somebody else did, right? And that someone else would be from around here. He'd be living around here playing possum.'

Walker groaned at the thought. 'Oh, my God.'

Fellows nodded agreeably. 'It opens up some interesting possibilities, wouldn't you say?'

'Somebody from around here? You got any ideas?'

Fellows' eyes were very sharp and he spoke slowly. 'Well, yes, Mr. Walker. We think Mrs. Sellers had a lover.'

Walker started visibly at that. 'A lover?'

Fellows felt his interest quicken. 'A lover,' he said amiably. 'She was all but naked when she was killed and she was killed in a rage. Struck down from behind, as a matter of fact. It adds up, wouldn't you say?'

Walker wet his lips and almost, but not quite, looked at the doorway again. 'I suppose so,' he said in a strained voice and cleared his throat. 'But I thought it was the husband.'

'So did a lot of people, Mr. Walker, but we're looking at the case a little differently now.' He gave Walker the smile again. 'So the question is, who was Mrs. Sellers' lover? Which of the men living in the neighborhood at that time might have been involved with her?' He looked brightly at the man. 'Any ideas?'

Walker croaked a little. 'No. No, I don't have any ideas.'

Fellows showed no surprise. He thumbed back through the notebook pages a little and went on. 'In the course of the last three years—in the time since the killing—nine men who were presumably known to Mrs. Sellers moved out of the area. James Benton is one. Then there's Robert Strauss, Richard

144

Kligerman, John Davins, Sherwood Spencer, Jeffrey Roberts, Carl Hensen, George Williamson, and Howard Justin. You know those people, Mr. Walker?'

Walker breathed a little easier. 'Some of them,' he said.

'You know anybody else who moved?'

'No.'

'Any of those men strike you as possible lovers?'

Walker wet his lips again. 'No, I wouldn't say so. I don't know the people around here that well.' He hesitated. 'Maybe if I knew what kind of a man you were after I might be able to tell better.'

'The kind of man who'd cheat on his wife—if he had a wife. The kind who'd cheat on a husband if he was a bachelor.'

'Davins was a bachelor,' Walker said quickly. 'He and his sister were around the corner. Only about four houses from the Sellers as a matter of fact. Maybe he's the man.'

'Know why he moved?'

'No, he didn't say. I didn't really know him.' He swallowed. 'Come to think of it, though, it wasn't long after the murder. Right after the trial, I believe.'

'I see,' Fellows said, making notes.

'Sort of what a person might do,' Walker volunteered. 'I mean wait till after the trial. So it wouldn't look funny, I mean.'

145

'He wasn't called on to testify, as I recall.'

'Well, who'd know? I mean about him and Sheila Sellers?'

'That's a good question. Would it be hard for her to keep a love affair quiet in this neighborhood?'

Walker shrugged. 'Not too hard.'

'People talk, I understand. If he was seen going to her house just once, well, it'd be all over the neighborhood.'

'He could go to her back door after dark. The yards all run into each other and there're very few fences.'

'You don't think it'd be hard?'

Walker said, 'No. I don't think it'd be hard.'

Fellows seemed satisfied. He wrote a little more and then said, 'Now what about Mrs. Sellers? You think she played around?'

'Well, if she had a lover, she must have.'

'She seem like the type to you?'

'I really didn't know her.'

'You danced with her at a block dance as I recall, and got punched in the nose for it by her husband.'

Walker looked uncomfortable again. 'Well, maybe you don't know about him. He gets hysterical. There wasn't anything to it. All I did was dance with her. It came out at the trial that that's all it was.'

'It also came out at the trial that you saw her on other occasions.'

146

'I ran into her, that's all. Sellers knew about it. It was all perfectly innocent.'

Fellows smiled. 'I'm not questioning that,' he said. 'What I mean is, seeing her on a number of occasions you must have formed some opinion about her. Was she the type to play around would you say?'

Walker concentrated. After a bit he said, 'I would think so. I wouldn't know, of course, but I'd guess she was—well let's say she wasn't one who was out looking for anything. She couldn't the way Ernest kept his eye on her. But if something came her way she wouldn't knock it back. Put it that way.'

Fellows accepted that. Then he said, 'Did you find this out by personal experience, Mr. Walker?'

He blinked and licked his lips again. 'No. Certainly not.'

'She was a pretty attractive woman. You danced with her. She must have had *some* appeal for you.'

'That was just a block dance, a get-together party. Everybody danced with everybody. I just grabbed her and danced with her. I'd never seen her before. I don't pal around with the people here so I only know them a little by name.'

'You didn't find her attractive?'

'Well, sure. But that doesn't mean anything. I mean, she's married to this guy and he gets upset about men dancing with

147

her. I'd steer clear of her, believe me.'

'But she struck you as a pushover?'

Walker shook his head quickly. 'No, no. Nothing like that. I mean if some guy really went after her, why I think she might be persuaded to play around.'

'Davins strike you as the type?'

Walker hesitated again. 'I wouldn't really know. I never knew him except by sight. All I can say is, living with his sister, well, he's got to do *something*. Whether he did anything with Mrs. Sellers—well, I wouldn't have any idea.'

'Is there anybody you like better for the role?'

Walker shook his head. 'No. I don't know people around here much. It could be anybody. It could be several people. I wouldn't know.'

'Several lovers?'

'Well, who knows about women? If one guy could make the grade with her probably others could.'

Fellows said somberly, 'This is quite a different picture of Mrs. Sellers that we've been getting before this.'

'Well, you can't tell about women. She shows one face to other women and a different face to other men.'

'So you think Ernest Sellers had good reason for his jealous tirades?'

'Well he had them, didn't he? If he'd

punch a guy just for dancing with his wife and make a big scene at a party because another guy so much as talked to her, it'd stand to reason he must know something about her.'

'And you noticed it just dancing with her?'

'Well, you can tell.'

Fellows glanced at the doorway this time. He said, 'To be personal, how come you passed up something like this? I understand you're quite a ladies' man.'

'Me?' Walker expressed great innocence. 'Where'd you ever hear that kind of talk?'

'It's floating around the neighborhood.'

'But I'm not that kind of guy. What d'ya mean? That shows the way people talk when they don't know what they're talking about.' He pointed a finger earnestly. 'That's what you get. You live in a neighborhood and you mind your own business. You don't associate much with the rest of them and that makes you the oddball. The first thing you know they're making up stories about you.'

Fellows nodded and smiled faintly. 'You know, that's very interesting. The Sellers were oddballs that way too, but quite different stories came out about Mrs. Sellers. Nobody had any idea she played around.'

'Well, that's all right. Maybe Sheila Sellers played a role. She made it look good. I don't bother and it makes me look bad.'

'I see.' Fellows went on, musingly, 'It still

beats me, though, a single man like you walking away from something like that.'

'I told you,' Walker answered heatedly. 'Her husband got hysterical. You think I'd go looking for trouble? Who knows what he might do if he found out she had a lover. He might kill the guy.'

'Weren't you running a risk even talking to Sheila after he'd punched you that time?'

'But all that was was running into her or them in the store or someplace and being polite.'

'Were you polite to him?'

'Well, I don't know that I ever talked to him after that. But if I talked to her, he knew about it. There wasn't much he didn't know the way he watched her.'

'But he didn't know she had a lover.'

'Maybe he did.'

'If he did, then why didn't he kill the man? Didn't you say that's what you were afraid of—that if you fooled around with his wife he might kill you?'

Walker swallowed and hesitated. 'I don't know,' he finally said. 'You got me all confused.'

'And if he knew about the lover he'd know who killed his wife. Don't you think he'd have been blabbing the guy's name all over the place instead of getting sentenced for the murder himself?'

Walker said heavily, 'I suppose so.'

150

Fellows switched subjects suddenly. 'How did you feel when you heard about the murder?'

'Me? I was shocked.'

'Did you believe he did it?'

'Not at first. Not till they arrested him. It never occurred to me.'

'You thought somebody else did it? Who, for instance?'

'Nobody from around here. Some robber or something.'

'When did you find out about it, by the way? You remember what you were doing that day?'

'I heard about it when I came home,' Walker said. 'I went down to Pittsfield on business when I left the office. Ate down there and didn't get back till around quarter of twelve. I saw the police cars there and a lot of people around outside so I went up and the people there told me what had happened. Dick Castle next door. Him and his wife. It was unbelievable.'

'The police ever talk to you about the case?'

Walker nodded. 'Oh, sure. They talked to everybody. What were the Sellers like? Did we see or hear anything that night? I couldn't give them any help. I hardly knew the Sellers and I'd been away all day. They poked through all the garbage pails on the block and dredged the sewers looking for the weapon but they never found anything.'

Any hopes Fellows had that he was talking to a murderer were pretty well dashed. The police apparently hadn't overlooked the obvious after all. It spoke well for the police but it also said the digging would have to be much deeper than Fellows had been probing. There was going to be no quick and easy answer. 'You mention Davins as a possibility,' he said, turning the subject back again. 'Who else in this neighborhood, in your opinion, fills the bill?'

'Who're the ones who moved again?'

Fellows re-read him the list and said, 'Of course it might be somebody who's still here. Name me anybody still around who might be possible.'

'I don't know these people too well,' Walker complained. 'I don't even know who lives around here.'

Fellows said, 'I'll read them off one by one and you tell me what you think. All right?'

'All right.'

The chief started with the ex-residents again and got Sherwood Spencer's name to add to Davins'. As for the ones still around, Walker was decidedly uncertain. He thought Gordon Henry, the bachelor who lived with his mother, might be possible. Then there was Horace Blackstone, Robert Franklin and William King on the back of the block. Along Wellington Street he nodded at Carsten

DeWitt, Frank Temple and Richard Maynard. He shook his head, however, at the five teen-age boys and knew nothing about store clerks.

Finally he was seeing the chief to the door and he closed it with silent thanks for his good fortune. The policeman had not embarrassed him by insisting on meeting the attractive woman who was at that moment waiting things out in the kitchen.

CHAPTER SEVENTEEN

Fellows hit two more houses before it got too late to go barging in on people's evenings and then he parked his car on Xavier Street, behind Wellington, to pick up Raphael Jones from whatever house he'd next appear.

Jones came out of the King place, seventh from his corner, which meant he'd either worked fast or sketchily. Fellows rolled the car forward and honked and Jones turned around, walked over and climbed in. 'Quits for tonight?' he asked in surprise. 'It's only half past nine.'

'These people aren't private detectives. They go to bed.'

'They watch television, you mean. Channel three from Hartford. Channel three is invading every house.'

'It's time to leave them alone at any rate.'

'I'm all for that. This is my idea of work. Let's go hit a gin mill somewhere.'

Fellows made a face and Jones caught the distaste. 'Come on, man, who the hell wants to go back and sit around a dead motel room? Hotels and motels give me the creeps unless you've got a broad or somebody to pass the time with. Relax and live a little, Fellows, before you get old. Oh, pardon me. You already are old. I forgot.'

'All right,' Fellows said. 'We'll go to a gin mill.'

'Now you're talking. Only remember, you're going in there as a customer. Don't try to raid the place.'

They found a dimly lit dive in the center of town called 'Bert's' and Fellows walked in like a man entering an unexplored cavern. He accustomed his eyes to the darkened interior and found his way to a booth which had a dim, shaded yellow light protruding from the wall. He said glumly, 'I don't know if I can read my notes in here,' but Jones, looking happily at home, wasn't bothering about notes. He caught the bartender's eye and said, 'Hey, two stiff whiskeys here. My father is paying.' He turned and shook a cigarette from his pack and lighted it. 'Now this is living, man.'

'It is?' Fellows raised his eyebrows. 'I thought this was a funeral parlor.'

'That's just the embalming fluid they serve, but one develops a taste for it.' He looked up at the television set over the door facing down the long room and said, 'If they'd turn that thing up a little we might be able to hear what they're saying about that soap they're showing. Hey, Mac!'

Fellows said, 'I thought we came here to work.'

Jones said, 'Yeah, I was afraid you thought so.' He waved at the bartender. 'Never mind, Mac. Just pour the drinks and remember Christmas is only five months away.'

Fellows tightened the corner of his mouth. 'If you can come down out of orbit, Mr. Jones, I'd like to know what you've got. I already gather it isn't much but I'd like to hear it all the same.'

Jones leered at him. 'Isn't much? That shows how good a detective you are. Why you start those people thinking there's a murderer loose in their block and they'll rat on their own family. Believe me the rumors are flying. I'll bet everybody in the development knows we think there's a murderer loose. Tonight's the tough night though. Tonight they aren't so willing to talk about their neighbors to strangers, but you wait. They're going to think about things in bed and start wondering which of their friends beat Sheila Sellers to death. By tomorrow they won't look each other in the eye and they'll start turning to us with all the dirt they know. They'll be so scared the others will squeal on them they'll fight to do it first. Man, I'm telling you, when we leave this place, whether we catch anybody or not, nobody'll be speaking to anybody.'

'It's unfortunate,' Fellows said, 'but I'm afraid it's likely.'

'Unfortunate? We're in luck. How else could we hope to get what we need?' He paused as the bartender served the drinks. 'Yeah, man,' he said, lifting his glass to the little bit of light. 'That's my favorite color of brown.'

Fellows lifted his own glass, took a tiny sip and felt his hair start to curl. 'What is this stuff?'

'Whiskey. At least that's what the bartender calls it. You can weaken it by letting it sit in the ice but you'll lose the flavor.'

'I hope so.' Fellows placed the glass on the pad and said, 'Suppose, now, we forget about all the information we're going to get tomorrow and talk about what you got tonight. You did get something, didn't you?'

'Sure, sure, sure. I called on five suspects, skipping only the Kligerman and Spencer houses. I figured the people who moved in after them wouldn't know from nothing.'

'And what about the ones who should?'

'Yeah, all right. Just let me get a taste of

156

the drink, huh? Man, you have the singlest track mind I ever met.' He dug into the glass with a big swallow and licked his lips. He sighed with pleasure, put down the drink and started. 'First there're the Pennys on the corner.'

'Don't you have a notebook?'

'Never learned how to write. Keep it in my head.'

Fellows said, 'Wait,' and got out his own. 'All right. Let's have what's supposed to be in your head.'

'First, you can scratch Mr. Penny. He's in his sixties and arthritic. It'd take a better girl than Sheila to make a man out of him. Next—'

'Hold on,' Fellows interrupted. 'What did you do, look at him and walk out? Didn't you ask him any questions?'

'Sure. I got no cooperation, though.'

'Didn't you mention what you were there for?'

'Sure, but like I just told you, tonight's the tough night. He didn't dig me. He thought that spiel was an opening wedge to sell him a set of encyclopedias or something. Hit him tomorrow and he might shovel some dirt. That is, if he knows any. I think it's all he can do to remember his own name.'

'What about his wife?'

'Motherly type. "Time for your medicine and pills, dear." That sort of thing. She's too busy hovering over him to hover over the neighborhood.'

'Is that a conclusion or do you have some evidence?'

Jones cocked his head at the chief. 'You know, Fellows, you're about as fussy a guy as I ever ran into. I'll bet you nail your furniture to the floor. Can't a guy have instincts without you wanting everything spelled out?'

Fellows said. 'What you mean is, it's a conclusion.' He made a note.

'Yeah, it's a conclusion. So there you have it. Now how about taking a slug of your drink? Take it all, why don't you?'

'You trying to get me drunk?'

'What, and have to carry you? You'd fall and crush me to death. No, I just want to corrupt you a little. All that virtue you got! What do you do with it? You can't eat it.'

'I'm making angel wings out of it. Now let's move along. What about the Blackstones?'

Jones had more of his own drink and said, 'Now you're getting warmer. Fortyish, black hair. Moved into the house the year before the murder. He has a very homely wife.'

Fellows scribbled and said, 'Go on.'

'Go on? I didn't ask him if he had an affair with Sheila Sellers, you know. Or maybe you think I should have.'

'What does he do on Thursday nights?'

'I didn't ask him that either. He was bigger

than me. But I did get from him that Penny never did anything Thursday nights or any other nights. I also got it out of him that George Williamson, one of those guys who moved, was sent to California to open a branch office of his company. He doesn't know where Kligerman went, though, which I figure is significant since Kligerman lived next door. He didn't know Kligerman's business either.'

'Anything else out of him?'

Jones reflected. 'Let's see. Husky, good-looking guy. Works for Savage Electronics Company. Engineer. Likes a drink in the evening along with his skinny wife. Knows a lot of the neighbors but doesn't know much about their private life. Neither does his wife, unfortunately.'

'O.K., then next after Kligerman comes Herbert Rogers.'

'Hey, slow up. Aren't you going to ask me my opinion?'

'I'm looking for facts but if you want to give me an opinion—'

'Man, you aren't going to find this lover guy with facts. It's all going to be opinion. So, my opinion is that Blackstone makes a good suspect. He moves into the house, meets the neighbors, and Sheila catches his eye. I think whoever did it moved in no more'n a year before the killing. He starts something and gets tired of it and finishes it with a bump on the noggin—several bumps.'

'All right. Now about Herbert Rogers?'

Jones sighed. 'I give up. All right, Herbert Rogers. Fourth house down.'

Rogers, Jones related, knew why the Kligermans had moved. They'd split up and another woman was involved. 'Unfortunately,' Jones said, 'not a woman from around here. And don't ask me what Kligerman did Thursday evenings.'

'All right. But what did Rogers do Thursday evenings?'

'Nothing. And he wasn't around the night of the murder either. He was in Colorado on a business trip and didn't even hear about the murder till the weekend.'

'Then next is Robert Franklin.'

'Him I like better. He's not best, but he's better.' Jones went on to explain that Franklin and his wife had lived there six years and liked a good time. They were the instigators of the block dances held once or twice a summer and they associated freely with the neighbors. 'Of course I don't know how free is "freely", whether it means wife-swapping or not but you never can tell. Anyway, they're buddy-buddy with the Castles who live next to Sellers. I can see Franklin playing around. I can very definitely see that.'

'On Thursday nights?'

Jones sighed. 'He and his wife are out most

nights but I didn't ask if they were always together. In fact, they were at the Castles' when the police arrived next door and that's how they learned of the murder.'

'Were they at the Castles' house between seven and eight-thirty?'

Jones said resentfully, 'Now can I go say to them, "Did you do it?" I asked as much as I could without getting them sore. Just keep him on the list of probables and let's go on to the real important family.

'Spencer?'

'Sherwood Spencer. That's right. Either him or his son. I got this from the Franklins mostly and a little from the Kings.'

'You got what?'

'First off, they moved in only four and a half years ago, or about a year and a half before the murder. And they moved out no more'n three months after the trial. I got it from Franklin that Spencer gave financial problems as the reason for moving. He said he had reverses and couldn't afford the place.'

'Know where he moved to?'

'That's the point,' Jones said triumphantly. 'Right over to the other side of Banksville. He's still right here in town at the same old job. So how do you like that?' He slugged his drink to celebrate.

'Find out anything about his character?'

Jones put the glass down. 'Playing it straight, huh, Fellows? O.K., his character.

161

He and his wife fought all the time. That much I got. But here's the interesting item. He talked about financial reverses but it came out after they moved that his son had been having an affair with some girl about three blocks away. So maybe he moved because of the girl, but maybe that wasn't the first girl the son had got mixed up with. You wouldn't think a guy'd pack up and shove off just because his son was playing around. You'd think he might have a better reason.'

Fellows had to agree. 'Got an address for him?'

'Franklin didn't know it but I guess he's in the phone book.'

Fellows made special notes about that and then got the report on William King and his son Junior. Junior was away in summer school till the end of July. The father was a homely, timid type, a chronic worrier. 'You can cross off the old man,' Jones said. 'I won't guarantee the son. So, now, what about you?'

Fellows shrugged. He allowed as how George Walker had the potential but seemed to be alibied for the murder time. 'At least I presume the police checked out the alibi.' As for Manny Bomstein and Sid Gary, both were apparently home all the murder evening and neither looked like suspects to begin with.

'So,' said Jones. 'You don't like me forming conclusions but you form them all over the place. What's that mean, yours are gold and everyone else's is brass?'

'Mine don't mean a damned thing. We're not really eliminating anybody, we're just feeling our way trying to size up the way things are around here.'

'So what do we do next?'

'We keep on doing what we did last. We ask questions and listen and hope that someone, somewhere, might give us a tip that'll point a finger in some direction.' Fellows picked up his drink and drained it in large gulps. He set the glass down and gasped, then shivered. 'Well,' he said, pulling himself together, 'if that's your idea of something good to drink, I'd hate to go with you across a desert.' He squeezed out of the booth and reached in his hip pocket for his wallet. 'Let's go get some sleep. Tomorrow's going to be a long hard day.'

CHAPTER EIGHTEEN

The morning paper was on sale in the motel cafeteria when Fellows entered it for breakfast Thursday. He pulled one from the rack when he picked up his utensils and then opened it on his tray at the counter while waiting for his order.

What he saw very nearly destroyed his

appetite. In large type on the front page was the headline, 'DETECTIVE SEEKS TO CLEAR SELLERS'. Above it was the kicker, 'Innocent, says Private Eye' and below, as a drophead, 'Claims Sheila's Killer Still at Large'.

Fellows angrily snatched up the paper and snapped it open to read the story. Mr. Raphael Jones, private detective from Springfield, Mass., was in town, so he had told the *Banksville Gazette* in their offices the preceding afternoon, to prove the innocence of Ernest Sellers, convicted, in Banksville's most sensational murder case, of slaying his wife Sheila three years before, come October 20th. Jones, according to the story, held the view that not only was Sellers innocent of his wife's death, he was also innocent of his wife's activities while she was alive. He refused to elaborate on this statement but announced his intention of digging up the true facts of the matter and exonerating an innocent man condemned to die. The rest of the story dealt with Jones' background, that he was partner in the firm of Jones & Strathmore, the 'well-known Springfield investigative agency'.

Fellows paid for his breakfast and glowered as he carried the tray to the table by the plate glass window in the rear. It was half past seven and only four others were eating that early, none of them being, of course, Raphael

164

Jones.

Jones didn't arrive until nearly eight, as the chief was finishing a second cup of coffee. The private detective waved gaily when he came in the door and, after going to the counter, brought cereal and toast and ham and eggs and coffee to the chief's table. 'Man,' he said, 'I thought I was early. You cops sure keep wicked hours. It's not even eight yet.'

Fellows said acidly, 'Where did you learn the private detective business? Out of Mickey Spillane?'

'Oh, oh,' Jones said, sitting down and spreading his napkin. 'The chief's got up on the wrong side of the bed today.'

Fellows pushed the paper across the table so Jones could see the story. 'What do you think this is, a game?'

'Oh.' Jones eyed it and looked pleased. 'Front page, too!'

He adjusted the paper to read and Fellows pulled it away again. 'Suppose you explain yourself, Mr. Jones. If you can explain something like this.'

'Oh,' Jones said, waving casually. 'I gave them that story yesterday afternoon when I was looking things up in the morgue down there.'

'I gather that. That's not telling me anything.'

'Well, what the hell,' Jones said, piqued. 'I

165

did that before we made our deal.'

'What deal?'

'About splitting the publicity.'

Fellows clamped the table edge with both hands. When he spoke his voice was under control, but only barely. 'I'm not interested in the publicity. I'm talking about you shooting off your mouth. Do you know what you've done?'

'Sure. Got my name in the paper. I told you. That's what I'm here for.'

'You got your name in the paper all right. You got it there by slapping all the police authorities in the county: the local police, the State Police, the Pittsfield police and the county detectives. You did it up brown, Mr. Jones.'

Jones said huffily, 'So what do you think, the sun rises and sets on policemen? You think a cop can't ever make a mistake? You think nobody ought to call attention to it if one of them or the whole mess of them do? *You* think Sellers is innocent. *You* think there's been a miscarriage of justice. Only you don't want anybody to come out and say so publicly because it might reflect on that most sterling of all occupations, policing your fellow citizens. You're like the AMA whitewashing the medical profession. Well, I'm not afraid to call a cop stupid even if you are.'

Fellows shoved back his chair. 'Have it

166

your way,' he said, getting up. 'But when the cops start throwing monkey wrenches, don't whine about it to me.'

'Now, listen, don't get sore just because your name didn't get in. I was going to tell you. I'm going to give the papers another scoop today and I'll tell them we're working on it together. Listen, hey, don't go I'm even going to tell them you're the boss of the operation!'

Fellows turned and came back. He gripped the back of the chair and leaned his weight. 'I don't think you've caught on yet,' he said. 'In a china shop you should be a pussy cat, not a bull. The trouble is, you don't even know you're in a china shop. Did you ever stop to think, Mr. Jones, what the reaction to that story might be? Did it ever occur to you that it might hamper an investigation?'

'All right, so it hampers. What are we investigating anyway? What do you really think we're going to find? It's not going to make a damned bit of difference whether we investigate or not as far as Sellers is concerned. They're going to pull the switch on him August eighth and you're kidding yourself if you think they aren't.'

'And who cares, right?'

'Come off it,' Jones said sullenly. 'It's not that. The fact is there's not one good goddam thing we can do about it no matter how much we might care. And if you were half as smart

167

as the papers make you out to be, you'd know it yourself. We're not miracle men, we're detectives and they had ten times as many detectives as us going over the case three years ago. There isn't anything there, Fellows. There just isn't anything there.'

'You thought differently last night.'

'You had me under your spell last night. So you know what happens? You go out and talk to people and you get carried along with it. And then you climb into bed and lie there in the dark and think about it and it comes to you that you're doing nothing but wasting your time. Nobody is going to know anything about a lover because they were all asked that three years ago and they didn't know anything then. And if they *did* know about a lover you still wouldn't have any motive for murder. And if you did have a motive you still would have to prove opportunity. It's all been done, Fellows. There's nothing for us to do but rake over the ashes and the ashes have been cold for three long years.'

'Not quite,' Fellows snapped. 'There's one thing we know that the detectives who investigated the crime didn't. We know who moved out of there when it was all over.'

'And what is that going to prove? Do you think a guilty conscience is something you can produce in court? Listen, I'm sorry about giving out the story. I did it before I met you. If you want to blame me, I can't stop you but

168

I wasn't expecting to find anything when I went after the publicity and it didn't matter to me how the cops felt about it. All right, it's done now. I can't take it back. If it louses you up, I'm sorry. If you want, I'll go down to headquarters and take the blame. Or if it'll free your hands, I'll lead the cops and the reporters a merry chase and give you a clear field to do the real work. Whatever you want is O.K. with me.'

Fellows made a face and let go of the chair. 'Hell, I don't know what's going to do any good. Maybe it's my fault. I should have called on the chief and taken him into my confidence yesterday. Now all I can do is go down there and see if I can square things.'

'You want me to come with you or anything?'

Fellows pointed his finger. 'I want you to get out to Wellington Street and see as many more people as you can before the cops start arresting you for vagrancy.'

CHAPTER NINETEEN

Police Headquarters in Banksville was a converted schoolhouse of ancient origin on a sidestreet in the center of town. It was half past eight by the time Fellows found the place, parked, and walked up the steps and

169

through the doorway of the nine-room, two-floored boxlike structure.

There was loud voices from the room on the right which bore the sign, 'Main Desk' and five men were there; the duty sergeant behind a cut-off desk, Chief of Police Dennis Acton, and three reporters. It was the chief doing most of the talking and the talking was about the front page story in that morning's paper. 'He's a headline hunter,' Acton was saying angrily. 'That's what he is. And if I lay my hands on him, I'll give him a few headlines.'

'Can we quote you?' one amused reporter asked.

'You damned well better not. You just get the meaning of what I'm saying and put it in right English. And I'll tell you this. No goddam sonuvabitch is gonna come into this town and scare the hell out of everybody with any line of crap about a murderer being loose. That case was solved three years ago. The State Police came in here and they solved it. And when the State Police solve something, they solve it. And you can quote me on that if you want! And besides the State Police, we had detectives from Pittsfield and we had the county detectives and we had our own men. We arrested Sellers and he was convicted fair and square and if you don't believe that, then you're a goddam fool because the courts threw out all the appeals. And if you don't think he was guilty, then you don't believe in the American system of justice and anybody who doesn't believe in America is a Communist and you can quote me on that!

'So what does that make that sonuvabitch bastard out of Springfield who can't mind his own business in his own goddam state but has to come down here to stir up trouble? Answer me that. He's a rabble-rouser, that's what he is. He's down here trying to frighten honest citizens. He's trying to get everybody upset.

'Now I'm telling you, he's not doing this just for kicks. There's an organization behind people like him and that organization is trying to stir up trouble and they're trying to get murderers like that Ernest Sellers out of jail. They're trying to frighten people and turn murderers loose on people. They want to empty our jails and terrorize us. Well, they're not going to do it. You put it in the papers that I say this guy is a nut or a spy or something. Anyway, he's a lousy sonuvabitch bastard, only don't you quote those words, and you put it in your papers that the people he goes to question should keep their traps shut and not tell him a goddam thing and if he gives them any trouble they should call the police and we'll have a squad car out there arresting him before he can get off their front steps. I run an honest town here and no sonuvabitch bastard is gonna come in here and frighten people. And no bastard outta

171

Massachusetts is gonna come down here and suggest Connecticut cops don't know how to solve murder cases neither, and you can quote me on that. On second thought, maybe you better not. Just say "bastards from *other* states". And you can also say that the Banksville police are launching an investigation into this man and we're gonna find out whether he's got a record somewhere and when we get through we'll know what he thinks he's doing coming in and messing up our town. And we're gonna find out who's paying him to do this and who it is wants to keep Ernest Sellers outta the electric chair where he rightfully belongs.'

Acton's eye caught Fellows leaning against the doorframe and he bellowed, 'What the hell do *you* want?'

'I'd like to see you when you've got a minute, Chief.'

'I'm busy.' He started to turn back to the reporters, then looked back again. 'I'm in a conference.'

'Yes. I'll wait.'

'This is a *private* conference.'

'With the press?'

'That's right. A private conference with the press.' He glared. 'Say, you ain't from around here. Who are you?'

'My name is Fellows. Fred Fellows. I'm chief of police in Stockford.'

'Fellows?' Acton's voice sounded slightly

strangled and the reporters whirled. 'Fred Fellows? *The* Fred Fellows?'

'I'm *a* Fred Fellows. I don't know how many others there are.'

'Are you here about the Sellers thing, Mr. Fellows?'

Fellows answered mildly, 'I'm here to see Chief Acton when he's through.'

'Yeah,' Acton said. 'Well, I'm through now. All right, you got your story, youse guys, only don't quote me where I said I didn't want to be quoted.' He brushed past the men and out the door, nodding Fellows along with him to the left rear of the four first floor rooms, which was marked by the sign, 'Chief'.

It was a large, forty-pupil classroom but Acton had it all to himself and it looked barren, the few furnishings lost in its size.

'Yeah,' Acton said, getting behind his desk and waving Fellows to the nearest of the few straight-backed chairs. 'Chief Fellows, huh? You addressed the Chiefs' Convention last year. I shouldda recognized you. Acton's my name.' He rose and held out a hand.

Fellows said, 'I know,' and shook it, then sat down again.

'Well, it's quite an honor. I mean, we get something like that Sellers case and we go to the State cops. We don't have the knowhow for nothing big like that. Down your way you do it yourself. And you really do it too! So what brings you here? I guess maybe you saw the papers this morning. That's what I was talking about to those reporter guys. Some joker trying to stir up trouble.'

'Yes,' Fellows said. 'And it seems that I'm here for something along the same lines.'

Acton blinked and scowled. 'You too? What are you trying to tell me, that Sellers is innocent?'

'No. I'm not trying to tell you that. I'm just not convinced that he's guilty.'

'Well if he isn't, then who is?'

'That's what I'd like to try to find out.'

Acton gripped the arms of his chair. 'Say what the hell *is* this? The case is over and done with three years almost and all of a sudden everybody and his brother shows up wanting to open the whole thing up again. Is everybody nuts?'

'I talked to Sellers and I talked to his lawyer and the prosecutor,' Fellows went on. He explained then about the letters that Sellers had sent out from his prison cell as a last resort to escape the chair. 'From what I've found out so far,' the chief said, 'I think there's a good possibility the man is innocent. If he really is innocent I'd hate to see him go to the chair, wouldn't you?'

He had Acton on a spot. 'Sure, of course,' Acton answered after a moment. 'Naturally. But who says he's innocent? That prosecutor shouldda set you straight. Lawyers know that

174

business and if you'd listen to him you'd know there ain't no doubt about it. He got convicted, you know.'

'I know, but I'm not convinced. So I thought I'd drop around and take you into my confidence. I'd like to work on this case a little, if you don't mind, and I'd appreciate any cooperation you can give me.'

Acton made faces at that idea. Finally he sat forward. 'Now look, Chief. I know you've proved yourself and you ain't no fool. You've done some pretty tremendous work down there in Stockford. In fact, you make the rest of us police chiefs look like bums. The police commissioners say to me, 'Fellows does it down in Stockford, why can't you?' and that ain't good. But those cases you solved, you started on 'em fresh. This time I got to tell you you're barking up a wrong tree. This guy Sellers is cold turkey. He did it and he's gonna pay. What you done is let him and his lawyer feed you a line and all I can say is, if you talked to Heligman like you say you did, I'm surprised you didn't get set straight on things. Sellers ain't leveling with you, Chief. He's feeding you crap and you oughtn't to take it. If you'd been at the trial you'd know and you wouldn't be making a mistake like this.'

'I wasn't at the trial,' Fellows told him, 'but I read the transcript. That's why I'm here.'

'Oh? So you read the transcript?'

'Of course. I wouldn't make a move till I'd done that much.'

'You read it but you ain't convinced?'

'That's right. The evidence was all circumstantial. If you look at it believing Sellers guilty, it all fits perfectly. But if you look at it believing Sellers innocent, it all fits too. The evidence fits both ways.'

'It fits best with him being guilty.'

'Best, but certainly not beyond reasonable doubt.'

'The jury said it did.'

'It may be beyond a reasonable doubt in the jury's mind and the prosecutor's mind and in your mind, but it's not beyond a reasonable doubt in my mind.'

Acton made more faces. Finally he said, 'So just what is it you want to do?'

'First I'd like to look through your file on the case. Then I want to dig around and see if there's any new evidence to be found. Evidence for or against. I want to set my own mind at ease.'

Acton glared. 'What you're saying is you don't think we looked hard enough. You want to go through the files to see where we slipped up.'

'That's not it at all, Chief. I'm sure you did everything possible.'

'Us and the State Police and the city police and all the rest. We looked, but you think

176

you can find something we didn't. You think there's something left to find.'

'There may be.'

'What, for instance?'

'The murder weapon was never discovered. The killer's clothes must have got blood on them. They've never been found.'

'There weren't any clothes. Sellers killed his wife naked. That was brought out at the trial and if you read the transcript like you say, you oughtta remember that.'

'That was only a theory. If Sellers didn't do it, there would probably be blood-stained clothes.'

Acton said testily, 'Well you ain't gonna find nothing because we looked everywhere. We dug up everything in the yard.'

'And the route Sellers would take to catch the bus.'

'Yeah. We looked everyplace he mightta gone.'

'But nothing was ever found. So what *did* he do with the murder weapon then? If, as you say, he killed her, he didn't have much time to wash up, get dressed and catch that bus. Yet he still has time to hide the weapon so you could never find it. That's kind of hard to manage it would seem to me.'

'He still couldda done it.'

'Sure, but so could a lot of other people and they could have taken their time about it. They could have done it better.'

It was getting a little complicated for the Banksville chief. He slammed both hands down on the desk top. 'Now listen, Fellows. You can twist things around all you want but Sellers did it! That's all there is to it. He did it! So don't come around trying to waste everybody's time.'

Fellows said quietly, 'No, Chief. I don't propose to waste your time. I'd just like to see the file and then go talk to people.'

'Well you're not going to see the files and you're not going to talk to people. I don't want you throwing scares into them like that sonuvabitch bastard who's trying to make everybody in the development think there's a murderer living out there.'

Fellows got up. 'I'll try not to scare them,' he said.

'I don't want you *talking* to 'em.'

'Aren't you taking rather a lot on yourself, Acton, trying to decide who's going to talk to who in this town.?'

'I can stop you from bothering people and if I get any complaints, believe me I will.'

'We'll leave it that way then. Thanks for your help.'

Fellows started for the door and Acton called him. 'Now look,' he said, rising. 'I don't want no trouble. It don't look good for police chiefs to be fighting each other. The newspapers latch onto something like that and it makes everybody look bad. Why don't

178

you and me issue a joint statement about something. You know. We could say you come up here to study juvenile delinquency in Banksville. They could take our pictures.'

Fellows, waiting patiently with the doorknob in his hand, shook his head. 'I told you why I'm here, Chief. I'd rather have your blessing than your curse but I'm here to find out what I can about Sheila Sellers' death.'

'All right,' Acton growled. 'I ain't gonna stop you, but I ain't gonna help you none either. I got enough trouble with the police commissioners now. What do you think it's gonna be when they hear you're stirring up trouble, especially when they hear you think Ernest Sellers is innocent? They're gonna wonder what I done wrong.'

'Nobody's done anything wrong that I know of.'

'I'm gonna worry that you'll find somebody did.'

'Then you should want to help. That would cover you.'

'You're trying to confuse me. I'm not sticking my neck out. It's bad enough you rocking the boat but I'm damned if I'm gonna help you. Go on out and do whatever you damn well like. But you find something, you bring it in here before you go to the damned newspapers, O.K.? I mean if we did something wrong we oughtta get a chance to correct it. I gotta think of my men.'

'I will if I can count on your support.'

'Well I ain't stopping you from going out and messing things up. I guess that's pretty good support all right.' He sat down and growled to himself, 'What do they let guys like Sellers send out letters for in prison?' Fellows closed the door. He stood grimly for a moment, then relaxed. If Acton wouldn't help, at least he wouldn't oppose and that was, perhaps, as much as one could hope for after the newspaper story. He went to the water fountain for a drink and walked out of the building.

CHAPTER TWENTY

Fred Fellows spent the rest of the morning in the shopping center where the eight storekeepers and clerks whom Sheila Sellers was supposed to know sold their wares. He was there from quarter past nine till half past eleven explaining that he wasn't a private detective named Raphael Jones but a policeman in plainclothes and asking for all the information they had on Mrs. Sellers. He found that Nick Daggett, the delivery boy for a dry-cleaning establishment who'd had a run-in with Ernest, was long gone from that job and nobody knew where, least of all Sam Weiss, the proprietor. Two others on the list were also no longer there and those that were were not helpful. They remembered Mrs. Sellers, of course, for they could hardly forget a murder victim, but the passage of time had grown her bigger than life. She was the most beautiful woman they had ever seen, the most charming, the kindest and nicest, the warmest, the pleasantest. They defended her virtue and murmured bitter words against the husband they believed had killed her, but none of it meant anything. Fellows' questionings only revealed that not one of them would admit knowing her in any capacity other than as a customer and all were quick to assure him that lecherous thoughts about her never entered their minds. She wasn't the type one would have such ideas about in the first place. She was too pretty and sweet and faithful.

Fellows questioned Weiss about Daggett's difficulties with Mr. Sellers but the old man was no help. Daggett had never mentioned the incident and though he learned about it much later, after the killing, he didn't know anywhere near as much as had been brought out at the trial. As for other information about the boy, Weiss could only relate that he quit the job eighteen months ago. He was twenty by then and ready to seek an occupation promising a better future.

Fellows drove over to Wellington Street at noon and saw Jones' white Anglia among the scattering of cars lining the curb. He proceeded around the corner away from that block and parked in front of the house belonging to Kenneth Landon, the man who'd very nearly been punched for chatting with Mrs. Sellers at a party.

A teen-aged girl answered the door and called her mother. Mrs. Landon appeared, gray-haired and firm. 'Are you another reporter?' she asked by way of greeting.

'Not a reporter, a policeman.' Fellows introduced himself and showed her his gold badge.

'More about the fight my husband had with Mr. Sellers?'

'Is that what the reporters were inquiring about?'

'Yes, ever since that story came out in the papers this morning. Reporters have been calling on everybody in the neighborhood. But I can tell you right now, before you go any further, that my husband knows nothing whatever about that woman's death. We only met the Sellers that once at a party. The Strausses had the party and it was ten years ago when we were new in the neighborhood. We were all in the living room, standing and sitting and having drinks. The Strausses had invited a lot of people to help get us introduced. My husband and Mr. Strauss were classmates in college and they had the party and my husband was talking to Mrs.

182

Sellers on the couch, perfectly publicly, about books when Mr. Sellers came over there and told my husband to leave his wife alone. Bob Strauss got between them because the accusations Mr. Sellers were making was getting my husband mad and they were about to come to blows. Bob broke it up and the Sellers left right after that and that's the last any of us ever had to do with either of them. Mr. Sellers was a nasty, unpleasant man with no background and no education and even less manners!'

'And you believe he killed his wife?'

'I believe he was perfectly capable of such an act though whether he did or not I wouldn't know. I can only tell you that my husband did not.'

'Nobody has suggested that he did.'

'Then why are the reporters coming around asking if I've been cross-examined by that detective yet and hinting that everyone is wondering right now who did kill the woman? My husband did not and we don't know who did.'

'You've never heard any gossip about Mrs. Sellers then?'

'No. And I wouldn't listen if I had. Is there anything else?'

Fellows couldn't think of anything. He thanked her and received a cold nod. Then he came down off the stoop and walked back around the corner to Jones' car.

Jones was beside it talking to two men and he waved the chief on. 'Couple of reporters, Fellows,' he said. 'They're helping us do our work. Right, you jokers?'

'We're looking for a story,' one of them said. 'So you're the chief from Stockford?'

Jones said to Fellows, 'I been giving you publicity and don't go bite my head off. Reporters are thick in this neighborhood and they're calling on more people and picking up more rumors that I am.'

'What kind of rumors?' Fellows asked the pair.

'Who's not speaking to who, what kid's dating what girl, a lot of junk.'

'What do they tell you that for?'

'We're asking questions about how they feel about the case opening up again and if they have any ideas on who did it. So they tell us what all the neighbors are doing instead of telling us who they suspect now. They're leaving it to us to put the pieces together and come up with our own answer.'

'You coming up with any?'

One of the men laughed. 'How can we come up with answers when we don't know what we're looking for?'

The other said, 'Yeah, Chief. What's the angle? What's the real story?'

Fellows rubbed his chin. 'The kind of rumors I want to hear about is who made passes at Sheila Sellers.'

'Oh, so that's it!'

'That's the general idea.'

A car with a dome light came up the street and one of the reporters said, 'Oh, oh. We've got the cops for company.'

The car slowed to a stop close by the Anglia and the uniformed driver leaned out. 'O.K.,' he said. 'You've had your fun. Now break it up and clear outta here before I run you in.'

One reporter said, 'Can the crap, Dillon. We're minding our own business.'

'You're sticking your nose into other people's business, that's what you're doing, and they don't like it. Now scram outta here.'

The reporter stepped off the curb towards the car. 'Listen, Dillon, we're looking for stories and you and the whole damned police force aren't going to stop us.'

'We got three complaints about you guys ringing doorbells and pestering people and you're damn well gonna cut it out.'

'What do you think you're going to do to make us?'

'I'll run you in, by God.'

The policeman sitting beside Dillon in the passenger seat leaned across. 'Crack wise, Buster, and you'll see what we do.'

'On what grounds are you going to run us in, huh? You want a nice fat suit for false arrest you just try it.'

'We'll have grounds,' Dillon said. 'Don't you worry about that.' He reached an arm out the window and motioned to Jones. 'You. Come over here!'

Jones looked at Fellows for some sign that he should ignore the summons. Getting none, he reluctantly stepped into the street and halted a few feet from the car. Dillon looked him over. 'Who're you?'

'Jones,' Jones said. 'One of the Jones boys.'

'You're the one started this mess. If you know what's good for you, you'll get outta this town.'

Now it was Fellows' turn. He advanced towards the car himself, looming formidably. 'Your name's Dillon?' he said. 'Did Acton send you here?'

Dillon looked up at Fellows. The big man wasn't chief of police in Banksville but he was a chief of police and Dillon knew what chiefs of police were and what they could do. 'The dispatcher sent us out,' he said. 'The complaints are pouring in down at headquarters and they don't like it. They sent us out to make it stop.'

'You said three complaints. Who're the three who made them?'

'I don't know. All I know is they got made.'

'And I want to know who made them. You've got a radio there. Call in and find out. I want their names.'

Dillon hesitated and looked to his companion. The companion, however, chose

186

to stare through the windshield. Fellows said impatiently, 'Come on, come on. That's a legitimate call. You come out here in answer to a complaint and you don't even know who's complaining. You can find that out.'

Dillon picked up his mike sullenly and muttered, 'Headquarters from Dillon.' A staticky voice answered and he made the request. The voice said, 'Hold on,' then returned again after a moment. 'Mrs. Robert Franklin, Mrs. David Coxe and Mrs. Gordon Manners.'

Fellows recorded the names in his notebook and said, 'Manners? She's a newcomer. She didn't even live here when the murder took place.'

Dillon said, 'Now look, Chief, these people don't like being bothered. You got no right pestering them.'

Fellows said sharply, 'There's a guy in a death cell in Midland Prison who may not belong there. I'm not going to let him rot just to avoid inconveniencing a few people.'

Dillon said gruffly, 'Well, all right, but what am I supposed to do?'

'You can stop interfering.'

'But these complaints come in and the dispatcher sends me out.'

'All right, you went out. You've done your job. If these people around here want more, let them swear out a complaint.'

Dillon shrugged. He said, 'O.K.,' sourly,

gunned the motor and took off.

Fellows watched them go and Jones said, 'Well, the power of a gold badge.'

'They'll report to Acton for instructions,' Fellows said. 'It's his gold badge that counts around here.'

'So, back to work?'

'Yes, and get as much done as you can. You know what facts you're after. When did these people move in and who might have played around with Sheila Sellers.'

'I know, I know. So what are you going to do, supervise?'

'I'm going to take the houses you don't take. And let's stop wasting time gabbing with reporters. I don't know what Acton's going to do and I don't want to wait around to find out.'

CHAPTER TWENTY-ONE

The day's effort brought meager results in the way of useful information and nothing at all that could be termed a clue. Too many reporters had been pumping the people and they were less and less cooperative by the time Fellows or Jones got to their door.

In the middle of the afternoon the evening paper appeared and that made matters worse. Most of the front page was devoted to the resurrected murder case and right in the most eye-catching spot was Chief Acton's blast. If the neighborhood had been unnerved by the sudden suggestion that a killer was loose, the residents were getting themselves under control again and Acton's urging that they not answer questions was all they needed to clamp the lid down tight. Once the paper was delivered, Fellows and Jones might as well have quit. Many people stopped answering the door and the few who did came with epithets and threats. Raphael Jones, when they got back to the motel, was mumbling about 'how to get hated' and seemed soured on the whole thing.

Fellows, sweaty and tired, had borne the ordeal more stoically. He was used to being hated, to getting grudging answers to his questions, to a general lack of cooperation. It was an integral part of a policeman's occupation, but even his great face was tight and grim.

They ate together in the cafeteria after the chief had a shower and Jones a swim in the pool. The swim had cooled the detective but it hadn't lightened his mood and he was bitter during the meal. 'These damned people in this town don't care what happens to Sellers,' he growled. 'Let him rot. Just don't come around asking questions. I hope that stinking killer, whoever he is, murders the lot of them.' He looked over at Fellows who had his notebook open on the table beside his plate and was frowning over what he'd written. 'Pack it in, I say,' Jones went on. 'It's a waste of time.'

Fellows raised his eyes. 'You going to let Sellers rot too?'

'What the hell can we do about it? Our hands are tied.'

'And you're going to throw in the sponge? Some detective you are.'

'Detective? I came down here for publicity, remember? I've told you all along they're going to pull the switch on him. But this publicity isn't doing me any good. I'm not going to paste any of this crap in my scrapbook.'

'You need another swim.'

'I need another hole in the head to go with the one that brought me down here. Pack up, Fellows. Go home. That's what I'm going to do.'

Fellows folded his notebook and put it away. 'You sure ride a rollercoaster, don't you, Jones? Up one minute, down the next. When things go well you can't lose. Let someone slap your face and you can't win. No wonder your business is bad.'

Jones pointed with his fork. 'Now don't you get after me, Fellows. I've had enough for one day. Just leave me alone.'

'Sure. I'll leave you alone. I should have from the beginning. You're not the man for the job. You're nothing but an anchor.'

'I said lay off,' Jones growled, digging harshly into his food. 'You think your men are so much better, go get some of them up here. Let them get the doors slammed in their faces for the next two weeks. You think that's going to do so much good, go right ahead.'

Fellows ignored him. 'Acton's the one to win over,' he said. 'If we can get him on our side—'

Jones tossed his fork on the table. 'Oh for Christ's sake.' He leaned on his elbows. 'All right. You win Acton over. What's that going to get you? What're you going to learn if nobody'll talk to you? Suppose you had his whole force at your disposal. What would you do with it? You saw what happened today. Everybody clammed up. So now what're you going to do? Just tell me what your next move is. I'd love to hear it.'

Fellows said, 'Well, first off, this is Thursday night. If I had a man working with me, I'd send him down to that chess club—'

'To do what? Find out how Sellers lost three games in one night?'

'Find out if they keep attendance and anything else that might be useful.'

'What's useful about attendance?'

'I'd like to know how often Sellers showed up at the club.'

'And what's that going to do?'

'I don't know. But if it was a ritual, then a

191

lover could be pretty certain the coast would be clear on Thursday nights. If he missed going very often, then Sheila Sellers would have had to have some kind of signal or means of letting the lover know when he could and could not come. There'd have had to be some communication.'

'Like the telephone, for example? She calls him while Ernest is away at work. What good's that going to do?'

Fellows shrugged. 'I don't know. I won't know what's going to do any good so I just collect whatever I can.' He looked Jones in the eye and spoke deliberately. 'Then this helper of mine would ask any questions of the people there that would come to mind and find out just as much as he could about Sellers, his habits, what kind of a guy they took him to be, things like that.'

'Yeah. This is the little job you've got picked out for me. So meanwhile what do you do?'

'I call on Sherwood Spencer, the one man who moved out of the area but still lives in town.'

Jones made a face. 'So go call on him.'

'You'll handle the chess club?'

'Yeah,' Jones growled. 'Like the damned fool I am.' He pointed with his fork again. 'But that's going to be the end of it, Fellows. This is my last night in this stinking burg.'

Fellows, with the aid of the phone book and a few requests for directions, got to the Sherwood Spencer home a little after eight and this time his luck was better. Not only did Spencer himself come to the door but, after the introductions, he let him in.

Spencer was a lithe, dark-haired man in his mid-forties who was particularly handsome and, with the slight graying at the temples, becoming distinguished looking. He shook hands with Fellows when he learned his identity and said, 'This is something of an honor. I've been reading all this to-do in the papers tonight and it must be quite something to get you up here on your time off.'

He brought the chief in, introduced him to Mrs. Spencer and to the three teen-age daughters who were around. 'My son Dick is out on a date. He'll be sorry to have missed you.'

Fellows took the chair that was offered when the females withdrew and said, 'Your son is how old?'

'Twenty. He's a junior in college. He's working in the foundry for a summer job and how he has the pep left to go out on a date, I don't know. These kids, they're inexhaustible.'

Fellows brought the subject around to the murder and Spencer said he remembered it well. 'The neighborhood was shocked. They seemed happy together. You never think of anything like that happening in your own neighborhood—to people you know.'

'You know them well?'

'I hardly knew them at all. I knew who they were but never was formally introduced.'

'Someone pointed them out to you?'

'They pointed themselves out. I was at that block dance when he took the punch at the salesman.'

Fellows asked his version of the story and it fitted the others he'd collected. Spencer hadn't known anything was happening until people were separating the pair and he'd drawn closer and heard the words that followed.

'What's your own view of the case?' Fellows asked.

Spencer shrugged. 'I always figured he killed her. What else?' He gestured. 'Of course I don't know anything about it, really. I saw in the papers tonight that you think otherwise, that you think there's a lover involved. If it was anybody else but you I'd say you were crazy but you're supposed to know what you're talking about and if you say there was a lover, then there probably was. She sure didn't look like the type to me, though.'

'You think you can tell by looking at her?'

'I think if she'd done any playing around

she'd have been the talk of the neighborhood, and she was one person nobody ever said anything about—except to pity her being stuck with Ernest for a husband.'

Fellows nodded and, for a moment, felt lost. It was the same refrain he'd got from nearly everyone else. Even when the neighborhood had been startled by the idea that someone other than the husband might have killed Mrs. Sellers the idea of there being a lover still failed to come out. The neighbors apparently had such an effective grapevine going that nobody believed anything like that could have happened without its being discovered.

Finally the chief said, 'Suppose there had been a lover. Whom would you pick for the job?'

Spencer shrugged again. 'I suppose George Walker.'

'Why?'

'He's the only bachelor.'

'Gordon Henry lived on that block. I understand he's a bachelor.'

Spencer laughed. 'Have you met Henry? He's a mama's boy so far as I could make out. Henry doing a thing like that is ridiculous. Walker at least played around. He had a harem, or so the story goes.'

'And that's why you pick him?'

'That's right. The rest of us were all married.'

'Married men play around too.'

Spencer smiled and sat back against the couch. 'I suppose some of them do. But not that crowd.'

The smile widened and Fellows said, 'What's so funny?'

Spencer laughed. 'I'm just trying to think of some of those men as lovers. The idea is very amusing.'

'About as amusing as the idea that Sheila played around?'

'I suppose so,' he said, the smile fading a little. 'I can't see her in that role either.'

'Not the type, I believe you said.'

He shook his head. 'Not the type.'

Fellows braced himself and plodded ahead though there seemed no place to go. 'Sometimes the most unlikely people do the most surprising things, Mr. Spencer. Mrs. Sellers was thirty-two when she died. That's an age when a woman who's been married for a long time might be tempted by boredom to see what else there is in life. That's a reaction that often strikes husbands too, after they've been married for a long time.'

'Seven year itch?' Spencer asked with a smile.

'That's right.'

'That's a pipe-and-slippers neighborhood, Mr. Fellows. Walker's the only one I can see doing any playing around and I frankly doubt he'd pick on someone like Mrs. Sellers. There

196

were too many easier fish in the sea.'

'Mrs. Sellers was a very attractive woman.'

Spencer shook his head. 'Nice to look at, maybe, but she was a mouse. I can't see her attracting anyone like George Walker. I can't really see the lover bit at all, Chief.'

'How about the boys in the block?'

'Boys?'

'Teen-age boys—like your son, for example.'

Spencer came up straight. 'Now listen, leave my son out of it. He doesn't do things like that.'

'Didn't *you* play around with girls at his age?'

'Not with married women I didn't, and neither does he. We have *some* ethics, you know.'

'Any of the other boys have fewer ethics, Mr. Spencer?'

His temper had been touched and the friendliness had left his face. 'I don't know about the other boys. Ask them. Just leave my son out. Way out. He doesn't fool around with married women and if he did fool around with married women, he certainly wouldn't murder them. I know what you're up to. You're looking for a lover to find a killer and you're not going to snoop around trying to pin anything on my family.'

'Somebody killed that woman, Mr. Spencer.'

197

'Her husband killed her. Don't go looking elsewhere because none of the rest of us are killers. You can take my word on that.'

'You mean you can't *believe* any of the rest of you are killers.'

'I mean they aren't!'

'You would have said that about Mr. Sellers, wouldn't you?'

'No. Not necessarily. He was a trouble-maker. He's the only one in that neighborhood, if you want my opinion, capable of doing something like that to his wife. I don't think you know what you're after, if you want to know what I think. I think you're nosing around to get Sellers off the hook and you don't really have any evidence for a lover at all. I don't think there ever was one and I think you know it. I think he killed her and that's that.'

Fellows said patiently, 'If there was a lover, Mr. Spencer, is there any time that lover could have come to the house and found Sellers away—other than on Thursday nights?'

'I wouldn't know and I couldn't care less.'

'Would you know what other people in the neighborhood, besides Sellers, had business on Thursday nights?'

'No.'

'No one?'

'I didn't concern myself with what other

198

people did weekday evenings. I don't know anything about anybody.'

'Well, you know if *you* had business appointments on Thursday nights, wouldn't you?'

Spencer sat forward stiffly. 'I don't like your insinuation, sir.'

'I take it, then, that you didn't work nights?'

'No, I did not.'

'And your son was home every Thursday night?'

'Yes he was home every Thursday night,' Spencer said tightly. He got up. 'I've had enough of this. I try to help and I get accusations. If you want my opinion, you're trying to frame somebody for this murder. I should have known better than to have anything to do with policemen. You will kindly leave now.'

Fellows rose. The term 'frame' always made him see red but this was one time when he could only swallow and be silent. He was looking for a lover when all the evidence said there was none. He was trying to get a man cleared of a murder that the evidence said he committed. He couldn't point to a single clue in favor of his own theory and that meant his neck was way out. He had no grounds on which to defend himself and he took the crack about the frame with a flush but he held his peace. 'Thank you for your cooperation,' he said through taut lips and walked to the door.

CHAPTER TWENTY-TWO

Raphael Jones didn't get back from the Banksville Chess Club meeting until nearly eleven and Fellows had spent the intervening time working with a pad and pencil making endless calculations with his fragmentary material.

When Jones knocked and was told to enter, he found the Chief sitting on one of the twin beds writing on the tiny bedtable between, with the lamp shifted to the other bed. He said, 'You're going to ruin your eyes, old man. Didn't your mother ever tell you about the value of eyesight?'

Fellows rubbed a hand over his discouraged face and said, 'This display of cheer doesn't become you, Jones. Somebody must have spelled your name right in the newspaper.'

'Yeah, and the gloom doesn't become you either. Where's the old up-and-at-'em attitude you were foisting off onto me at dinner? Spencer must have petered out and the old man needs a drink.'

'I can think of other things I could use more. What happened at the chess club to buoy you up? They serve liquor?'

'You really are in a bad way, aren't you? Well, the chess club was kind of interesting if you like chess. I discovered something. They make a record of the moves they make so they can play a whole game over again after it's done.'

'They do it with baseball games too, only more so.'

'And they also have a chess ladder there.'

Fellows sighed. 'Is this supposed to have anything to do with anything?'

Jones sat down on the bed opposite the chief. He put the lamp back on the table, on top of Fellows' papers, and lay out, stretching himself full length. 'I think it might.'

'Well that's something. And do they also keep an attendance record?'

'Yeah, that they do.' Jones quoted from memory. 'Ernest Sellers was a dyed-in-the-wool enthusiast. You can rest assured that Mrs. Sellers didn't need any elaborate signal arrangements. Ernest missed only three meetings in four years. One, in February of 1957 when he was down with the flu, one in May of 1959 when his wife was sick and one in June of 1960 when he had a touch of grippe.'

'What date in 1960?'

'The ninth of June. Why?'

'If there was a lover, that was one Thursday night he couldn't have come around.' Fellows made a note.

'And what good is that going to do you?'

'If we could find a man who was busy every Thursday evening except June ninth it would mean a little more than finding a man who was busy every Thursday evening including June ninth.'

'So what? We haven't found anybody who was busy *any* Thursday night, including the night of the murder.'

'Thanks for reminding me. Now did you talk to those guys there? You get any impressions?'

'Yeah. As a matter of fact, I'm coming around to your view, Fellows. I don't think he did it. I think Sellers is innocent.'

'Why?'

'One of the things at the trial, according to what the newspapers said anyway, was that the night of the murder Sellers lost three straight games of chess. And he was supposed to be one of the top players in the club.'

'Yes, I know that.'

'The prosecution made a big thing of that. I won't say that that alone convinced the jury but it must have weighed pretty heavily in their minds. The guy who usually wins gets clobbered on the night of the murder. Sounds funny, doesn't it? Well, it so happens that the guy who usually wins wasn't usually winning. Sellers was in a slump. He'd been in a slump all through the summer, in fact, and had dropped from number two on the ladder in

June to number five in October. The three guys who beat him that night hadn't taken one in ten from him before June, but either they improved, or they got hot and he went cold, or whatever happens to chess players and listen to the record during the summer. In five games with one, Sellers won three and dropped two. That's not counting the loss on the murder night. With another, Sellers won four, drew one and lost one. With the third, Sellers won four, lost two and drew two.'

Jones waved a hand. 'Now with a record like that, and that record wasn't brought out at the trial, his happening to lose to all three in the same night isn't so impossible after all. In fact, it's quite likely it'll happen some night. Tough luck for Sellers it was the night his wife got killed.'

Fellows said, 'Yeah,' slowly. He clapped his hand on the bedtable. 'By God,' he said, 'and here I'd reached the stage where even I was thinking of throwing in the towel, of saying I'm nothing but a sucker, that there is no lover, that there never has been, that Ernest Sellers is using this as a desperation measure to try to beat the chair.'

'And now?'

Fellows said curtly, 'Jones, I think that guy is a victim of circumstance. Losing those chess games was the only thing that was hard to explain away and you've just done it. I think Sellers has been roped into the chair by

203

a series of bad breaks. I think he had nothing to do with his wife's death and I was a damned fool to even think about giving up.' He pointed a finger at the reclining detective. 'Somewhere out around Wellington Street a murderer lives or used to live. He's a slick character, Jones. He's so slick he made love to the wife of the most jealous and eagle-eyed man in a neighborhood full of gossips and got away with it cold. Then, when he tired of this and the wife tried to hold him by threatening to tell, he walked in and murdered her and left the husband holding the bag. He's one sharp son of a bitch, Jones. He's so sharp I almost decided he didn't even exist. I almost went home and let Sellers take the rap. Well, he does exist. I'm certain of it. And I'm staying right here and I'm going to find him.'

'Before the eighth of August?' Jones asked.

'Yeah. Before. Way before.' Fellows retrieved his papers from under the lamp and looked them over. 'We haven't got much to go on,' he said. 'But we'll get more. We'll get a lot more.'

'What're those papers supposed to be, Dad?'

'I've been cataloguing what little information we've picked up so far on the men on the block, how long they've lived there, when those who moved moved and where to, who was out Thursday nights, who was doing what the night of the murder, plus any pertinent information about them as potential lovers.'

'You make it sound lousy. What about your probables and improbables, or should we say possibles and impossibles?'

'You make it sound good. What've you got?'

'Mostly blank spaces.'

'The only impossibles,' Fellows said, 'are Herbert Rogers who was in Colorado at the time of the murder and the Polins who were in Florida.'

Jones grinned. 'There're your men, Fellows. That's just the kind of alibi a real slick murderer like you describe this guy would come up with.'

'Don't make it harder. It's hard enough already.'

'All right, let's hear the breakdown or don't you have it broken down?'

'It breaks down into this,' Fellows said and picked up the sheets. 'Of the six people who have moved, we know where three went. Williamson to California and Roberts to Cincinnati, both on job promotions, and Spencer to the other side of town. We have definite claims that Penny, Rogers, Gary, Bomstein and Temple did not go out Thursday nights. Franklin goes out many nights, but with his wife. Spencer denies he went out but his son does because his son is out tonight. The rest are blanks. As for the night of the murder, Rogers and Polin are, as I said, completely alibied. Walker was in Pittsfield and we can figure he's off the list. The Franklins were at the Castles' so presumably they're off. Baxter and his son were home, supposedly, and that's all we've got on alibis. As for your theory that the lover moved into the neighborhood only shortly before starting the affair, Blackstone, Spencer and Coxe are the only ones we know about yet who moved in the year before the murder. Everything else is a blank.'

'So far it's a blank,' Jones said. 'How many people are there on that block that you don't have any information for?'

Fellows consulted his pages again. 'Kligerman,' he said. 'We still have to find out where he moved. Justin, another who moved. Maynard, Coxe, Collins and Bruce. A number of others all we know about them is how long they've lived in their house.'

'So who are your impossibles, your possibles, your improbables and your probables?'

Fellows made a wry face. 'I haven't got that far. We've got to fill in more blanks to get to that point.'

'And you hope,' Jones said, 'that when all the blanks are filled in, presto, the finger of guilt will point to somebody, huh?'

'I hope some kind of finger will point to some kind of a direction—to a group if not to an individual.'

'And if it doesn't, then what? Do we go after the delivery boys and the families across the street? Or do we go back to Sellers' co-workers in the print shop?'

'We?' Fellows lifted an eyebrow. 'You've decided not to quit?'

Jones got to his feet and said, 'What the hell. There's nothing doing in Springfield. I called my partner tonight. I might as well be working here as loafing there. Without any dough involved it's the same difference.' He turned and gave an imitation smile. 'Besides, who knows what might happen with Fred Fellows on the case? You might even turn up something and if you ever did, wouldn't I be one damned fool to be back home in Springfield reading about it?'

CHAPTER TWENTY-THREE

The week that followed was a fascinating one for the gossips of Wellington Street. The newspapers, after the first flush of enthusiasm, gave up reporting the dull ploddings of the two detectives and with the dwindling interest of the press the hostility of the neighborhood thawed. It was the rash of reporters that had got the people's backs up but now they almost regretted the fact they were no longer important.

Meanwhile, they appreciated the drama implicit in the detectives' wanderings and were titillated by the thought that a friend of theirs, someone who had supped in their parlor, played bridge at their table or danced with them had killed a woman. Perhaps a hand they had shaken had wielded the weapon that had beaten out Sheila Sellers' brains. Perhaps some calm pair of eyes that looked into theirs had watched the blood fly.

Thus the presence of the two strangers roaming the neighborhood held a fascination and gossip was almost solely limited to the latest rumors about Fellows and Jones. Did they have a lead yet? Who'd told them what? Whom did they suspect? Around Wellington Street the grapevine was so effective that everyone who cared knew exactly where the detectives were and whom they were interviewing every minute of the day.

What made it really enjoyable, of course, was that it was all perfectly safe. If was fun to speculate on who, other than Ernie, might have committed the crime, to giggle and laugh at the idea of so-and-so being Sheila's murdering lover, but there was no real fear that it was actually true. For one more week the detectives would scour the neighborhood and keep the housewives tingling. Then the eighth of August would come, the switch would be thrown and the detectives would go away, leaving behind a delicious memory. Now that their first outrage had passed, the gossips in the area wouldn't have missed it for anything.

For Fred Fellows and Raphael Jones, however, the week was just the opposite. For them there was no suspense. For them there was nothing but the grinding millstone of disappointment. They filled in most of the gaps in their knowledge. They found out just how long everyone on the block had lived in his house. They found out what most of the people were doing the night of the murder—or at least what they claimed to have been doing. They finally even found out, through other sources, where the missing families had moved to. But they could not find out a single thing that really mattered—who cheated on his wife, who had business appointments that weren't concerned with business, who had an eye for Sheila Sellers and who might have wanted to see her dead. If the women in the neighborhood were gossips and if they spiced their lives with such tidbits, they didn't choose to spice the lives of policemen. Fellows and Jones were beyond the pale and Fellows, at least, knew it. He knew that what he heard was the no-account stuff, that the stories that mattered passed him by when they made their lightning rounds. He got what he didn't need and never heard what he

209

did and he was powerless to change the situation. The people were almost friendly now. They liked to see him around but they were in an unspoken conspiracy against him. They had banded into an alliance bent on self-protection so that even their earlier stories were contradicted. George Walker, the ladies' man bachelor, was now two steps from sainthood. The Kligermans' divorce was no longer thought to involve another woman. Dick Spencer mixed up with a girl? That was a malicious rumor with no truth in it at all.

By the night of the first of August Fellows had hit pretty close to bottom. Though he tried to keep it out of his voice when he called his wife, she picked it up right away. 'It's not going at all well, is it?' she said and he confessed it wasn't. 'We can't get a lead. Everything we turn up is negative. Sheila Sellers would never cheat on her husband. None of the husbands would cheat on their wives. None of the youths would touch a married woman. Everybody was indoors watching television when the murder took place.'

'Where else would people be that time of night, Fred? Of course they'd be indoors watching television.'

'Except for one man,' the chief reminded her. 'Except for one man.'

'Or a woman, Fred. It might've been a woman, mightn't it?'

'It might if I could think of a motive for a woman to kill her.'

'But do you have a motive for a man killing her? I know you think it's a lover and all but really, Fred, why would a lover have to kill her? I mean, what could she do to him?'

Fellows had to smile. 'You've been living with me too long, Cessie. You're getting to be a detective yourself.'

'Now you're laughing at me, but I mean it. What could she do? She'd never tell her husband. She'd never do that.'

'No, but she might pretend she was going to. I'll grant you a point there, though.'

They talked a little longer and Fellows felt better when he'd hung up. Cessie wasn't the smartest woman in the world, he knew, but she was possessed of good common sense and conversation with her helped clear the air. He went out of the phone booth in the motel cafeteria and back to his own room and, instead of picking up his sheaf of notes, lay down on the bed and stared at the ceiling.

Raphael Jones knocked a few minutes later and came in with liquor on his breath. 'Loafing, huh?' he said. 'A week to go and he's loafing.'

'Take a chair,' Fellows said without moving. 'Make yourself comfortable.'

'Sure thing. There's no way I like to pass the time better than sitting around watching tired old policemen rest.'

'I've been thinking,' Fellows said. 'The work we've been doing hasn't been getting us anywhere.'

Jones flopped into a chair. 'I'm a week ahead of you, Dad. I came to that conclusion *last* Thursday.'

'It's basic stuff,' Fellows went on. 'It's work that has to be done and usually it's the kind of work that eventually pays off. In this case it hasn't.'

'And you should have known damned well it wouldn't.'

'It hasn't,' Fellows continued patiently, 'because we can't be sure of our source. The people we've talked to tell us whatever they want and we have no way of knowing whether it's true. We've got alibis for everybody except the people who moved. We've finally found out where all of them have gone, but Davins is the only one who didn't move more than a hundred miles away. He's down in Pittsfield and we'll have to go see him—'

'You go.'

'And quite apart from whether the stories we've gotten are true or not, we're trying to fill in the wrong blanks. All those questions about how long have you lived in the house, what did you do Thursday nights, where were you the night of the murder. Even straight answers wouldn't turn up a lover.'

'But you sure have been plugging away at asking them, Dad.'

'We had to find out, Jones.'

'The cops found out three years ago. They didn't turn up any lover either.'

Fellows sighed. 'So now let's backtrack a little,' he said. 'We've been looking for a lover—'

'You're telling me?'

Fellows sighed again. 'I wish you could listen instead of talk. The search for a lover gets us nowhere. The reason is because nobody and everybody fills the bill.'

'Everbody? Pardon me for talking some more but do you mean *everybody*?'

'Anybody then. A lover can be a married man or a single man. he can be in his teens or his dotage. Out of our original list of fifty-one people we have arbitrarily eliminated better than half but the elimination has been totally arbitrary. Outside of three or four people who are definitely alibied for the time of the murder, all the others we've removed from the list have been for reasons that have nothing to do with their potential as lovers. We eliminated all those who didn't live on Sellers' block for example. That doesn't mean the lover couldn't live on another block, it only means we've been arbitrary.'

'So what are you trying to do, widen the scope of this investigation? You haven't enough to do sorting through the people who live on the block so you want to enlarge the list of suspects again?'

213

'No. As I said, nearly anyone can fill the bill of lover. But we aren't looking for a lover, Jones. We're looking for a murderer.'

'And nearly anyone can fill that bill too, Dad. You just pick up any newspaper—'

'So,' Fellows interrupted, 'let's pay a little more attention to the murder angle. Why would a lover kill his mistress?'

'What's this going to be, Twenty Questions? All right, Mr. Bones, why would a lover kill his mistress?'

'I'm asking you.'

'To get her off his back.'

'Any other reasons?'

'She's taken up with another guy.'

'Her husband, for example?'

Jones blinked and sat up a little. 'What the hell are you driving at?'

'I'm looking for motive, Jones. We've more or less assumed without thinking much about it that she was killed by a lover because she wouldn't let him go. The point is, how can she hold him? Would she threaten to tell Ernie? Maybe, but could she scare a guy so much with a threat like that that he'd risk the electric chair to get rid of her? Then let's take the way she was killed. It was in a rage. If he killed her to get rid of her, there's a lot more to it than just the threat to tell her husband. She would have to have him bound to her so he can't get away. She was killed with the hatred of a prisoner for a captor.'

Jones shrugged. 'So what about it?'

'I can't figure out what such a hold could be.'

Jones clasped his hands behind his head and stretched his legs. 'Why don't you put first things first, Dad? I thought that was your forte. We're looking for the guy, not the motive. The motive comes later.'

'You ever hear the story of the lad who hung around the supermarket?'

'What lad, what supermarket?'

'This lad kept hanging around the supermarket. Young lad, he was. Well, it seems the supermarket did a big business and the manager was constantly worrying about being robbed. So he told the cops about this kid and the cops started trailing him. They kept a watch on him twenty-four hours a day waiting for him to meet with his gang or something. So while they're watching him and he's not meeting with anybody, the supermarket gets knocked off. Now the cops didn't know how the guy did it—how he got his information to the gang, so they arrest him and haul him in to make him tell. The lad confesses and it turns out that he had no connection with any gang whatsoever. All he hung around the supermarket for was because he had a secret crush on one of the checkout girls.'

Jones said in satisfaction, 'The cops goof again!'

'Yes, the police department goofed and the reason was because they overlooked the fact that there might be other motives for the guy's behavior. Now in our case, we've been looking for a lover. First things first, as you say. But that's not getting us anywhere so let's pay a little attention to motive. Maybe there's some other reason for the lover killing Sheila besides escaping from her clutches.'

'Such as?'

'Maybe it was the other way around. Maybe she wanted to get him off *her* back.'

Jones was silent for a moment. Then he said slowly, 'Yes, I suppose. Or, of course, if you're looking for motive, there are any number of reasons why people who live together intimately kill each other.'

'Let's just stick to this one, shall we?'

'All right. So why does she want to get him off her back? Ernie doesn't like it?'

'Ernie doesn't know about it.'

'She's afraid he'll find out?'

'How?'

Jones said sourly, 'God, this really *is* Twenty Questions. I'll bite. How?'

'I don't know. Try something else.'

'You're getting lazy, Dad. You want me to do the work for you. All right, maybe she started rejecting him and he was so smitten he couldn't stand it. Guys have killed the girls they love for rejecting them.'

'And,' Fellows added, 'to keep someone

else from having them.'

Jones said, 'Say, I really do believe you think she was starting to take up with another man.'

'As I said before, her husband possibly.'

'And the guy kills her because she's throwing him over for her husband?'

'Let's just suppose she's throwing him over. Let's just suppose that's the motive. What kind of a guy would kill a woman for that reason?'

'A lunatic.'

'How old a lunatic?'

'About a fourteen-year-old lunatic, I'd say.'

'Possibly sixteen or seventeen?'

Jones sat up slowly. 'So that's it. You think a kid killed her?'

'The kind of person who would kill for that reason, it would seem to me, would most likely be a youth she seduced. The first love, the first flame of sex. You'd be most likely to find the fiery passion and the emotional instability required to kill in someone like that, wouldn't you?'

Jones shook a cigarette from his pack and said, 'Yeah,' thoughtfully. He lighted up, sat back and blew a lungful of smoke towards the ceiling. 'Only one thing wrong,' he said. 'She's rejecting him, right? He comes with a weapon for the purpose of killing her, right? But she opens the door to him in a costume that suggests acceptance, not rejection. Being stark naked under a bathrobe is a come-on in my book.'

'But she was naked because she was going to take a bath,' Fellows reminded him.

Jones leaned forward with his elbows on his knees and stared throughtfully at the floor. 'And,' he said slowly, 'she opens the door to him because she's forgotten to be modest around him. He follows her into the living room, pleading his cause one last time. She rejects him but he's so aroused by her nudity he can't stand it and whacks her. That what you're thinking?'

'It fits the conditions, doesn't it?'

'So who're the kids around?'

'Mike Baxter, who lives next door. Robert Bruce around the corner. Dick Spencer and William King Junior on the back side of the block. And I think we should also include a lad named Skip Hopworth who lives directly across the street.'

'You've got them memorized, haven't you? So, the Spencer kid was playing around with girls and the family moved shortly after the murder trial. Is he your bet?'

'If the moving had anything to do with it, then the father is as guilty as the son. I don't have any real choice but I do want to study those boys and see if they can make the pick for me.'

'Yeah. And one thing. The kids ought to make it easier for us than the grownups. We ought to be able to open them up like a bottle of beer.'

CHAPTER TWENTY-FOUR

Fellows bearded Dennis Acton in his office first thing Friday morning. For Acton the week had not been the horror he'd feared and he had long since got over his rage at Jones' newspaper story. Now he could be almost patronizing and when he looked up from going over arrest records with a police reporter, he grinned. 'Well, now,' he said. 'You making progress?'

Fellows, glancing at the reporter, said, 'Maybe.'

'You don't have much time left. I suppose you know that.'

'Yes. I have a calendar and a clock to remind me.'

The reporter, leaving the reports, said, 'Come on, give me a quote, Fellows. Give me something to make the readers happy.'

Fellows shook his head. 'My only quote is I have nothing to quote.' He waited and Acton said, 'All right, Willie. See you later.'

When the reporter was gone and the door closed, Acton tilted back in his chair. 'Is that right, Fellows? You don't have a thing?'

'I have some leads.'

'Leads? Do you have one single shred of tangible evidence that Sellers didn't murder his own wife?'

Fellows shook his head. 'But I've narrowed the field. It's down to five now.'

Acton snorted. 'You know something? We narrowed the field right down to one three years ago.'

'Only maybe you got the wrong one.'

'Maybe,' Acton said, still smiling. 'Only you ain't got nothing that says so, right?'

'I'm trying,' Fellows said and sat down. 'What I need right now is your help.'

'Fat chance.'

Fellows' mouth tightened. 'So it's still like that, huh?'

Acton brought his chair upright. 'I don't mean it that way, Fellows. I've got no objection to helping. The commissioners, they've taken this whole thing pretty good and I don't think I'd be out of line. The trouble is I can't. What do you want, men? I don't have them. I don't know what your police force is like down in Stockford but here we're shorthanded. We're always shorthanded.'

'Mostly I want information.'

'The files?' Acton deliberated over that for a bit and finally shrugged. 'Well, I guess I got no objection.' He pressed a buzzer and sat back. 'Anything in particular you want from them?'

220

'Alibis. Did you take alibis from people around there when you were investigating?'

'Of course we did. What do you think? Cleared everybody except Sellers himself. He didn't quite come off.'

A sergeant stuck his head in the door and Acton waved. 'Get me the file on the Sellers case.' The door closed and Acton said, 'You really think he's innocent, don't you?'

Fellows said, 'I guess I do.'

'Why?'

'I don't know. Just a feeling that I don't know the whole story.'

'But you haven't got one single goddam thing to back up that feeling. Is that right?'

'I'm groping, but I'm hoping for a break. That's why I want your help.'

Acton sat back and drummed his fingers on the desk. 'I don't like the sound of that. You want the files. What else?'

'A couple of detectives for some interviews. It would be more official if the interrogators came from the police department.'

'Oh no. Oh no.' Acton waved his hand negatively. 'That's out. That's definitely out. The moment I send out a couple of my men that makes your whole project official. I'm not so dumb. People have been keeping quiet around here because you and that Jones guy are just a couple of harmless jerks who're more amusing than bothersome. But the moment I send just one of my men out to give

221

you a hand, even if it's only to change a tire, then it's a completely different matter. Then the Banksville Police Department is saying it's buying your theory. It's saying this ain't a game, it's for real. And then the public and the police commissioners and the mayor are all going to be on my neck and what'm I gonna tell 'em? You answer me that. Am I gonna say, "Chief Fellows has a hunch"? Am I gonna say, "When Fellows says Sellers is innocent he's innocent because Fellows has solved some tough cases down in Stockford"? I think I done plenty for you just by leaving you alone. Don't try to make it my neck.'

'But if there's any doubt about Sellers' guilt, Acton—'

'Juries decide guilt, not policemen. And personally, I ain't got no doubts about this case. You produce some cold, hard evidence and I'll talk about doubt. Otherwise I'm not sticking my neck out.'

The sergeant came in with a thick folder and laid it on the desk before the Banksville chief. Acton opened it and said, 'Any special alibis?'

'I want to know what the teen-age boys in that neighborhood were doing the night she was killed. I also want to know what kind of search was made for a murder weapon.'

'Teen-age boys? Are you serious?'

'I am.'

Acton pushed the file across the desk.

'Here, you look it up. Everything's there, either original or carbon. You can use that table there and browse to your heart's content. But don't take nothing out of there.'

That was the best Fellows could get for himself for the time being and he settled at the table and, for the first time, had the actual case-file in his hands. It was the one connection with the murder that he hadn't seen before and he took full advantage. He read every page of every report, the results of every interview, the details of every police action from the time the phone call came in announcing that a woman was dead in a pool of blood at 36 Wellington Street.

He worked without lunch and well into the afternoon, making notes, studying and pondering, all against the backdrop of Chief Acton's comings and goings, the phone calls and visitors.

When he was finally finished, he turned the back cover, rose and carried the thick bundle of papers back to Acton's desk. Acton, on the phone, gestured, said his goodbyes and hung up. 'Help you any?' he asked.

'Maybe a little.'

Acton shook his head. 'You know, I oughtta resent your coming in and trying to open up a case that's been dead and buried for three years, but I got to say I admire your guts. You've got no easy task. I thought you'd be gone long before this. I guess I'm really sorry you couldn't find anything. Sit down and shoot the breeze. What're you looking for? Maybe I can clue you in on anything that's missing. I know that case well. It's the biggest this town's ever had. So it's teen-age boys, huh? Why is it and what're you after?'

Fellows sat down and said, 'This is to be confidential, Chief. It wouldn't serve any purpose to let it out.'

'You're telling me? I want to keep this town quiet.'

Fellows related then his latest theory that one of the five boys in the neighborhood might have done Sheila Sellers in and said, 'What I've been trying to find out is what those boys were doing that night, how they behaved under questioning, and where the hunt for the murder weapon took place.'

'And what did you get?'

'Not very much.'

'What do you mean?'

Fellows pointed at the file. 'There isn't much about alibis in there. For instance, you've got the Castles and the Franklins saying they were at the Castle house all evening. But you've got George Walker coming up and being questioned and saying he just got back from Pittsfield but nobody ever verified it.'

Acton placed his hand down on the bulky folder. 'And why should we? He wasn't under

224

suspicion for anything. We can't go sending men all over creation running down facts unless we got a reason.'

'And,' Fellows went on, 'most of the people on the block weren't even asked what they were doing that night.'

'What the hell do you think, Fellows?' Acton said in exasperation. "We ask all the people close by where they were and what they were doing so's we can find out if somebody heard anything or saw anything. Then we start asking questions about the victim and who she associated with. If we could've found anybody she did more'n say hello to we'd've gone after their alibis but good. We can't go dig into the alibi of everybody in the neighborhood. Half of those people probably wouldn't even have a good one. So what's the point of going around asking for one?'

'I know that,' Fellows said. 'No complaints. I just hoped there might have been more.'

'Is that how you're working it? Seeing who's got alibis and who hasn't?'

'That's part of it. It may be working things backwards but it's about the only thing we can do.'

'You get much on the kids?'

'It says in the file that Mike Baxter ate supper about half past six and then went upstairs to his room and studied until his folks asked him to get the stepladder for Sellers.'

'And you think maybe since nobody saw him studying he might have sneaked next door?'

'Not really. Discovery of the body very nearly put him in a state of shock. And I can't find anything in his reported behavior afterwards that indicates a guilty conscience, remorse, glee, or something other than what you'd expect from a seventeen-year-old kid who's discovered the dead body of the woman next door.'

'I could've told you you wouldn't,' Acton said. 'Don't you think these interviewers weren't looking for signs? It wasn't till they eliminated everybody else that they turned to Sellers himself. The Baxter kid was the first one they wondered about. The man who discovers a body is always suspect. And I can tell you the Baxter property was searched but good for the weapon.'

'So I found out.'

'All the sewers were searched, the rubbish heaps, the garbage pails of all the houses around, everyplace a guy'd be likely to hide a weapon.'

'Including,' Fellows said, 'the route to the bus.'

'Yeah. Personally I think Sellers took it on the bus with him and got rid of it downtown somewhere.'

'Only you couldn't find any place downtown either.'

'That don't make him innocent, it only shows he was slicker than we were. So what else did you find?'

'The boy across the street, Skip Hopworth, was visiting Robert Bruce that night from about half past seven on. He's pretty well knocked out.'

'Like I say, we investigated everybody near by before we turned to Sellers.'

'But you didn't do much with William King Junior or Dick Spencer over on Xavier Street.'

'Well, after all, like I say. There was nothing to show those kids knew more than who she was.'

'But the Spencer boy was cutting quite a swath with girls around that time.'

'Yeah?' Acton perked up just a little. 'Didn't know about that.'

'That's a rumor we picked up. You probably wouldn't have learned about it without investigating him. The rumor goes that that's why the Spencers moved from the neighborhood.'

Acton stroked his chin. 'You think there's anything in that? I mean that he could have been playing around with Sheila?'

'Either one of them might have. There's no alibi for them and their yards weren't searched more than sketchily for the weapon.'

'We didn't have the manpower to dig up every yard in the neighborhood, you know. We did a thorough job on all the most likely places and thinned it out from there. There're a lot of places on that block where we didn't look, I have to admit.'

'I'm not criticizing, I'm just saying if either one of them did it, there was no investigation conducted that would have revealed it.'

'And so now you're going to see if they did or not?'

'I'm going to try to talk to them, yes.'

Acton said, 'Listen, Fellows, if you really wanted, I suppose I could send a detective along with you.'

'That's something I'd appreciate.'

'Of course, they wouldn't have to talk to a detective any more than they'd have to talk to you, but it might straighten them up a little and make them lay it on the line a little better. You know I'm sticking out my neck, of course.'

'I know. It's a tough spot.'

'I oughtta have my head examined but I got to admit you're beginning to make me wonder a little myself. Who the hell knows what kids do these days? Come on in after supper and I'll have Sam Wiggin here waiting for you.'

CHAPTER TWENTY-FIVE

Sam Wiggin was a short, bulky man with a low forehead, a beefy face and a thick crop of black curly hair. He wore a gray slack suit and a bow tie and he shook Fellows' hand with an iron grip. 'So you want to talk to a couple of kids,' he said. 'That shouldn't be hard.'

Fellows allowed that perhaps it wouldn't and Wiggin said, 'This here that other detective, Jones?' He squeezed Raphael's hand and made him wince. 'All right, let's go. I don't know what the chief's up to but he assigns me and I do the assignment but there ain't no point in wasting time about it. I don't like working after hours.'

They took off in Wiggin's car, a battered sedan that looked more as if it belonged to a junk driver than a policeman, but the only apology he made was to say, 'We'll go in my heap because I get mileage.' They drove out to the Sherwood place with Fellows directing and pulled up across the street and one house away. 'Never park in front of where you're going,' Wiggin said. 'It tips off the suspect.'

Fellows replied very soberly, 'I'll have to remember that.'

'Now this punk. Is he guilty or nor guilty?'

'That's what we want to find out.'

'That's no help. What do you think he is?'

'Why?'

'It depends on whether he's guilty or not guilty how I question him. There's no point roughing up a suspect to make him talk if he don't know nothing to talk about. It's like beating a dead dog.'

'You'd better consider him innocent then,' Fellows said.

'And what's the point of questioning an innocent man?'

Fellows, in the back seat with Jones, smiled faintly. 'One thing about you, Mr. Wiggin. No beating around the bush.'

'Let's get with it. That's my motto. Hey, a car's coming out the drive. That the kid driving?'

'I haven't seen the kid but they don't have two that age. You'd better stop him.'

'Nuts to that. Let's see where he's going first.'

The sleek new car with the young man inside wheeled into the street and leaped off. Wiggin had his motor going and picked up the trail, following at a distance and varying it. 'The kid's going too fast,' Wiggin said. 'I can run him in for speeding right now if you want him questioned at headquarters.'

'Let's follow your first idea and see where he's heading,' Fellows suggested. 'So long as you can keep with him.'

'He won't lose me. I ain't been in the

230

business twenty years for nothing.'

The sleek car led them to another residential section of town and stopped in front of a house. The youth went inside and came out again five minutes later with a girl in tow. Wiggin, parked half a block away, said, 'Friday night. It figures.'

They watched the couple climb into the car and start off again. Wiggin took up the pursuit. Fellows said, 'I hope he doesn't tumble he's being tailed. This car of yours is rather distinctive.'

'You mean it's a piece of junk. I'll tell you, it took three years to pay off the mortgage on it and I'm gonna get my money's worth. But don't worry about the kid. He ain't gonna tumble. Look at the way they got their heads together. He's probably giving her a big feel while he's driving. I can arrest him for not keeping both hands on the steering wheel if you want.'

They followed the car out of town as it rolled at a leisurely rate. It swung onto a back road and loafed along and Wiggin said, 'He's heading for Lonergan's farm. Lover's lane stuff and it ain't even dark yet. Probably told the dame's folks they were going to a movie, too, the punk.'

The sleek car slowed, cut sharply and rolled off into a field. Wiggin stayed on the road and drove past. 'We'll find a place to turn around and come back unannounced.

They won't be going anywhere.' He went on to the Lonergan farmhouse, reversed course in the drive and headed back. When he swung into the field the couple were still in the car, parked under a tree fifty yards from the road.

Wiggin pulled up alongside and the boy, by that time sitting in the corner of the driver's seat, turned as if he hadn't known they were coming. The girl was busy doing something with her dress.

The bulky detective hopped out, went around the front of his car to the boy's window and said, 'All right, punk, let's get outta the heap.'

'Why? the boy asked. 'What for?'

'Because I said so. You want an engraved invitation?'

'Who are you?'

'I'm a policeman, that's who I am.' Wiggin flipped open his folder with the badge in it for the lad's benefit and tucked it away again. 'Now do you wantta come out like a nice punk or do you wantta make it tough on yourself?'

The boy said, 'We weren't doing anything,' but he opened the door and climbed out. He was in shirt sleeves now with his jacket in the back seat and he was tall and good looking with neat, cleancut features. 'What do you want, anyway?'

Wiggin didn't answer. He led the boy

around the other side of his own car, away from the girl who sat quietly and didn't even turn her head to watch. 'Now,' he said, close to the open window in Fellows' door, 'You'n me are gonna have a little chat. You're gonna tell us about a woman you used to know. Sheila Sellers.'

The boy blinked and stared at Wiggin. He turned and scowled at Fellows and Jones. 'Say, what is this? Sheila Sellers? I don't know any Sheila Sellers.'

'You're Dick Spencer, ain't ya? You used to live on Xavier Street, didn't ya? What d'ya mean you don't know about no Sheila Sellers?'

'Oh, *that* Sheila Sellers.'

'Yeah. You know some others?'

'Well, no, but I just didn't—you said somebody I used to know and I didn't know her.'

'She only lives a couple of backyards away from you and you don't know her, huh? You'd better think up better answers than that, punk.'

'I knew who she was if that's what you mean.'

'That's what I mean.'

'Well, that's all I knew.'

Wiggin growled. 'Don't give me that, punk. We happen to know better. You were playing around with the dame. Admit it.'

'Playing around with her?' Spencer's voice

233

came up. 'What're you talking about? I don't even know what you're talking about.'

'We know about her, punk. You don't have to try to hide nothing. She had an eye out for young boys and you were a young boy with an eye out for the girls. Tell us about it and it'll go easier.'

'There's nothing to tell,' he said steadfastly. 'I don't know why you think—I didn't even know her to say hello to.'

Wiggin made a gesture as if he'd only barely been able to resist striking the youth. 'Now cut out the crap,' he said, his growl getting more threatening. 'You aren't no dumb kid where girls are concerned. You got an eye out for a pretty face. Look at you right now. You gonna try to deny it? And she had her eye out for a good-looking boy. So don't try to feed me that "I didn't know her" crap. You knew her all right and we know you knew her. Come clean and you won't get in no trouble. Admit it and stop trying to protect her reputation. We already found out about her reputation.'

'But you're crazy,' the boy pleaded. 'I didn't know her. I swear it.'

Fellows leaned out the window then. His face was stern, backing up the detective's. 'You remember the night she was murdered, Spencer?'

Spencer turned. He nodded and wiped his mouth. 'Yes, sir.'

'What were you doing that night?'

'I was—I was out with a girl. We had dinner at her house and then we went—ah—dancing. I got home about half past twelve and my folks were still up. They'd heard about the murder and they were talking about it.'

'What was the name of the girl?'

'Why? What difference does it make? What's this all about, anyway?'

'Was it Sheila Sellers?'

The boy's eyes bugged for a moment and he said in astonishment, 'What? Are you kidding?'

'We want the name of the girl. We want to verify you were at her house when the Sellers woman was killed.'

The youth blanched. 'Oh my God. You don't think—Listen,' he pleaded. 'I didn't know Mrs. Sellers. I don't think I ever saw her more than a couple of times in my life.'

'That was a Thursday night you were out with this girl. That was a school night.'

'Well, so?'

'So who's this girl who can go dancing with you on school nights?'

'She was out of school.'

'You'd better give us her name.'

'But what for? If you want to ask her was I with her that night she probably won't remember. It was almost three years ago. I only remember because of the murder.'

'She might remember.'

'But, listen, she doesn't live here any more. She got married and she moved away. I don't know who she married. I don't know where she is. I don't know anything about her any more.'

Fellows said severely, 'That's not too good, Spencer. Is there anybody else who might remember what you were doing that evening?'

Spencer swallowed. 'Maybe her parents. But I took her out a lot and they wouldn't recall any special day. I'm sure they wouldn't.'

'What's their name?'

'Capstan. Oliver Capstan. 44 Turnquist Road.'

They asked him a few more questions then told him to take off and they waited till his car was gone before Wiggin started his own. On the way back he said, 'You're too soft on the punk. You spoiled the whole caper. If you'd let me talk to him we'd have him admitting right now that he knew one hell of a lot more about that Sellers dame than he let on.'

Fellows leaned wearily against the cushions of the back seat. 'Do you think,' he said dryly, 'that you could have got him to admit he murdered her too?'

CHAPTER TWENTY-SIX

They didn't get to William King Junior till late that night. He was back from summer school but at the movies and Fellows dismissed Detective Wiggin, preferring to tackle the lad himself. He and Jones intercepted him outside the house when he returned home and in two minutes' questioning had lost him as a suspect. On Thursday, October 20, 1960, he was in the hospital recovering from an automobile accident. This was something to be checked, of course, as was Spencer's story, but Fellows had now abandoned the whole idea of a neighborhood youth being the culprit.

'It didn't make much sense anyway,' he told Jones on the way back to the motel. 'A kid committing a murder? The guilt would have been all over his face. The police would have had a confession out of him within twenty-four hours.'

'Which brings us right back to Ernest Sellers again, right?'

'Let's say it means we start over again.'

'Yeah,' said Jones. 'Just like those games where you take the wrong turn and end up at a square which says "go back to the beginning".'

Fellows went back to the beginning again

when he got into his bed and when Jones finally joined him at the breakfast table the next morning he had the next trail laid out. 'Look at it this way, Jones. Knock out the kids in the neighborhood and the youngest men left are in their middle thirties.'

'Bingo,' said Jones digging into his pancakes. 'That's the greatest deduction I've seen in my whole time in the business.'

'It's not likely that men that old would beat a woman to death in a fury because she denied them her body. They're wiser, stabler, and their sex drive is less pronounced.'

Jones shook his head, 'Man, you never give up, do you? The clobbering you've taken on that lover theory and you still stick with it.'

'I'm stuck with it. Let's put it that way.'

'Well, be stuck with it. I made up my mind after last night's fiasco that from now on I'm playing this strictly for laughs.'

'Go laugh it up with Ernest Sellers then.'

'Do I detect a note of bitterness because your best audience is deserting you? Come on, man. How long do you think you can pull these fancy ideas out of thin air and sell them? One after another they dissolve into nothing but you keep them coming and you keep expecting somebody—namely me—to take them seriously.'

'When you've got nothing to work with you have to manufacture something.'

'And that's worked for you in the past, I

gather, so that makes it surefire.' Jones said, 'Go ahead, old man. Unburden yourself. I'll pretend to listen.'

'Don't bother. Pack up and go back to Springfield. You aren't going to get any more publicity here.'

'No point in quitting now, Fellows. It's only five more days. I'll go along for five more days. I'll keep on being your legman. Like, for instance, I'll verify those alibis we got last night for you. Gotta leave you free to think up new avenues, you know.'

'You can save yourself the time. I don't need you. I didn't come up here to work with anybody in the first place.'

'Real bitter. Amazing what poverty will do to strain the closest friendships. Now we're starting to snap at each other. By tomorrow we'll be throwing things.'

Fellows said roughly, 'All right, let's forget it. Maybe I am edgy, but I'm not giving up.'

Jones laughed. 'No, I guess you don't know how. I'll tell you, man, I'd hate for you to be after me. You wouldn't even rest in your grave.'

'Let's get on with it,' Fellows grumbled. 'Only don't pretend to listen. Either listen or leave me alone.'

'Sure I'll listen. You tell very fascinating stories.'

'Then get this fascinating one. The girl was killed in a rage. There was hatred there. If it

239

wasn't done by a kid, then the hatred wouldn't be rejection.'

'You're reaching there, man. That's not a justifiable conclusion.'

'Then say it's more *likely* to be something else.'

'It's more likely if you're dealing in generalities. What you're forgetting, old man, is that the person you're after is an individual, not a statistic. He can be the exception to all the rules you're going by. He could be sixty years old. He could come from another block. He could be somebody you don't even know she knew—that nobody knows she knew.'

'Don't tell me things like that. I know that. I've known that from the beginning. What do you think police work is? Why do you think some murders are never solved? But we don't have time to consider specific individuals. The only thing we can do is work in generalities and hope the man we're after fits some of them.'

'O.K., O.K., I get the picture. What makes you sore is the fact you know yourself how flimsy the theory is. That makes us both even. Go on with the rest.'

Fellows made a face. 'All right,' he said gruffly. 'We can guess the lover's motive for murder isn't rejection by Sheila. That brings us back to him trying to reject her. He's desperate to get away and she won't let him. Now why would a man be desperate to get away?'

'He hates her.'

'But he once loved her.'

'So maybe he's got a new love.'

'Maybe. And if he has, isn't it likely then that he's a bachelor?'

'Not necessarily. He might have a wife in the kitchen while he plays in the bedroom.'

'If he did, that would hardly be a secret in that neighborhood and we'd have heard about it.'

Jones shrugged. 'And then, of course, it might be that his wife found out and threatened him if he didn't break off.'

'If so, then what hold could Sheila possibly have on him?'

'What hold could she possibly have on a bachelor in the first place?'

'She might be able to queer things with the new girlfriend.'

Jones took a sip of coffee. 'Pretty weak, old man. I guess you know that.'

'It's weak, but it's better than nothing at all.'

'So you figure it's going to be a bachelor. Since there're only three of them, I'm all in favor of investigating bachelors.' Jones sat back and mused. 'Let's see, there's Gordon Henry. He lives right around the corner. He's not supposed to go with girls. Mama wouldn't like. So if Mama wouldn't like, Gordon Henry might be unhappy about Sheila talking. That ought to make him a good suspect. Then there's George Walker. He got punched by Sellers for dancing with Sheila and cuckolding Sellers might be a good revenge. What he forgets is that Sheila might not want to let go when he's had his vengeance. Good suspect number two. Then there's John Davins who lived with his sister. All we know about him is he moved to Pittsfield and that makes him an automatic suspect. Who's your choice, Fellows?'

Fellows said glumly, 'That's the trouble. None of them are very good.'

'That's supposed to be my line. What's wrong with them?'

'From what we've found out about Gordon Henry, it's hard to see how he would get together with Sheila. She'd practically have to seduce him and nothing we've found out indicated she was the type.'

'Nothing we've found out indicates she'd have a lover, man, yet that's the whole basis for your thinking.'

'My thinking is that she might be seducible rather than seducing.'

'So there's good old George Walker who's doubtless very good at that.'

'I know and he's the man you're going to check on. He claims to have been in Pittsfield but it's never been verified. I think it's time it was. And check it carefully, Jones. George Walker is the only person in the whole neighborhood who thinks Sheila Sellers might have played around. He may have a reason for wanting to plant that idea in our mind.'

'O.K., boss. Your legman will get to work. And what are you going to do meanwhile?'

'I'm going down to Pittsfield to call on Jim Davins. He's supposed to have moved because he changed his job but there are some interesting things about him. Walker saw him as a lover and Ernest Sellers didn't have him on his list of men Sheila knew. That makes him one man Ernest didn't have his eagle-eye on. It's barely possible there was something more than a change of jobs that led him to move after Ernie's trial.'

CHAPTER TWENTY-SEVEN

If Fellows had any expectations on the subject of Jim Davins, he wasn't to get them satisfied on Saturday August third. He didn't locate the Davins house on Elgin Street in Pittsfield until late in the morning and when he did there was no answer to his ring. In fact, the shades were drawn and the place was locked up tight.

He tried the neighbors on both sides and the second one gave him the bad news. Jim Davins and his sister had gone off on vacation on the first and wouldn't be back till the fifteenth. The woman didn't know where the Davins had gone nor did anyone in the half dozen other houses he tried. None of them knew Davins very well nor did they know anyone who did.

Fellows drove slowly back to Banksville pondering what to do about this new turn of events. Davins and his sister could be traced, of course, but it would take time and time was short. With nothing really pointing to the man, Fellows' problem was should he take the time?

He ate lunch alone in the motel cafeteria for there was no sign of Raphael Jones. He thought about things fruitlessly in his room for an hour thereafter and then, because Jones still hadn't shown up, he rented a bathing suit and took a dip in the pool.

The water was cool and refreshing but he didn't notice it. One of the four other swimmers was a pretty girl with a luscious figure but he didn't notice her either. Right then the chief was in real trouble and for the first time in the whole case he didn't know what to do.

It was when he was returning, soaking, from the pool to his room that Raphael Jones finally turned into the motel lot and pulled up alongside. Fellows saw him coming but only reluctantly came to a stop. Jones looked too cheerful to bear just then.

'Loafing as usual,' Jones said by way of

greeting. 'Only five more days and he's loafing.'

Fellows turned, bleak of eye, and looked in at Jones' perspiring figure. 'And I suppose you've been working all this time?'

'Busy as a buzzsaw and you ought to appreciate the fact. I'm cutting down your list of suspects for you.'

'Who've you cut off the list today?'

'George Walker. Wasn't he the one you scheduled?'

'Yeah. About five hours ago.'

'You wanted his alibi verified. "Check it very carefully," I recall your saying. That takes a trip to Pittsfield. Which reminds me. You were down there. From your face I gather Davins fell on his.'

'Yes. And from yours I gather Walker did likewise.'

'He was down there all right. It was on a wild goose chase but it was verifiable. Lucky for him he stopped to phone or he'd have no alibi at all.'

'What are you talking about?'

'He went down to see a man who wasn't there. Fortunately he made a phone call and the woman remembers.'

'What man who wasn't there? Make sense.'

'All right, all right, maybe he didn't tell you. It seems he got a call to go down there to see somebody who wanted insurance only it was a phony address. He—'

'What?' Fellows said, suddenly awake. 'Come again?'

Jones began over. 'He remembers that night because when he got back he saw the police cars and the ambulance at Sellers' place. He claims he had a few beers down in Pittsfield before driving home again. Probably he was trying to pick up a girl in a bar. Anyway, he was teed off about the phony phone call.'

'The phony phone call. That's what I want to hear about.'

'Look,' Jones said in exasperation. 'Walker got a call—or rather his answering service got a call. I checked with the answering service and they had it in their files. A Barry Rogers called and said he lived at 232 Emmett Street and would Walker come see him that evening at nine o'clock about an insurance policy? So Walker, when he left his office, drove down to Pittsfield and had dinner in a restaurant there and drove out to Emmett and there wasn't any two hundred and thirty-two. There wasn't anything past a hundred and eighty, in fact. He rang doorbells in three of the houses around but nobody had ever heard of a Barry Rogers. So Walker thought maybe the street was wrong. He borrowed a phone book at one house and there wasn't anybody by the name of Barry Rogers listed in Pittsfield. He called his answering service from that house and got it that that was the name and address all right. So I talked to the people who let him make the call and they remembered it. They didn't remember the date but they remembered it happened. The answering service, though, they had the date and it was October twentieth, the day of the murder. He was down there all right.'

'He was down there at nine o'clock,' Fellows snapped. 'He wouldn't have had to leave Banksville before quarter past eight. That's no alibi. He only thinks it is.'

'He went down there from work. He ate in a restaurant.'

'Who says he did?'

'Come off it,' Jones said. 'What the hell are you trying to say, that he'd kill a woman and then hop out and see a client? You don't make sense at all. If he'd wanted to kill her he'd wait for another time.'

'Unless he put the call in to himself,' Fellows said. 'Don't you see it? There's our break. George Walker was Sheila's lover. I'm sure of it.'

Jones shook his head. 'Man, if you don't go off the deep end. How you can jump to that conclusion just like that—'

'What conclusion do you jump to? Why do you think anybody'd send George Walker on a wild goose chase? It wasn't April Fool's Day.'

'Maybe the answering service got the message wrong.'

'Maybe, but I hope you asked Walker if Barry Rogers ever called back.'

'I did. He didn't,' Jones confessed.

'And there it is—the one freak thing that happened in that neighborhood on the murder night—'

'That doesn't prove there's any connection, you know.'

'No, but I'll lay you odds there is. That's too coincidental, something happening like that. Where's Walker, is he home now?'

'I wouldn't know. He was home this morning when he gave me this story. You really think he's the one?'

'Don't you?'

Jones shrugged. 'I'd hate to try to get him to admit it.'

'That's my department, just as soon as I get dressed.'

CHAPTER TWENTY-EIGHT

No one answered Fellows' persistent ringing of George Walker's bell at half past three that afternoon and the chief, who was ready to eat Walker whole, didn't get his chance to pounce. 'We'll set up a watch,' he told Jones returning to the car. 'He's probably out with a dame.'

Jones said, 'You know, don't you, that all

he's going to have to do is say "no" to everything and you can't touch him.'

'I'm not going to let him say "no" unless no is the right answer.'

They waited for an hour, parked down the block. They talked for a while then lapsed into silence. Boredom began to sit with them and it got so that the actions of a three-year-old child playing with a doll carriage on the sidewalk engrossed them. Finally Fellows said, 'Call me if he shows,' and got out of the car. He went to the Bomstein house next to Walker's, rang the bell and was admitted. He came out again three minutes later, walked past Walker's to Polin's on the other side. This time he was inside nearly half an hour. When he reappeared, he came down the steps from the stoop and strode briskly back to where Jones sat behind the wheel of the Anglia. 'I've got the motive now,' he said. 'A girl, of course.'

'Spell it out in words of one syllable, will you?'

'The Bomsteins didn't know anything and Mrs. Polin didn't know much more but I was able to get her to recall the important things I needed.'

'Which are what?'

'The girl I saw in his place last week is a girl he's had around off and on for about a year now. Before that, though, there was another girl. Mrs. Polin didn't know her name, of course, any more than she knows his present flame's name. But she did recall when she first saw the former girlfriend. She first saw her around Labor Day three summers ago—six weeks before the murder.'

'So that's the girl he started to take up with after Sheila—that is, if he ever had anything to do with Sheila in the first place, which you haven't proven yet.'

'I haven't proven it, but more and more I'm expecting to. I'm building up a case against this guy, Jones, and when I throw it at him I'm going to break him with it. For instance, before that girl, who happened to be an attractive blonde, Mrs. Polin didn't see any women around for about six months. There'd been one before that only she'd stopped coming around—or he'd stopped bringing her around. My guess is it was Sheila Sellers' turn during that period, only he went to *her* instead of vice versa.'

'A once–a–week proposition while hubby's playing chess?'

'Yes. And then there comes a new girl and Sheila finds out. He can't have a girl around without the neighborhood knowing about it.'

'So he tells Sheila to go to hell. What can she do about it?'

'She must have been able to do something.'

'Name one good thing. Name one thing worth killing for.'

'I'd rather let Walker name it.'

250

They lapsed into more silence and did some more waiting. Finally, at six, Fellows suggested they stagger the watch. 'No telling how long before he shows up. Take me back to the motel. You can grab something to eat and I'll come back in my car and sit. You can relieve me when you're through so I can eat and then I'll take over again say about ten o'clock.'

'Sure, only this time I'm going to bring a newspaper along. Say, why don't you get that detective—Wiggin—to help out? He could probably force a confession out of Walker faster than the First Army. He looks like he's got the technique.'

'We'll try it my way first. If he wants something official I'll get Acton in on it.'

They returned to the motel and Fellows came back but the Walker house was still empty. Nor had Walker returned when Jones relieved, and he was still not in when Fellows pulled up behind the Anglia at ten o'clock that evening. The two men talked for a few minutes on the sidewalk and Jones said, 'You don't suppose he's waited till now to take that powder he should have taken three years ago, do you?'

'He'll come back,' Fellows said confidently. 'Nothing's happened to scare him away. He gave you an alibi you could verify. He wouldn't suspect we'd see it differently from the way he meant it.'

'Maybe.' Jones climbed into his car. 'When do you want me back?'

'No more tonight. I'll stick it out for a reasonable time and then call it quits till tomorrow.' The chief stepped away and let the Anglia go. He turned and eyed the dark house, then climbed into his own car and took up the vigil once more.

CHAPTER TWENTY-NINE

It was half past twelve when headlights turned the corner and swung into the driveway at Walker's house. Fellows, half dozing behind the wheel of his old coupe, came alert. He yawned and stretched and got out, closing the door quietly. There were few lights on in the houses around and the Bomstein and Polin places were as black as Walker's own.

Fellows strode quietly around to the driveway where the red beacons of Walker's taillights were moving into the garage. All the lights cut off and the whole yard went black. There was the sound of the car door slamming and then the garage doors coming down.

The garage was not a part of the house but set some twenty feet behind and Fellows was waiting when Walker's footsteps sounded crossing the pavement. 'Walker,' he said softly when the insurance salesman was close to the back door and Walker whirled as if shot. 'What?' He peered but could see nothing in the darkness. 'Who's there?'

Fellows moved closer. 'Fellows,' he said. 'I've been waiting for you.'

'Well, Jesus, you don't have to scare the hell out of a guy.' Walker went to the back door and started fumbling for his keys. He paused and turned to the chief who was close enough to be visible now. 'Wait a minute. What do you mean you've been waiting for me?'

'I want to have a talk with you.'

'This is one hell of a time to think about having talks. Don't you cops have office hours?' He clicked a key against the lock seeking the slot.

Fellows said, 'You went through the back yards, didn't you?'

'Back yards where?' Walker turned the key and opened the door and stopped again. 'What're you talking about?'

'You went to her house through the back yards, didn't you? After dark nobody could see you unless they stumbled over you.'

'Say, what are you after? What're you talking about?'

'I'm talking about Sheila Sellers and her lover. Do you want to discuss it with me out here or do you want to go inside?'

Walker hesitated. Finally he said, 'Come on in.'

Fellows allowed himself a faint smile in the darkness. George Walker's invitation was not a confession but it suggested something less than innocence. Sheer outrage on Walker's part would have thrown the chief off but he hadn't expected sheer outrage. He had expected just what he got.

They moved into the house with Walker throwing the switch that lighted the kitchen. He went through into the living room and put on two lamps there. 'This is one hell of a time to come calling,' he said but the angry note in his voice had a false ring.

Fellows followed him and remained standing. Walker brushed past him back to the kitchen and said, 'You want a drink?'

'No thank you.'

'I can tell you I'm going to have one.' There was the clap of a bottle on the counter, the click of the icebox door and the rattle of an ice tray.

Fellows went to the doorway to watch the proceeding. 'Go right ahead,' he said patiently.

'Yeah,' Walker retorted bitterly. 'Police technique isn't it—get the guy drunk?'

'Truth serum's better. You want to tell me about it or are we going to have to play games?'

'I've got nothing to tell you about anything.

Speak your piece and then get out and let me get some sleep.'

'Speaking of sleep, Walker, how well do you sleep these nights?'

'Like a baby.' Walker broke the ice from the tray and dumped cubes into a tall glass. He poured liquor around the cubes and topped it off with a splash of water. He started back to the living room and on second thought brought the bottle along too. He pushed past the chief without a word and settled himself on the couch, clumping his feet onto the coffee table.

Fellows followed slowly and just as Walker got himself settled, said. 'It was hard to figure how you could get away with it without the neighbors finding out but when I see how dark it is out back I can understand. Nobody suspected a thing, did they?'

'Nobody suspected what?'

'That you were seeing Sheila Sellers on the sly. What was it, every Thursday night?'

'You're out of your mind. I never knew the woman.'

'What made you go after her? Do you usually tackle married woman?'

Walker put his feet down and sat up. 'Listen, if you've come here to insult me—'

Fellows' voice got harsh. 'What about it, Walker? Are married women usually your dish?'

'Oh, you want to get tough about **things**?'

255

'That's right. That's exactly right. Maybe we should go down to the station. It's a little tougher there.' He pointed. 'Put down the drink and come along.'

'What for?'

'The atmosphere here doesn't make you cooperative. Down there it will.'

Walker sat back a little. 'What're you trying to ride me for?' he complained. 'I'm minding my own business. I come home beat and you start giving me a hard time. What're you after?'

'I want the truth out of you, Walker. I want to know all about you and Sheila Sellers.' Fellows held up a hand and interrupted when Walker started to protest. 'And don't give me the innocent business. You try it and I'll take you down to headquarters. If you cooperate we can talk here. If you won't, get on your feet and come with me.'

Walker brushed a hand over his face. 'Jesus, what're you so hot about? What do you want? Didn't that guy Jones tell you where I was the night of the murder? I wasn't anywhere around here for Christ's sake.'

'I'm not talking about the night of the murder. I'm talking about the other nights when you *were* around—when you were around and Ernest Sellers was off playing chess. I'm talking about the way you lied to me the last time. You tell me just one lie this

256

time, mister, and that's it. You're going downtown and we'll put you under the lights till we get the truth.'

'Well what are you after? I don't get it. I thought you were looking for who murdered the woman. What do you want to know about all this other stuff for? What's that got to do with it?'

'Where do you think we get our leads from—people lying to us the way you did? You made love to her. How many others did?'

'How would I know?'

'She might have told you.'

'Woman don't talk about things like that. Christ, what do you think they are, dumb? I don't know who killed her. I always thought that jerk Sellers did till you come around.'

'When did you take up with her?'

Walker expostulated, 'Who says I took up with her at all?'

'I say it and I happen to know. Stop beating around the bush. Are you going to cooperate or aren't you?'

'How the hell could you know? Nobody knows.'

'You only *think* nobody knows. Let's get on with it, Walker.'

Walker held up a hand. 'No, no. Wait a minute. Where did you get the information? I want to know how you found out. Nobody *could* have found out!'

257

'Save it. I'm not going to tell you. Just know it's been found out.'

'Then the one who found out is the son of a bitch who sent me down to Pittsfield the night she was killed. He wanted to get me out of the way.'

'Very likely,' Fellows said by way of invitation. 'We'll get to that later. First, when did you take up with Sheila?'

Walker shook his head and plunged into his drink. 'I still can't get it,' he said. 'I still don't know how the hell—'

'When did you take up with Sheila?'

'He shook himself. 'In the spring,' he said bitterly. 'She was a girl who needed comforting and I comforted her.'

'Let's have it from the beginning. Had you ever known her before you danced with her the summer before?'

'No.' He had some more from his glass. 'I just saw her and she was a neat looking dish so I danced with her. So then that cockeyed husband of hers punched me. I would've broken his jaw but the rest held me back. That was the first time I ever laid eyes on her.'

'And you wanted her?'

'I wanted her bastard husband. That's who I was out to get.'

'And you got him through her?'

'That's about it. Not that she was any hardship, but no sonuvabitch is going to take

258

a poke at me and get away with it.'

'When did you start after her?'

Walker waved the glass. 'Well, not right away. This was something in the back of my mind when the chance came along. So next I ran into her in the store by accident. She was in there buying food and she was embarrassed to see me because of what her husband had done but I set her mind at ease and she was grateful. I had one strike on her to start with because of the way her husband behaved and she felt she owed me something. I offered her a ride home but she was afraid—because of the way her husband was and if she was seen riding with me it'd be all over the neighborhood in an hour and it'd make her look bad.' He gave a bitter smile. 'The neighbors think I'm not fit company for women.'

'So you started running into her at the store?'

'I started planning my shopping by her schedule, that's right. And I loosened her up a little with conversation. I found out she liked books and her husband didn't read so I talked books. That got her interested and it got her relaxed. Then it got so we tried to arrange shopping so that the other neighbors wouldn't be around and we could talk longer without anybody noticing. Then, when the time was ripe for the next move, I went to her back door one Thursday night after her

259

husband had gone to chess to lend her a book I'd been talking about.

'Of course she was panicked and she didn't want to let me in for fear somebody'd find out but I persuaded her I hadn't been seen and I stayed an hour. She was nervous but she was kind of excited and she liked the idea of our being able to talk a little without having to cover up every time somebody came down the aisle of the supermarket. She wouldn't keep the book for fear her husband might find it and made me take it back but I told her when I left that I was coming again the next Thursday. She told me I shouldn't, that she was frightened, but she didn't make it stick and she knew she hadn't and she knew I knew it and she was expecting me the next week.

'It grew into a weekly habit and, of course, the conversation got away from books after a couple of times and onto other things and it wasn't too long before I had my revenge on her husband.'

'You used her, in other words?'

Walker held Fellows off with his glass. 'Now wait. I admit that was what made me pay attention to her in the first place but by the time what happened got around to happening it wasn't him I was thinking about, it was her. She was really a sweet kid—well she wasn't exactly a kid—and she was much too good for that jerk husband of

260

hers. I really liked her.'

'Do you mean by that that you weren't in love with her?'

'Of course I wasn't in love with her. What's love, for Christ's sake? And what would be the point of falling in love with a married woman? We liked each other, that's all.'

'Oh? She wasn't in love with you?'

'No. We were friends. We enjoyed each other. She got from me what she couldn't get from her husband, that's all.'

'And this started in the spring?'

'Late April, early May, somewhere around there.'

'And what about her husband?'

'Him?' Walker took a swig from his glass and gestured with it. 'He never knew a thing.'

'Then what was the point of deceiving him if he didn't know about it?'

'Oh, hell. Who cares about him? I started off with the idea of getting back at him but he doesn't have to know it so long as *I* know it. It was *my* ego I was doing it for, not his. Besides, by the time we reached that stage I'd forgotten about him anyway. It was Sheila I cared about. We had a good thing going. It was in our own interests to keep him in the dark.'

'How long did this Thursday night habit last before you got tired of it?'

'Got tired of it? I wasn't tired of it. It lasted

right up till she got killed and if I hadn't got that phony phone call getting me out of town, whoever killed her might not have done it.'

'You were going with another girl at the time Sheila got killed. A blonde.'

Walker started and looked up. 'How the hell do you know that?'

'I've been spending the last couple of weeks finding out a lot of things. What about that girl? How did Sheila react to that news?'

'I didn't tell her about it. It was none of her business.'

'The neighborhood gossips found out fast enough. Don't tell me she didn't hear the news.'

Walker shrugged. 'She probably didn't. She wasn't a gossip herself and she didn't circulate.' He looked up. 'Leastways, she never said anything to me about it.'

'What if she had? What do you think her reaction would have been if she had found out?'

'It wouldn't have mattered to her. After all, she was married. She had her personal life. I had a right to mine.'

'That might be the way you'd look at it but I suggest she'd take a different attitude.'

'Dog in the manger like?' He drank some more and said, 'I doubt it.'

'And if she tried to hang onto you?'

'Hang onto me? I wasn't going anywhere. I wasn't trying to break it off.'

'What about the blonde? She didn't want you to break off?'

'She didn't know about Sheila.' He scowled at Fellows. 'Say, what kind of a jerk do you think I am?'

'Then it's your claim that you weren't trying to break off with Sheila when the new girl came along?'

'Absolutely.' His voice fuzzed suddenly and he shook his head. His eyes came momentarily unstrung and he forced them back into focus. He stared at his glass which was nearly empty, made himself drink the last of the liquor and set it down on the coffee table extra loudly. 'No shir. Sheila wush a nice girl.'

'Did she have any other men on her string?'

Walker shook his head heavily. 'Naw. I don't think she was that clever. She wouldn'tta known how to go about it.'

'She fell under your spell. She might have fallen under another man's.'

'She could've. Yesh. But she never told me. Not little Sheila. She never told me about any other men.'

'You don't think there were any?'

Walker's head was lolling slightly. He forced himself to think. 'Any more men? Little Sheila wouldn'tta done that to George Walker. She was a cute little girl. She was a nice little girl, Sheila was.' He looked up.

'You know something?'

'No. What?'

'I forget. But she was a nice girl. She was too good for that stinking Ernie. I saw Ernie a couple of times. You know what I'd do? I'd shay hello to Sheila right in front of him and y'know what he did? Nothing. That's what he did. Nothing. He just didn't like me dancing with her, that was all. So I'm sleeping with her and I say hello to her on the street and he doesn't do nothing. He didn't know I was sleeping with her. He only knew I wasn't dancing with her. How'sh that for a laugh?'

Fellows said carefully, 'When did you call your answering service?'

Walker didn't answer. He stared at his glass and picked it up. 'I really poured myshelf one. I really poured myshelf a big one. I been drinking gin all evening. I shouldn'tta changed.'

'When did you call your answering service?' Fellows asked again.

'Called who?' Walker stared up at him stupidly.

'The answering service, to give them the message about Barry Rogers?'

'Barry Rogers? I don't know any Barry Rogers. Oh, yesh. He's the little man who wasn't there. There ain't no Barry Rogers. He's a myth. He'sh a nonexshistent male. That's Mishter Barry Rogers.'

Fellows stepped closer and grasped Walker

by the shoulder, shaking him. 'The phone call,' he snapped. 'You made a phone call to your answering service the day Sheila was murdered. Remember?'

Walker looked up. 'No. Whaddid I shay?'

'You said your name was Barry Rogers.'

Walker grinned at the chief and waved a loose hand. 'Oh no I didn't! Oh no. I never said my name was Barry Rogers. He did it. Old Barry Rogers said his name was Barry Rogers.'

Fellows stepped back and scowled, unsure whether the man was really drunk or pretending. Walker reached for the bottle and missed. He reached again and Fellows took the bottle away. 'You've had enough,' he snapped. 'We're not through talking yet.'

'Just a little one,' Walker begged, smiling foolishly. 'Pretty please?'

Fellows took the bottle out to the kitchen and set it on the counter. He came back and Walker was sprawled face up on the couch, his eyes closed, one arm dangling.

The chief shook him vigorously but there was no response. He thought momentarily of throwing water on the man but decided against it. Instead, he went to the telephone in the corner and dialed the operator, turning to watch Walker's recumbent figure.

The figure stirred slightly, a hand rubbed the face and flopped again. When Fellows said into the mouthpiece, 'Would you connect me with the police, please?' Walker's eyes opened and focused. He struggled to an elbow and said thickly, 'What're you doing?'

Fellows ignored him but his right hand slid unobtrusively under the tail of his sport shirt.

Walker struggled to a sitting position and said, 'Hey, you can't arrest me.' He pushed himself unsteadily to his feet.

Fellows took out his service revolver and pointed it at the man's chest. 'Stay where you are,' he said. 'I don't want any trouble.'

Walker blinked and shook his head dazedly. 'Whas going on? Just because I'm drunk? You can't arresht me for being drunk. It'sh my own house.'

'I'm arresting you on suspicion of murder,' Fellows said, 'so mind yourself.'

Walker gasped and sank, his body falling heavily against the cushioned back of the couch. 'You can't,' he said, staring incredulously.

Into the phone, Fellows said, 'Sergeant? This is Chief Fred Fellows of Stockford—'

CHAPTER THIRTY

Fred Fellows beat on Jones' motel door at quarter of eight the next morning. For at least a minute nothing happened then, finally, the door was pulled inward and the sleepy-eyed detective said, 'Don't you have a calendar, Dad? This is Sunday morning.'

'And a hot one,' Fellows told him. 'Stop sleeping your life away and get dressed. There're things to do.'

'My turn to stand watch? Listen, I got a little head—'

'I thought you wanted publicity. The bird came back to roost last night. Right now he's sleeping it off in a cell.'

Jones came into wakefulness in an instant. 'He did it?'

'He did it, but we have to make him say so.'

'No wonder you're so bright and cheerful.' Jones retreated into the room and turned for his clothes. 'How do you know he did it?'

'He admitted the lover part,' Fellows said, following and closing the door. 'We've nailed him for that on his own admission. Now all we have to do is make him admit the rest.'

Jones shed his pajamas and started dressing. 'What happened? How come he didn't admit all of it? Why stop at just being a lover?'

'You can't get electrocuted for being a lover, that's why. He didn't mean to admit the first part and then he pulled a drunk act to shut himself up. He'd been drinking but he wasn't that drunk. So I hauled him off to the station and Acton and a couple of detectives came down to question him for a couple of hours.'

'And he didn't admit anything?'

'He tried not to. He tripped himself into the lover bit again but he clung to the alibi he was down in Pittsfield when Sheila was killed. Along about three we gave up and put him in a cell.'

'When does round two start?'

'As soon as we can get down there and start nudging things along.'

They left the motel room as soon as Jones had shaved and Fellows had enough compassion to permit the detective a cup of coffee. He had one himself and started chewing tobacoo impatiently while Jones went through a bit of Danish pastry. Finally, at eight-thirty, they were on the road to headquarters.

Questioning of George Walker had not yet begun when Fellows and Jones arrived. In fact, there was no immediate prospect of further questioning for the press was there in force and Acton, bright and shiny despite the Sunday, was holding court. 'Always thought there was something funny about the case,' he was saying when the two came in. 'They didn't have no evidence against Sellers. Only reason Sellers was convicted was because nobody could find out about the lover.'

'Who do you mean by "they"?' one of the reporters said.

'The State Police and the Pittsfield police

and all. It wasn't my case. We don't have the equipment to solve things like that. We have to get help. Mind you, I'm not knocking the police. Things like this happen. It's practically impossible to find a lover in this circumstance. That fellow Walker was real slick.' He saw Fellows at the rear of the group and added, 'Matter of fact, the chief there is responsible and he'll tell you it took a lot of real digging.'

That switched attention to the Stockford chief and Fellows answered questions for another fifteen minutes. He was polite and he mentioned Jones' part in things but he did not answer more fully than he had to for he was chafing to get to Walker.

When he explained, with Acton's confirmation, that the interrogation of Walker would get under way again as soon as the press was through, the reporters brought their interview to a quick close and prepared to wait for the confession that would make their big headline. 'You think it'll take long?' they asked.

Fellows turned that one over to Acton who parried it. 'We don't know. Depends on Walker.'

Fellows, Jones and Acton left them then, Acton saying to the sergeant, 'Send the prisoner up to the interrogation room.'

The interrogation room was on the second floor of the old school building and contained a large table, a dozen straight chairs, a swivel chair under a metal lamp in a corner, and equipment lockers. Acton went around drawing shades and turning on the metal lamp which flared like a searchlight. He adjusted the lamp to glare on the swivel chair and studied the arrangements like a maitre d' checking a table setting for VIPs.

One of the two doors opened and the detectives came in. Leader of the two was Sam Wiggin looking grim and primed and Jones muttered to Fellows, 'If Wiggin takes over we ought to be through in ten minutes.'

Walker came next, handcuffed to one guard and followed by another. He was sullen and disheveled and his eyes, when they met Fellows', glared with outright hate.

They sat him down in the swivel chair under the hot blaze of the lamp and removed the cuffs. The two guards stepped back and stood at the ready against the walls. Walker looked up, squinting. 'Pretty tough,' he said bitterly. 'Seven against one.'

Another policeman came in, wheeling a stand with a stenotype machine on it. He pushed it close to the table and took a chair. Acton, watching, said, 'That everybody?'

Walker, peering at the newcomer, said, 'What's that, dictation?' He raised his voice. 'Save it. I'm not talking without a lawyer.'

Wiggin moved in on him then. 'Crack wise,' he said, leaning close into the light, 'and I'll belt you one.'

'I didn't do anything,' Walker told him bluntly, 'and you aren't going to make me say I did.'

'You'll say it all right,' Wiggin replied and backed off from the heat.

Acton interrupted then. 'Let the record show,' he said, 'that the prisoner has been informed of his rights. You know your rights, Walker?'

'What rights?' He looked past, to the man at the stenotype whose fingers moved methodically and evenly in response to speech. 'Let the record show that I don't have any rights.'

Wiggin caught a handful of Walker's hair and jerked his head back. 'Now we'll have no more such talk or I'll cut out your tongue.' He shoved Walker's head hard and let go.

Acton, speaking as if from another world, said, 'Under the Constitution of the United States, Walker, you are not required to testify against yourself. You do not have to answer any question you don't want to but everything you say here can be used against you. Is that understood?'

Walker said, 'Listen, Chief, you've got the wrong guy. I was eating dinner in Pittsfield when Sheila was killed.'

'Do you understand your rights, Walker? Do you hear me?'

'Yes, I hear you and I'm not going to

answer any questions till I have a lawyer.'

'That's your privilege, Walker.'

'I want to call a lawyer.'

'You can call him after we talk. Now suppose you tell us again everything you did on October 20, 1960.'

'I told you I'm not going to answer questions.'

Wiggin moved in and took Walker's face in one hand, twisting it around. 'That's not a question, that's a request. Now you be a good little boy and do as you're told. Tell the man what you were doing that day.'

Walker's face was white under the light and it was already dripping sweat. He swallowed when Wiggin released him and put his hands over his eyes. 'I told you,' he said dully. 'I checked my answering service when I came back from lunch and they told me a Barry Rogers had called up from Pittsfield leaving a message saying he wanted to see me that evening at nine o'clock. I left the office about five and drove down to Pittsfield where I had dinner—'

'What was the name of the restaurant?' Wiggin put in.

'I told you before I don't remember. I never even noticed the name.'

'Then what? Snap it up.'

'I left the restaurant about half past eight—'

'That's one hell of a long dinner. Come on,

272

Walker, admit it. You never were in Pittsfield that night.'

'I was, I was. And it wasn't long. I killed an hour in the cocktail lounge part of the restaurant first. I didn't even go in to eat till quarter past seven.'

Wiggin looked up at Acton. 'What should we do with these liars, Chief? Do we have to listen to this bull?'

'Let him go on,' Acton said mildly.

Wiggin turned. 'You heard the chief. Talk.'

Walker swallowed. He took his hands away from his eyes to test the light. 'I went to the address,' he said, 'and there wasn't any such address. I asked the neighbors and they never heard of Barry Rogers. One couple looked it up in the phone book for me and there wasn't any Barry Rogers in Pittsfield.'

'How come you didn't check that before you ever went down there?' Wiggin demanded.

'Why would I? How was I to know there was no such place?'

'Pittsfield's quite a ways from here. That's a long trip to make when you don't even know what the guy wanted.'

'But I didn't have a Pittsfield phone book.'

'So the operator could look up his number, couldn't she?'

Walker turned towards the silhouette of Chief Acton. 'Can I please have a lawyer?'

273

'You'll get a lawyer when we say you can get a lawyer. Go on with your fairy tale.'

Walker wiped his perspiring brow. 'I got home around quarter of twelve and saw the police up at Sellers' place. I—'

'What were you doing between nine o'clock and half past eleven?'

'I stopped at a bar.'

'What bar?' Wiggin shot at him.

'I don't know.'

'You don't know much, do you?'

'If you could let me go back there I might find it.'

'Wouldn't that be just dandy? I'll bet you'd find the restaurant too, wouldn't you?'

'I think I could.'

Wiggion snarled and made a gesture that caused Walker to cringe. 'What do you think we are, stupid? Suppose you back up your alibi with names instead of places, Walker. Who saw you at that restaurant? Who were you with when Sheila Sellers got killed?'

'I wasn't with anybody. I was alone. I was in the—'

'In the restaurant,' Wiggin sneered. He turned. 'Come on, Chief, how much longer do I have to listen to this crap?'

Acton said patiently, 'He'll get tired.'

'I'll make him tired.'

Walker said with tears in his eyes, 'Please let me call a lawyer.'

CHAPTER THIRTY-ONE

Shortly before twelve o'clock they put Walker back in his cell. He had shriveled considerably but he hadn't broken. He had finally, in stubborn desperation, fallen back on his refusal to answer questions and was making it stick.

'We're gonna have to let him call a lawyer,' Acton grumbled. 'We can't stall that off much longer and once he has that we can kiss the chances of a confession goodbye.'

'Anybody taking a look around his house?' Fellows asked.

'Not yet. I'll have it turned inside out this afternoon.'

'Better get a search warrant.'

'I can't. It's Sunday. I'd have to locate the judge.'

'Any evidence you find won't do you much good if it's illegally obtained.'

'Yeah,' Acton sighed. 'I guess I'd better try to find the judge.'

Wiggin came up and said, 'Why the hell didn't you let me handle him my way, Chief? I wouldda made him talk.'

'It wouldn't stand up in court, that's why.'

'It wouldn't anyway. At least then we'd know where to look for the evidence to convict the sonuvabitch.'

Fellows started off and Acton said, 'Where're you going?'

'I want to call Sellers' lawyer and let him know what we've got.'

'You can't. It's Sunday. He won't be in the office.'

'He's got a phone in his home, doesn't he?'

'Yeah, but it's not listed. You can't get him before tomorrow unless you drive down there.'

'I'll drive,' Fellows said. 'Sellers has waited long enough.'

A phone call to Heligman when he got to Pittsfield was enough to get the chief Mills' address and it was Leonard Mills himself who answered the door. He was in golfing costume and a look of impatience crossed his face when he saw who was there. He said, 'I'm sorry, I have an appointment.'

Fellows nodded. 'So I see. However, I have some news.'

Mills' lips tightened. 'Mr. Fellows, I don't know about the police department and your twenty-four hour shifts but today is Sunday and I don't conduct business on Sunday. If you have something to say it can wait till tomorrow.'

Fellows didn't budge. 'This has to do with Ernest Sellers.'

'I'm sure it has.'

'The least he gets is an extension. If we're lucky, he gets set free.'

276

Mills' expression didn't change. He showed no surprise and no less irritation. 'There's nothing about this that has to be told me today,' he said tartly. 'Perhaps you don't understand that this is Sunday.'

Fellows' voice took on a harshness of its own. 'One day more or less may not mean much to you, Mr. Mills, but a day means a lot to Ernest Sellers. He's only got four of them left. I'd appreciate it, therefore, if you'd listen to me.'

Mills studied the chief for a moment and decided the quickest way to get to the club would be to let the man talk. 'Very well,' he said stiffly. 'Come in.'

He led the way through a large foyer into a spacious and expensively furnished living room. 'All right,' he said, gesturing at the couch. 'But please be brief.'

Fellows sat but Mills remained standing, clasping his hands behind him. Fellows looked up 'We've found a lover,' he said.

'Sheila Sellers had a lover?'

'That's right.'

Contempt crossed Mills' face. 'And am I supposed to leap with joy at that unexpected disclosure?'

Fellows' tone could be biting too. 'I thought you might,' he said.

'And who is this lover?'

'George Walker, the man Sellers once punched in the nose.'

277

'And where is George Walker now?'

'In custody.'

'Has he confessed to the murder?'

'Not yet.'

'Nor is he likely to,' Mills said sarcastically. 'Not unless he's a bigger fool than I took him for. What evidence have you got against him?'

'As a lover? We have his own admission.'

'I mean as a murderer?'

'We don't have any except the fact that he was involved with the woman.'

'The fact he was involved with her is no evidence at all. What you mean is you've got nothing against Walker, isn't that so?'

'So far. We've only begun.'

'Begun? You've gone too far already. You should never have started.'

Fellows came to his feet. 'Now that's about enough, Mr. Mills. You perhaps forget that Ernest Sellers was scheduled to be executed next Thursday. If we can get a confession out of Walker before then, he'll be set free—'

'Not until Walker is tried and found guilty he won't!'

'Have it your way. If Walker is found guilty, Sellers will go free. The very least that happens is that the Governor will issue a stay of execution. If I hadn't begun, Sellers would die Thursday night. Don't tell me I shouldn't have started this.'

'A stay of execution?' Mills almost sneered.

278

'And what is that going to do except keep Sellers alive a few more weeks? What's a few weeks compared to the rest of his natural life? Suppose you tell me that, Mr. Fellows.'

'What are you talking about?'

'I'm talking about my appeal to the Governor. I had high expectations that he would commute Ernest's sentence to life imprisonment and this would eventually almost surely lead to Ernest's freedom on parole. The main strength of my appeal, Mr. Fellows, my request for clemency, was the lack of motive for Ernest to kill his wife. This is what my whole defense was built on—that Ernest had no reason to want his wife dead. Now you, with your ceaseless meddling, have very effectively produced a reason. Anyone who knows Sellers knows that his behavior was such that he could be deemed capable of anything should he learn of such an affair. You've wiped out my whole argument to the Governor and we can now kiss any hope of executive clemency goodbye. Yes, we can get a stay of execution for Ernest but, unless you can prove George Walker is a murderer, you bought that stay of excution at the cost of his life.'

'You're only assuming the Governor would have granted clemency in the first place.'

'That's a fair assumption, Mr. Fellows. And it's an even fairer one that he won't grant it now that you've produced an

A-number-one motive for Sellers.'

'It's only an A-number-one motive if Sellers knew about it. But he didn't.'

'Can you prove that? Can you prove he didn't know his wife was carrying on with another man?'

Fellows hesitated and Mills lifted his chin in bitter triumph. 'All you've got,' he said, 'is a theory that George Walker might have done it instead. But you have no evidence. You don't even have a motive. Why would he kill Sheila Sellers? There's a big difference between sleeping with a woman and killing her. And what about opportunity? Can you prove he was where he could have done the deed?'

'I can show you the weirdest alibi in the world,' Fellows answered and went on to tell about Walker's supposed phone call from 'Barry Rogers' and the resulting trip to Pittsfield.

Mills snorted at that in derision. 'Am I supposed to make something out of that? That's not weird, it's stupid.'

'I made out of it that Walker was Sheila's lover and I was right.'

'So therefore it's going to make him out her murderer too? That alibi is too stupid to be anything but true. If he really wanted an alibi, why wouldn't he set up a real appointment with a real man?'

'He'd have trouble with the timing.'

'You think he doesn't here? You can theorize about it if you want but you've got nothing there you can go to court with. Have you any proof there is no real Barry Rogers, for instance? Have you any proof Walker made that call to himself? Can you produce the answering service woman and get her to swear that she recognized George Walker's voice when he made it?'

Fellows said testily, 'Of course not. That was three years ago.'

'That's right. Of course you can't. So if you can't prove *he* made it, the possibility remains that someone else made it. And who else could that be but Ernest Sellers himself—or do you suggest that Sheila had other lovers and someone else sent Walker away so *he* could sneak in and murder Sheila?'

Mills glanced at his watch and then put his hands on his hips. 'I'm going to tell you something, Mr. Fellows. You've put Ernest Sellers in the soup. There's only one way you can save him now and that's by proving that either George Walker or someone else killed his wife. I don't mean that they *might* have done it but that they *did* do it. Because if you can't, Ernest Sellers is going to die.

'Now I'll be in court tomorrow but Tuesday I'll contact the Governor and get that stay of execution you've been so anxious for. Whether it does Sellers any good or not is up to you.'

CHAPTER THIRTY-TWO

Fellows drove back to police headquarters in Banksville grimly. He knew that Mills was heavyhandedly trying to blame him for Sellers' plight but he also knew that in one respect Mills was right. The only way to get Sellers in the clear was to build a case against Walker. That meant a strong motive—something more than the mere acquisition of a new girlfriend—and some solid evidence.

He checked in with Acton and learned that George Walker wasn't helping things along in either of those directions. He not only wasn't confessing, he wasn't answering any questions at all. He had finally been allowed to contact a lawyer and the lawyer had told him to maintain absolute silence till he could get to him. The burden of obtaining evidence, therefore, lay completely on the police. They were, Acton said, getting started on that and an investigating party, assisted by Raphael Jones and armed with the legal aid of a search warrant, had gone off to Walker's house to see what could be found.

'I don't suppose it'll be much,' Acton said dispiritedly. 'Not after all this time.' He leaned his elbows on his desk. 'I don't mind saying, Fellows, I'd feel a lot happier about the whole thing if we could figure a good motive for him killing Mrs. Sellers. I'd go for him as the guilty party a lot better if I could see why he might want her out of the way. I can't see why getting a new girlfriend would lead him to murder the old. You got any ideas about that?'

Fellows had to admit he did not. 'If we could only talk to him long enough it might slip out.'

'Fat chance. The next time that guy'll open his mouth will be on the witness stand in his own defense—that is if a Grand Jury indicts him. Right now we don't even have a damned thing to take before a Grand Jury. And when that lawyer of his gets after us we may even have to let him go.' Acton shook his head. 'All I can say is he's going to be a tough one. It takes a pretty cool character to stick it out in that neighborhood. It was a long shot that nobody'd know about him and her in the first place and then to stay around where there's always the chance he might trip himself up—well, I don't like the spot we're in and I don't mind telling you so.'

Fellows felt bad enough without letting Acton depress him further. He left the chief and drove out to Walker's place to see what, if anything, was turning up.

When he arrived, he found the front door of the house wide open behind the screen. Out back two probing figures were visible and, in front, a patrolman paced the sidewalk. Further away, at a respectful distance in both directions, small groups of neighbors watched.

Fellows parked in the nearest available space and crossed the street to identify himself to the patrolman on guard. The officer passed him through and he mounted the stoop and entered the house.

Raphael Jones, thumbing through magazines in the living room, was the first to see him and said, 'Well, Dad, did you get Sellers sprung?'

'Not yet. Is that your idea of searching for clues?'

'The pros don't like us amateurs meddling. They only let me come because you weren't around to baby-sit.'

'What have they found?'

'Just what you'd expect them to find three years after the fact. Nothing.'

'What about women?'

'You mean spending the night? If they come they bring their own things. There's not so much as a powder puff in the bedrooms upstairs.'

One of the detectives climbed the cellar steps and came in from the kitchen. He saw Fellows and said, 'Nothing down there. That tears it, I guess, unless there's something in the garage.'

The three went out to see and another detective there gestured in the negative.

284

'Empty as a politician's head,' he said.

'You look over the whole yard?' Fellows asked.

'I didn't, but Bratton's been poking around behind the garage.'

They walked out and around to where untended bushes grew and old dead cuttings lay in the narrow gap between the rear of the garage and the low back fence. Bratton was kicking the things around as his means of seeing what was there. Beside him, out in the open, lay an eighteen-inch length of dirt-encrusted lead pipe.

'Ain't nothing here,' Bratton said, turning to come out.

Fellows pointed to the pipe. 'What's that?'

'Piece of pipe. It was buried there just under the surface at the base of the garage.'

'Bring it out.'

Bratton said, 'Hell, it's only an old piece of pipe. I stepped on it. That's how I found it.' He picked it up and pushed through a bush to hand it to Fellows.

One end was only soiled but the other was caked with earth. Fellows looked it over closely and hefted it. Bratton said again that it was only an old piece of pipe but Jones and the two detectives peered closely. Fellows broke away some of the soil. It had been glued to the pipe by a dark, dirty substance which stained the other end. One of the detectives said, 'Well I'll be damned. So that's what he brained her with!'

Fellows rubbed a little more of the dirt away. 'Nobody searched here after the murder, I guess.'

'Not way over here. Only the garbage pails and rubbish containers. We didn't think—we couldn't look everywhere!'

Bratton said, 'Hey, you mean I found something?'

'Don't get a swelled head,' the detective told him. 'You wouldn't have mentioned it if we hadn't come out.'

'Well, what the hell. I was looking for—well how would I know an old piece of pipe—'

Fellows said, 'Well, shall we get this thing over to a lab and find out if that dark stuff is what we think it is?'

'Yeah,' said the detective. 'And wait'll Walker hears what we found!' He grinned at Fellows. 'I guess you'll be hanging over the lab technicians' shoulders tomorrow, sweating your baby home.'

'I'm going to Midland Prison tomorrow,' Fellows answered. 'There's a guy in the death cell up there who's doing a little sweating of his own. It's about time somebody told him what's going on and I'm not going to wait for his lawyer to get around to it.'

CHAPTER THIRTY-THREE

The apprehension of George Walker was the big story on the front pages when Fred Fellows picked up the Monday morning paper in the motel cafeteria and sat down to his breakfast at eight o'clock. Walker was being held on suspicion of murder the article said but the other story, the one about the discovery of the ominous piece of pipe, made it clear that 'suspicion' was only a technicality. Walker's lawyer, when asked about the pipe, had said the substance on it hadn't been tested and the pipe therefore had no meaning. Walker himself was saying nothing.

Raphael Jones plopped a tray down on the chief's table as Fellows pored over the paper and he slid into the facing seat saying, 'Well, Dad, for a hero of the hour you're wearing a pretty damned long face. Don't you ever smile?'

Fellows folded the paper and laid it aside. 'Sometimes I do. Whenever there happens to be something to smile about.'

'Worried about Walker's motive?'

'No. I'm worried about that piece of pipe.'

Jones sat back and regarded the chief. 'Now don't tell me you're afraid it won't be the woman's blood!'

Fellows raised his eyes. 'Look,' he said. 'If George Walker was having an affair with Sheila, could somebody else have been?'

Jones gaped at him. 'What?'

'Could she have had more than one lover?'

'You're off your rocker. No.'

'That's what I'd say too, but.'

'But? But what? Say, what the hell's eating you, Dad? Don't you like to solve cases?'

'I like to solve them right.'

'Right? How right can you get? This one's tied up in pink ribbon. You suspected there was a lover. You found him. Now you've found the murder weapon practically in his pocket. What's there to bother you?'

'Finding the murder weapon in his pocket bothers me.'

Jones waved that aside as nothing. 'It happens all the time. Criminals get caught with the goods on them more often than not.'

'Not after three years they don't.'

'Hell, man, it's easy. Walker goes to the house and kills her, see? He's got to get rid of the weapon—'

'Why?'

'Why leave clues? Maybe the pipe could be traced. So he buries it—'

'In his own back yard?'

'Just temporarily. He can ditch it somewhere else later.'

'But he didn't.'

'He forgets about it. That's one of the ways

288

killers trip themselves up. The heat's on Sellers. Nobody even looks at Walker.'

'We looked at him. For two weeks we've been prowling the neighborhood. That ought to have made him remember it in a hurry. And why should he bury it so shallowly in the first place?'

'I can think up answers but all right, Dad, let's hear what yours are.'

'Maybe he didn't know it was there.'

'How the hell would he not know it's—' Jones broke off and said, 'Oh,' softly. 'You think somebody else might have killed her and planted it on Walker? Now I begin to see why you're wondering about another lover.'

'Precisely.'

'Oh, Jesus. Are we going to have start this all over again? We've got nowhere to look.'

'We'd know one thing. This other person would know about Walker.'

'Sheila kisses and tells, huh? But Walker didn't know about anybody else.' Jones shook his head and dipped into his bacon and eggs with distaste. 'You've spoiled my appetite, Fellows, I suppose you know that.'

'And, of course,' Fellows went on, 'Walker's lawyer would use that "plant" idea to the hilt. That pipe won't convict Walker of a damned thing.'

'And you've got to produce a murderer to get Sellers off the hook? That's just great. You still going up to see him?'

'Yes. I arranged it with the warden last night.'

'Maybe he knows something,' Jones said hopefully. 'I know he doesn't know about lovers but if he learns there've been a few he might be able to point a couple of fingers.'

'That's what I want to find out.'

Jones looked up. 'Say, how about me going with you? Two heads and all that. Besides, I'd kind of like to meet the guy I've been working so hard for for the last couple of weeks.'

Fellows said, 'Curry might let you in if you're with me. But you let me do the questioning.'

'I'll be as silent as a grave—and just about as grim.'

CHAPTER THIRTY-FOUR

Warden Joseph Curry was still at breakfast when Fellows and Jones arrived at his home inside the walls of Midland Prison. He sat them down for a cup of coffee which the 'missus' served and he said, 'You've been going great guns. It's all over the papers. You found the weapon and all. Looks like I'm going to lose my star boarder. He don't know nothing about it yet, you know. We don't let him see controversial pieces in the newspapers, especially something that might get his hopes up falsely.'

Curry was hesitant when the chief asked permission for Jones to accompany him to the condemned man's cell but finally decided it would be all right. 'Hate to see you make the trip for nothing,' he told the detective, 'and I guess, in light of what's been happening, Sellers is entitled to special favors.'

Could we see Sellers now?'

'Sure thing. I'll call McCarthy.'

Once more Chief Fellows followed the guard to the heavy door that opened onto Death Row and once more he found Ernest Sellers lying on his bunk staring at nothing, not moving at the sounds.

'Company, Sellers,' McCarthy said and unlocked the barred door to the condemned man's cell.

Sellers turned his head a little but didn't roll over to look. Instead, he waited till Fellows and Jones actually entered the cell so he could see without craning for there was little curiosity in him.

When he saw the chief, however, his brooding ceased and he came quickly to a sitting position. 'It's you,' he said. 'You didn't forget me.'

Fellows shook his head and said, 'This is Raphael Jones, another of those you wrote to. He didn't forget you either.'

Sellers got up and wrung Jones' hand and

the chief's in turn. 'I'd about given up,' he said gratefully. 'I haven't heard about the reprieve from the Governor or anything. My lawyer—I think he's forgotten I'm still alive.'

Fellows said somberly, 'The Governor turned you down.'

'Oh.' Sellers sat slowly down on the bunk again. He brightened a little. 'But you're here. You've got something. You found something?'

Fellows shook his head. 'I'm afraid not, Mr. Sellers.'

It took a moment for the news to sink into Sellers' brain and Fellows gave Jones, who was scarcely able to control himself, a sharp and quieting elbow in the ribs. Then Sellers leaned forward. 'But that's impossible,' he said. 'There has to be something. Somewhere there has to be something.'

'I'm afraid not,' Fellows went on. 'At least if there is we couldn't find it.'

Sellers bit his lip. 'But you *got* to have. You're a detective!'

'That may be, Mr. Sellers, but if there's nothing to find, the best detective can't find anything. We questioned everybody and nobody knew a thing.'

'They must have,' he almost shrieked. 'They're lying.' He sank back and started to sob. He looked up again almost immediately. 'Today's Monday,' he cried shrilly. 'There's only three more days. They're going to kill

292

me in three days. Even the Governor won't help!'

'I know,' Fellows said soberly. 'But I'm afraid we couldn't uncover a single clue.'

'What about a lover? Did you investigate about a lover?'

'She didn't have any lovers, Mr. Sellers. You told me that yourself.'

'Not that I knew about,' he said frantically. 'But maybe she had one I didn't know about. Maybe it was a lover that killed her.'

'Maybe it was a man from Mars, Mr. Sellers. There's no evidence to point to her having a lover. You and all the neighbors defend her purity.'

Sellers ran a hand over his face. He wet his lips. 'Listen,' he said desperately. 'I've been thinking about that. You know? You lie here with nothing to do and you think. I'm thinking maybe she had one. I'm thinking it's quite possible she could've had one.'

'How?' Fellows said skeptically. 'You watched her like a hawk.'

'Yeah, but you see.' He waved his hands in little pleading movements. 'I play chess, see? I'm away every Thursday night. I'm not watching her on Thursday nights. It'd be easy for a lover to sneak into the house behind my back on Thursday nights.'

Fellows remained unpersuaded but willing to be convinced. 'You have any reason for thinking such a thing could have happened,

293

Mr. Sellers? I know, at this point, you'd like to believe this, but do you have anything that would make *me* believe it?'

Sellers wet his lips again. The sweat was standing out on his face and starting to run down his cheeks. 'I—ah—well, I'll tell you. She was different when I'd come home on Thursday nights. I mean sometimes when she was still up she'd be in a particularly happy mood. Kind of fulfilled, you might say. Or other times she'd be good and happy the next morning. There was kind of a glow about her.'

'You mean this was only after you'd been away on Thursday nights?'

'Yeah. There was this glow. She was extra happy, like. I didn't think nothing of it at the time but now that I been recollecting I can remember this. You know what I think now? I think she had a lover. I'm convinced of it. I think it was the lover who killed her.'

'I suppose that's possible,' Fellows said thoughtfully. 'I suppose that glow you mention might make one wonder about something like that—.'

'That's right. It's enough to make you wonder, isn't it? Right now I'm sure that's the answer!'

'A lover,' Fellows said, stroking his chin. 'Definitely a possibility. But who? It could be anybody. There wouldn't be a chance in the time left of finding out if there was one, and, if so, who.'

Sellers, almost frantic with excitement, said, 'Well, now, what about that fellow George Walker? He's a bachelor—leastways he was then—and he played around a lot of women.'

'Married women? Your wife?'

'Why not?' Sellers said, constantly gesticulating with his hands. 'Sheila was a beautiful woman. Remember when he danced with her at the block dance? He was starting something right then, I'll bet. He's just the one, Mr. Fellows. He's just the kind of man who'd do a thing like that. Have you talked to him?' He looked at Fellows' face and a stricken look came into his own. 'He hasn't moved, has he? He's still around, isn't he?'

Fellows nodded. 'Yes, Mr. Sellers. He's still around. We've talked to him, in fact, but he says he didn't know your wife. The only time he ever saw her was at that dance.'

'He's lying,' Sellers shouted back. 'He's a goddam dirty liar. He talked to her other times. I saw him talk to her. He talked to her, bold as brass, in front of me too. He saw her plenty of times.'

'Well, talking to her doesn't mean he seduced her and he says he didn't.'

'Did you search around his place? You can't be sure he isn't lying.'

'Search?' Fellows asked blandly. 'For what?'

Sellers waved his wild hands. 'I don't know. For clues. Maybe he hid the murder weapon around his place.'

Jones was eyeing both Fellows and the little shrunken man on the bunk warily. He scowled faintly as Fellows dismissed that idea. 'I doubt he'd do a thing like that,' he said. 'After all there's no evidence he was her—'

'But did you look?' Sellers insisted. 'Why don't you look?'

'Look where, behind his garage?'

'Sure. Why don't you dig behind his garage? That'd be the kind of place he might pick to hide a weapon.'

'Like what, a piece of pipe or something?'

'Sure, a piece of pipe, a wrench, any kind of thing like that that might've done it. Go take a look.'

'We already did.'

Sellers stared up at him. 'You mean there's nothing?'

'There's nothing behind Walker's garage.'

'Did you dig?'

'We dug.'

'Everywhere?'

'Wherever there was a place where something might be buried.'

'He's got junk back there, old prunings. Did you look around there?'

'That's where we dug. There's nothing there, Mr. Sellers.'

296

Sellers' face was ashen. He put his hands to it and sank back. 'Oh, no,' he said. He struggled up. 'He must have found it. He must have thrown it away somewhere else. Question him,' he said desperately. 'Ask him what he did with the murder weapon. Make him tell you where he hid it and then you'll know he did it.'

'Maybe,' Fellows said dryly, 'you buried it too deep.'

'No. It wasn't deep. He picked it up and—' He stared. 'What do you mean? You mean *he* buried it too deep.'

'No, Mr. Sellers, I mean *you* did.'

'Me?' He shrieked. 'You're outta your mind. What kind of a detective are you?'

'Not a very good one,' Fellows answered quietly. 'You led me a long chase, Mr. Sellers. You got me to follow the biggest red herring I ever saw. I fell right into your trap, Mr. Sellers. I got to believing in your innocence so much I broke my neck finding out what you wanted me to find out—that your wife was having a love affair with George Walker. I got so convinced the lover was guilty that I ignored the things that couldn't be explained, like why he'd keep on living in the neighborhood, like why he'd want to kill her in the first place. I did all that right up until we found the piece of pipe you buried. It wasn't till then that I finally stopped and took another look at things.'

'But I didn't bury any pipe,' Sellers protested. 'I didn't know he and Sheila were having a love affair. I swear I didn't'

'Oh yes you did, Mr. Sellers,' Fellows said bitterly, 'and you just now told me how. That glow business. That's what I needed to know to tie it up. That bothered you, didn't it? That made you suspect all kinds of things, you with your suspicious, jealous mind. Maybe you did other things to verify your suspicions, like sprinkle a film of powder in a doorway to catch a man's footprint or place a thread to see if the back door had been opened, but one thing I'm certain you did. You left to play chess one Thursday in June, only instead of going to play chess you stationed yourself in your yard or garage somewhere and waited. And what happened? Pretty soon who should come along through the dark back yards but George Walker, the man you'd punched for dancing with your wife. And now you knew not only that there *was* a man but who he was.'

'That's a lie,' Sellers shrieked. 'I didn't know anything. He talked to my wife and I didn't do anything, did I? That ought to prove I didn't know anything.'

'Just the opposite, Mr. Sellers. Usually you got violent when people paid attention to your wife, but now, suddenly, with George Walker you don't. Why? Because you had other plans for him and you didn't want to let on. Before, the men you fought with were innocent of any wrongdoing but now here was a man who wasn't. So you, with your chess-player's mind, concocted a subtle combination which was going to get rid of both your wife and George Walker. You were going to kill her and throw the blame on him.

'What you needed was a motive for him, right? He had to have a reason for killing Sheila. So what would it be? I'll bet you paid a lot of attention to Mr. George Walker that summer, Sellers. I'll bet you were waiting for him to tire of Sheila and take up with someone new. And when he did bring a new girlfriend around, you struck. You sent him to Pittsfield with a phony phone call. You came home and had your supper and when your wife got undressed for her bath you lured her into the living room and beat her to death. Probably you stripped your clothes off first. I don't know why she turned her back on you. Maybe she saw the pipe and turned to flee. Maybe she thought you wanted to make love and was rejecting the offer. But you killed her and dressed and went to your chess meeting, only you didn't go by the usual route. You went out the back and through the yards to hide the pipe in a shallow hole behind Walker's garage on your way to the bus. The rest of the story we all know.'

'You're out of your mind,' Sellers protested vigorously. 'You don't make sense at all.'

'Where don't I, for example?'

'If I knew George Walker was having an affair with my wife, I'd have pointed the finger at him! I wouldn't be sitting in this cell myself!'

'You couldn't point a finger, Sellers, not without giving yourself a much better motive than he could have. That's what I mean about your chess-player's mind and your little combination. Knowing that gossipy neighborhood, I'll bet you suffered all summer firmly convinced you were the only one who didn't hear how Walker was cuckolding you. I'll bet anything you thought all you had to do was play the innocent and everyone else would tell the police about Walker. They'd investigate, find the weapon, and send him to the chair. He probably wouldn't have been convicted even so but it would have seemed surefire to you. You knew nothing and he was the only other possible suspect.

'The only trouble was, nobody else knew about Walker and that left you holding the bag because you couldn't tell on him. So, when all your lawyer's attempts to beat the chair failed, you turned to us hoping we'd find out about Walker for you.

'Well, we did, Sellers, but it was three years too late because he'd never have left that pipe there all that time even if he'd put it there in the beginning. It was a plant and the answer to the question who planted it was obvious. All I needed to clinch it was some clue that you knew about him and Sheila. That's why I told you what I did and that's why I thought it was a good idea to have Raphael Jones come along as a witness.'

The sweat was dry on Sellers' face and his complexion was red now rather than white. 'You and your witness,' he snarled. 'You think you're going to get me to admit anything? I'm not saying one word. I'm not answering a single question without my lawyer!'

'You don't have to,' Fellows reminded him. 'We're not trying to convict you. You're already convicted. All we're going to do now is walk out.' He raised his voice and called the guard.

McCarthy appeared through the corridor door and fitted his key in the cell lock. There was a secret smile on his face and he said as he let the two men out, 'Lotta loud talking in here. Got your voices up pretty high.'

Sellers called the guard a series of foul names and when the door was locked on him again and Fellows and Jones were outside, he leaped from the cot to the bars, clutching them tight and pressing his face between them. 'You aren't going off and leave me like this,' he shouted. 'Get me out of here. You can't go and leave me to die!'

Jones looked back but Fellows touched his

301

arm. 'Come on.'

They passed through the door to the outer corridor and from behind came Sellers' screaming voice. 'I'll see you in hell,' he yelled. 'That's where you're going to go. You're going to hell with Sheila and Walker. You're all of you going to hell, hear me? Hear me? You're going to hell! You hear? ... You hear? ... You hear?'

Nor was it till they were outside in the open that they stopped hearing.

They walked slowly across the hot glaring yard towards the warden's house and Fellows' face was twisted wryly. 'I guess we'd better get on back and take George Walker off the hook,' he said. 'I imagine he's paid enough for his loving.'

'Yeah. And what are we going to tell the newspapers?'

'Then there's Mills. We've got to call him off from that stay of execution business and we've got to see that the Governor learns what happened. It may have a bearing on whether he commutes the sentence or not.'

'You mean he hasn't decided yet? You said—'

'I made that up to pin Sellers to the wall. And there are a few other things we've done that have got to be undone.' He turned and said dryly, 'I guess you know we've been double-decker fools and those who aren't going to be sore at us are going to be laughing

302

fit to kill. Maybe all that publicity you're so hot for won't taste so good. Maybe you don't want to take fifty-per-cent of the credit after all.'

Jones said, 'Listen, Dad, if you think you got the only pair of load-carrying shoulders in the business you can readjust your ego. I can stand being called a damned fool in sixty point type just as much as you can, and I mean even if they spell my name right. After all, two guys who've done all that we've done for *free*, for not even expense money, what the hell else do you think we ought to be called?'

Photoset, printed and bound in Great Britain by REDWOOD PRESS LIMITED, Melksham, Wiltshire